The Duke's Mercenary

The Duke's Guard Series,
Book Nine

C.H. Admirand

© Copyright 2024 by C.H. Admirand
Text by C.H. Admirand
Cover by Dar Albert

Dragonblade Publishing, Inc. is an imprint of Kathryn Le Veque Novels, Inc.
P.O. Box 23
Moreno Valley, CA 92556
ceo@dragonbladepublishing.com

Produced in the United States of America

First Edition June 2024
Trade Paperback Edition

Reproduction of any kind except where it pertains to short quotes in relation to advertising or promotion is strictly prohibited.

All Rights Reserved.

The characters and events portrayed in this book are fictitious. Any similarity to real persons, living or dead, is purely coincidental and not intended by the author.

ARE YOU SIGNED UP FOR DRAGONBLADE'S BLOG?

You'll get the latest news and information on exclusive giveaways, exclusive excerpts, coming releases, sales, free books, cover reveals and more.

Check out our complete list of authors, too!

No spam, no junk. That's a promise!

Sign Up Here

www.dragonbladepublishing.com

Dearest Reader;

Thank you for your support of a small press. At Dragonblade Publishing, we strive to bring you the highest quality Historical Romance from some of the best authors in the business. Without your support, there is no 'us', so we sincerely hope you adore these stories and find some new favorite authors along the way.

Happy Reading!

CEO, Dragonblade Publishing

Additional Dragonblade books by Author C.H. Admirand

The Duke's Guard Series
The Duke's Sword (Book 1)
The Duke's Protector (Book 2)
The Duke's Shield (Book 3)
The Duke's Dragoon (Book 4)
The Duke's Hammer (Book 5)
The Duke's Defender (Book 6)
The Duke's Saber (Book 7)
The Duke's Enforcer (Book 8)
The Duke's Mercenary (Book 9)

The Lords of Vice Series
Mending the Duke's Pride (Book 1)
Avoiding the Earl's Lust (Book 2)
Tempering the Viscount's Envy (Book 3)
Redirecting the Baron's Greed (Book 4)
His Vow to Keep (Novella)
The Merry Wife of Wyndmere (Novella)

The Lyon's Den Series
Rescued by the Lyon
Captivated by the Lyon

Dedication

DJ ~ You wrote it first in that note you left thumb-tacked to my parents' front door. Afterward, the notes we exchanged always ended the same way, because in our hearts we believed it.
I still do, my darling…

I love you,
More than yesterday,
Less than tomorrow,
Forever…

Acknowledgements

A special thank you to my wonderful editor Arran McNicol! I am so grateful for his innate ability to pinpoint where I've gotten lost in the plot, and highlighted where one sentence is enough—and two are too many.

Dear Reader:

I cannot believe I have finished writing book nine in *The Duke's Guard*! Dermott O'Malley's story is just over the halfway point in the series, and I'm more in love with these handsome-as-sin Irishmen than I was when they first appeared on the scene in **Mending the Duke's Pride**!

Thank you for joining me on this wild ride, and the biggest series I have ever written. Your encouragement and support—in reading, commenting, stopping by events and takeovers—means so much more than you can imagine. I am so grateful for each and every one of you.

CH.

PROLOGUE

LORD EGGERTON TURNED the card over and felt the blood rush from his head. Dizzy with it, he closed his eyes, praying to God the brandy was to blame for his poor eyesight. He could not have consigned his pride and joy, the light of his life, his daughter Georgiana, into the clutches of the ancient reprobate sitting across the gaming table from him.

"I believe this hand is mine." Viscount Trenchert gathered his winnings and pulled them toward him. Caressing the folded bit of foolscap on top of the pile, he licked his lips in anticipation. "I believe I shall enjoy living in your manor house in Sussex, adding the chit's dowry to my bank account...and plowing her virgin fields."

Eggerton surged to his feet. "You will never touch one hair on my daughter's head!"

Trenchert flicked an invisible speck of dust from his sleeve. "If you do not possess the skill at cards, you should not have wagered your homes nor your fortune," the viscount said, "nor your daughter's dowry and her hand in marriage to me."

"You must have put something in the brandy!"

Trenchert shook his head and glanced about the darkened room and the few gentlemen still gambling. "No talent at cards. No head for the finest French brandy. You are pathetic. Have my prize—*your daughter*—prepared to journey with me to my new home in Sussex tomorrow by teatime."

The thought of his lovely Georgiana married to the musty-smelling gargoyle sitting across from him scraped Eggerton's gut raw and had him surging to his feet. "She will not be going anywhere with you!"

Everything Eggerton valued in life was clutched in the man's hand. His heart sank when the other man curled the foolscap in his fist, snickered, and held up his hand, waving it in Eggerton's face. "You relinquished your rights in the matter." The old man rose from the table and, without a backward glance, in a voice that carried, barked, "Teatime tomorrow!"

Hot on his heels, Eggerton followed, grabbed Trenchert's arm, and shouted, "You cheated!"

Trenchert's expression darkened. "My seconds shall call upon you. Chalk Farm at dawn."

The blow of the man's final words cleared Eggerton's head. He staggered outside and signaled for his coach. He did not remember the short ride to Mayfair. Consumed with worry, he tried to devise a plan. What in the bloody hell would he say to his daughter? How could he explain that he'd been plied with heavy brandy and cheated? That was the only reason he had not won the hand where he confidently wagered their homes and fortune, her dowry, and her hand in marriage. Good God, he'd broken his promise to Georgiana that he'd never gamble again. She would never forgive him.

As the coach slowed to a stop outside his town house, Eggerton knew what he had to do. Head high, he stepped down from the carriage and yanked the door open, nearly plowing into his butler.

"Lock the door behind me and do not let anyone in!"

"Yes, your lordship."

He strode to the staircase, taking the steps two at a time, and shouted, "Georgiana!"

Her bedchamber door opened, and a vision of loveliness draped in her favorite forest-green dressing gown appeared, candle held high. "Papa? What has happened? What is wrong?"

He shook his head and motioned for her to follow him to his private study. The fire had been lit, anticipating his arrival, but the warmth did not penetrate the marrow frozen in his bones. "You shall never forgive me, but I beg you to understand…" His words failed him.

Astute as her mother had been, his daughter lost all expression. "You were gambling again, weren't you, Papa?"

"Aye, but it's not just coin that I lost tonight. Even if in your heart of hearts you should someday forgive me, I would not deserve it."

She set her candle on his desk, reached for his hands, and held tight. "Whatever economies we will have to make, I promise not to complain. We can send word to Madame Beaudoine that plans have changed and advise that I do not need the new ball gown."

He tugged his hands free. "You must pack a small portmanteau, and your jewels, and leave at once!"

"Leave? But why?"

"Your life is in danger, and by all that's holy, I am the bloody bastard who put you in his cross hairs!"

"Whose cross hairs? Tell me. Please?"

He raked a hand through his silver hair. "There is no time for explanations. Please trust me and someday…someway, I hope you forgive me."

And as her mother had done on many an occasion, she planted her feet firmly, met his gaze, and refused to budge. "Who is the blackguard, and why does he wish me harm?"

Anguish swept up from his toes as ice filled his veins. "Viscount Trenchert."

Her eyes widened, but instead of fear, he saw fire there. "Tell me you did not sit down at cards with him. He is a known cardsharp!"

He grabbed hold of her hand and tugged her through the door, then down the hall to her bedchamber. Opening the door, he motioned for her to precede him. He closed the door behind them. "Pack while I explain."

Finally, she obeyed and began tossing things into her portmanteau. "I'm listening."

"I've lost it all. The town house, our country estate, our fortune, your dowry"—his voice broke over the words—"and you."

She threw herself into his arms and hugged him tight. "You could never lose me, Papa. I love you. We have always had one another's backs ever since Mum passed. I won't leave you now."

Self-disgust twined with abject horror at what was in store for his daughter. He was reprehensible and had placed himself beyond the pale. He set her from him and confessed, "I've given your hand in marriage to Viscount Trenchert, along with the rest."

He would not tell her about his dawn appointment. Lord willing, the bloody bastard would die at his hand, and Georgiana would be safe. But he needed to know she was on her way to safety before he met the viscount on the field of honor.

While she stared open-mouthed at him, he added, "My carriage will be waiting out front. You must be dressed and ready to leave in a quarter of an hour!"

Before she could respond, he spun around and closed the door behind him. Events had been set in motion, and there was no time to alter them—or change his mind. He returned to his upstairs sitting room. Pulling the key from his waistcoat pocket, he unlocked the cabinet behind his desk and retrieved the mahogany box. Setting it on his desk, he lifted the lid and stared down at the dueling pistols. He had only used them once before. Though he took them out regularly to ensure they were well oiled and in working condition, he kept them locked away, never intending to use them again.

After checking both weapons, he returned them to the velvet-lined box, closed the lid, and prayed, "Dear Lord, if it be Your will that I die at dawn, I beg You to send a warrior strong enough to protect my daughter. Save her from that villainous viscount!"

Sixteen minutes later, he carried Georgiana's portmanteau

downstairs and whisked her into his carriage. He instructed his coachman, "Do not let her out of your sight when you change horses!"

"Aye, your lordship. You have my word."

He buried his emotions deep, leaned into the coach, and pressed his lips to Georgiana's forehead. "If anything happens on the way to Eggerton Hall, find your way to Lippincott Manor."

"But Papa, I thought you and the earl had a falling-out over your gambling."

"Nevertheless, he will not deny my request...or you, Georgiana. Promise me!"

Her frown was fierce, but she acquiesced. "I promise."

"The earl will see to it his brother's guard will protect you."

"I don't see why the duke's guard would—"

He stepped back from the coach. "Drive on!"

The last thing his saw was his gregarious daughter leaning out of the coach window waving.

The last thing he heard was *"I love you, Papa!"*

CHAPTER ONE

DERMOTT O'MALLEY SCANNED his surroundings as he rode the last few miles toward Lippincott Manor. The earl would be pleased to know that all was as expected on his dawn patrol from the manor house to the village and back. The air was crisp. Though still hidden behind the trees, the sun was breaking just over the horizon.

As he rounded a curve in the road, the sound of branches breaking caught his attention. Homing in on the sound, and the direction it came from, he urged his horse forward. A slip of a lass wearing a burgundy coat stood out among the dense green as she climbed onto the stone wall running parallel to the road. Her light brown hair was half up, half down, with leaves and twigs caught in it. Had she stumbled and fallen? Was someone pursuing the lass as she ran for her life through the forest? Before he could speculate further, she tossed her bag to the ground.

He'd guessed her intention before she struggled to her feet, hands extended to balance. He galloped toward the lass perched on the wall but knew he wouldn't reach her in time. "Don't... Ah, bloody *fecking* hell!"

He closed the distance between them, leapt off his horse and knelt beside where she lay on the dew-drenched grass. "Lass?" She didn't answer. He brushed the tangle of hair, dirt, and leaves from her nearly translucent, satin-smooth cheek. The gash high on her forehead, hidden by her hair, was deep and bleeding and required immediate attention.

She was breathing, but unconscious. First things first. The blood flowing from the wound high on her forehead was more urgent. Stanching the flow of blood had to be dealt with first. And a concussion was likely.

He whipped the handkerchief, and one of the spare cravats he kept in his frockcoat pocket for emergencies—in particular, binding a miscreant's hands behind their back when he'd forgotten to tuck lengths of rope in his pockets—out of his waistcoat pocket. Folding the linen into a thick square, he placed it against the wound, ignoring how quickly her lifeblood stained it. Dermott had to get her to the safety of Lippincott Manor! He wrapped the cravat around her head and tied it into a firm knot. Was she injured elsewhere? He prayed she was not, because checking for broken bones would have to wait.

He called to her again, but still no answer. He pulled her closer. Laying his ear to her breast, he listened intently, praying to hear a sound that would confirm she was still alive. Relief speared through him as he heard the beat of her heart and her ragged, indrawn breath. She must have knocked the wind out of herself. 'Twas a bit unnerving the first time it happened to him—mayhap she was too frightened to open her eyes as she struggled to breathe normally.

Thinking of the way she'd climbed up on the wall, then paused before leaping, he sensed she had more grit than a lass too skittish to scale a stone wall in the first place. Dismissing the idea that she was frightened, he wondered if she was in too much pain to open her eyes. He called for the third time, "Lass, can ye hear me?" Still no response.

Raised to believe that the Lord helped those who helped themselves, he began to check her limbs for broken bones. Miraculously, there were none. He said a quick prayer: "God, I could use Yer help." Omniscient, the Lord would know what Dermott did not have the time to say.

Carefully lifting the lass into his arms, he left her bag where she'd tossed it to the ground at the base of the wall. He'd retrieve it later.

As he approached his horse, the animal shifted uneasily, spooked by the scent of blood until Dermott soothed, "Easy now, laddie. We've a lass who needs us." The horse calmed at the tone of his voice, and he placed her on the animal's back. Bracing her with his hand, he quickly unbuttoned his frockcoat and mounted behind her. The limp weight of her had unease slithering up his spine. He trusted his faith and the makeshift bandage he'd wrapped around her head would keep her alive until they made it the safety of the manor house.

She was cold to the touch. No telling how long she had been in the woods, alone…or running from her pursuers. He gently drew her against the heat of his body, tucking the edges of his coat around her. His arm anchored her to him, and emotions he had not felt in too long to recall battered him from the inside. Silently cursing, he refused to be distracted by the curve of her cheek, the fullness of her lips, or the way she felt nestled against him. "Ye'll be fine, lass. I'll take care of ye," he vowed.

Giving the animal his head, Dermott raced toward help…and safety. Who was she? What, or whom, was she running from? She had not stirred since he swept her into his arms. He felt the flutter of her heartbeat against his own as they covered the short distance between the curve in the road and the wall she had jumped from. A voice whispered, *"Ask her."* Was it his need to have the answers, or a message from the lass's guardian angel?

The road leading onto the earl's land lay ahead. "Almost there, lass." He wondered, yet again, who in the bloody hell she was. His worry increased. Then he remembered his brother Emmett, the healer in the family, mentioning that even an unconscious and seriously injured person could still hear when spoken to.

Holding on to that thought, Dermott glanced down at the woman in his arms, and the bloody bandage around her head. His heart began to hammer in time with the pounding of his horse's hooves. Her face was pale as flour. Her thick, dark lashes fanned against her cheeks lay utterly still. She hadn't roused yet and was still unconscious. "Who's after ye, lass? Where are ye running to?"

He fought to control the worry slithering through him at her unnatural silence. Continuing as if she had answered him and asked who *he* was and where *he* was taking her, he introduced himself. "O'Malley's me name…Dermott. Not to be confused with me cousin, Sean O'Malley, who ye'll be meeting shortly. We're stationed at Lippincott Manor with our cousin, Seamus Flaherty. We're on assignment protecting the earl and his family, and are part of His Grace the Duke of Wyndmere's sixteen-man private guard. The earl is the duke's brother."

The eerie silence had the hair on the back of his neck standing on end as bright crimson continued to stain the bandage he'd wrapped around her head. It needed threads to close it. He dug deep for patience… Never his strong suit. Ma's voice echoed in his head, reminding him that patience was far more useful than worry. He'd need a boatload of it to keep his head and get the lass to safety and the help she needed.

He chanced another glance at the woman cradled in his arms and wondered aloud, "Where is yer escort?" The warmth of her blood seeped through the bandage and his waistcoat. His gut flipped over. He called on his steely control and clenched his jaw as his mount galloped toward the end of the long drive leading to Lippincott Manor. Needing to keep his balance—and his seat—he could not risk leaning down to listen to her breathing again. *Bloody hell!* He needed to know that she was still breathing! Sliding the tips of his fingers to her neck, he searched for her pulse and found it. Relieved, he rasped, "Nearly there, lass."

Confidence restored and flowing through him, he stole a quick look, noting the fit and quality of her coat. It was exquisitely made, as was the dark blue gown peeking from beneath it. "Ye're too finely dressed to be a servant on the run from a cruel master." His gut roiled as another possibility occurred to him. "Is it a cruel husband ye're on the run from, or have ye been jilted by yer intended?"

To curb the anxiety slithering inside of him, he murmured, "No matter. I'll protect ye." He brushed his lips to the top of her head as a childhood phrase slipped into his mind... *Finders keepers.*

Bollocks! He was no longer a lad. He shoved the thought from his mind, while his heart whispered, *You found her. Keep her!*

Dermott could not afford to let his mind agree with his heart. He'd taken a vow of honor to protect the duke, his family, and his extended family with his life. The lass in his arms could wreak havoc with that vow, and that he could not allow!

His decision firm, he made a vow he knew would not compromise the one he'd sworn to the Duke of Wyndmere: "I'll protect ye, lass."

Once his mind was made up, it was like a steel trap. His brothers and cousins had tried to change it over the years without success.

As he glimpsed the first of the outbuildings, Dermott solidified his pledge to the lass. "Whoever set ye to running—whether they be family, friend, or foe—they bloody well won't get past meself or me cousins! Ye have me solemn word, ye'll have the protection of meself and the rest of the duke's guard from whoever is hounding ye!" He pulled her closer to his heart and rasped, "Ye need not worry—as the duke's mercenary, I'll seek out and destroy yer enemies while ye're recovering."

He gave a sharp whistle as the stables came into view. His cousins, Sean O'Malley and Seamus Flaherty, came running. Flaherty held out his arms. "Hand her to me while ye dismount."

Dermott's mind rebelled at the thought, and his hands wouldn't cooperate or let the lass go. In a bid to cover the emotions rioting through him, he grumbled, "I've dismounted without aid carrying yer wounded hide more than once, Flaherty. I can manage on me own with this slip of a lass."

Flaherty smiled. "Aye, that ye can. But didn't our cousin,

Sean here, tell me ye had me draped over yer shoulder at the time...and not cuddled in yer lap?"

Dermott ignored Flaherty and told Sean, "Remind me to clip Flaherty in the gob later."

"Done!" Sean studied the young woman and the blood-soaked bandage. "I'll send for the physician." Turning toward the building where two stable lads stood watching, he sent one of them to summon the doctor, and the other ahead of them to the house with instructions to alert the earl, his housekeeper, and cook.

Dermott's steps faltered when fresh blood seeped through the bandage. She'd wake up soon—she had to! His heart chose that moment to remind him of his first reaction, and his silent vow about keeping her, and he nearly repeated it. Best to keep that thought buried, he told himself. Once spoken aloud, he would feel obligated to move mountains to keep the lass. And not because of some childhood phrase, but because of the soul-deep connection he'd felt the moment the lass leapt off the wall. Her courage and determination were rare in the Englishwomen he'd met since leaving Ireland. The curve of her lips and fullness of her curves were a temptation he could not afford. Her beauty...

Before his brain could finish the thought, Dermott shoved it aside. He needed to tell his cousins of his pledge. "I'd best be telling the two of ye now, lads. I'm the one who's found her—"

"Oh, for the love of God," Flaherty interrupted.

"*Bollocks*, Dermott," Sean scoffed. "Don't say it!"

"Ye don't even know what I'm going to say," Dermott griped, striding toward the manor house with his precious burden.

"We've known ye all our lives," Flaherty reminded him. "Of course we know what ye're thinking."

"She isn't a stray kitten," Sean said. "Ye cannot just keep the lass because ye found her unconscious on the side of the road."

"Let me finish what I was going to say," Dermott ordered them. "I'll beat the bloody *shite* of both of ye if ye don't shut yer gobs!"

"Finish it, then," Flaherty replied.

Dermot's hackles rose at his being told what to do, but the lass in his arms needed him to finish the ridiculous conversation. Her injuries required immediate care. "I pledged to protect her—and I will as long as there's breath left in me."

Sean grunted. "If that's all, ye can honor yer vow to His Grace, and add the lass to the list of those under yer protection."

Flaherty poked Dermott in the back of the head, irritating him. "What?"

"Aren't ye going to wax poetic and tell us ye're keeping the lass?"

Frustration twined with anger and filled him to bursting at the realization that he *did* want to keep the lass. But he'd go to his grave before admitting it to his cousins.

Flaherty grumbled, "I take it that ye've yet to make up yer mind on the matter. Now then, if ye did not find her on the side of the road, where did ye find the lass?"

Dermott's heart hammered in his chest as he recalled the sight of her frantic climb to the top of the wall before she leapt after her bag. Striding toward the house, he explained, "I heard someone moving through the trees, treading on fallen branches, on the other side of the stone wall a few miles from here. With the recent threats against the baron, and the bloody bastard who abducted our cousin Darby's wife, I was prepared to handle whoever was rushing toward the wall."

"Was anyone following her?"

Dermott was not surprised that Sean had reasoned out what he'd been thinking. Mignonette had been the target of attackers before Sean had rescued her…and married her.

"She was alone when I saw her climbing onto the wall," he replied. "The lass stood up, tossed her portmanteau onto the ground, and jumped after it."

Flaherty nodded. "Ye had to leave the bag behind, as the lass was unconscious and bleeding."

"Aye," Dermott answered as they arrived at the back door. "I'll fetch it after the physician's seen to the lass," he promised. The door opened as Sean reached for the handle.

The earl's cook was waiting for them inside by the back door. "Hurry now," Mrs. Wyatt urged, and beckoned Dermott into the room closest to the door. She clucked her tongue at the sight of the injured woman in Dermott's arms. "Bring that poor woman in here and lay her on the cot. Gently now!"

Dermott laid her on the cot and knelt beside her. He figured he was on good enough terms with the Lord that He would hear Dermott's silent prayer: *Send as much of me strength as the lass needs to heal so she can wake up!*

He heard the splash of water behind him and breathed a little easier. Mrs. Wyatt was washing her hands in the ceramic bowl kept for that purpose on the scarred oak table running the length of the wall. When he felt the cook's hand on his arm, he glanced up and saw the compassion in the older woman's eyes. She was a rare gem, just like the duke's cooks at his other properties: Mrs. O'Toole at the town house in London, and Constance at Wyndmere Hall in the Lake District.

"If you intend to stay, Dermott," she told him, "wash your hands."

He was hesitant to leave the lass's side, and knew he'd be summarily dismissed if he didn't do as Mrs. Wyatt bade him. He removed his frockcoat and rolled up his sleeves. Glancing down, he was horrified to see his hands were stained with her blood. He quickly washed them, ignoring the sight of the bowlful of bloody water.

"Where did you find the poor thing?" The cook's question interrupted his thoughts.

"A few miles from here, where the stone wall separates the woods from the road. I heard someone coming through the woods and rushed over to investigate."

Mrs. Wyatt nodded. "Wise, considering the recent troubles the family has had. What happened?"

Dermott was about to relay the story to Mrs. Wyatt when the housekeeper arrived with a footman in tow, bearing a steaming pitcher and spare bowl. Mrs. Jones instructed the footman to set the clean bowl and pitcher of hot water on the table along the wall. Pointing to the now-tainted water Dermott had used, she asked the servant to remove it. The housekeeper washed her hands before pouring hot water into one of the small bowls on the table. She grabbed a linen cloth and the bowl of water and brought them over to where the injured woman lay on the cot.

Mrs. Wyatt folded a length of clean linen into a smaller square and handed it to Dermott. "Press this to her forehead, Dermott, as soon as I remove this bandage."

She carefully untied the bloody cravat and lifted it. Dermott pressed the cloth firmly against the wound, which was smaller than he'd thought. "Head wounds bleed like a son of a—" He paused and looked at the cook. "Er...begging yer pardon, Mrs. Wyatt."

Her frown was fierce when she handed him another cloth. "Add this quickly now, and keep firm pressure against the wound." The housekeeper moved to stand beside them, studying the young woman. "I thought we would have a chance to cleanse the wound, but we'll have to stop the bleeding first."

Dermott heard people coming and going behind him, but ignored them while he continued to hold the cloth to the lass's forehead, changing it when instructed to, all the while willing the woman to open her eyes.

"I understand you rescued a young woman, O'Malley," a familiar deep voice said from behind him.

Dermott glanced over his shoulder to answer, "Aye, yer lordship." He turned back in time to see black-lashed eyes the color of the finest Irish whiskey staring at him. She was awake. *Praise God!* "Ye're safe, lass."

He expected her to react to the fact that she was safe, but instead she rasped, "Lordship?"

"Aye," Dermott answered, "Earl Lippincott."

Frustration marred her brow. She lifted a hand toward her head, but Dermott stopped her before she touched the cloth, by gently placing his much-larger hand atop hers. The size of her hand belied the strength the young woman had to possess to leap from that wall. Admiration for her surged inside of him as he quickly explained, "Ye were injured jumping off the stone wall. We need to stop the bleeding, lass."

The confusion in her eyes had him fearing her injury was more than a gash that needed to be sewn closed. Her next question confirmed it. "What was I doing on top of a wall?"

"Well now, 'tis the question I was about to put to ye, lass."

"As O'Malley told you, miss," the earl said, "you are safe here."

She glanced behind Dermott and stammered, "Th-thank you, your lordship."

Lippincott inclined his head. "No thanks necessary. Our door is always open to those in need."

Dermott could feel her uncertainty as she nervously licked her lips. "Ye can have some water, lass, if ye've a thirst."

Mrs. Jones poured a small cup and brought it to her. While Dermott eased the injured woman to a semi-sitting position to drink, he asked, "Do ye not remember running toward the wall and scaling it?"

Her eyes met his, and he noted her struggle to remember in their amber depths. "Nay."

Her soft reply had his heart going out to the woman. He'd been knocked on the head more than once during a bare-knuckle bout. Rattled his brainbox good and proper, too, but he'd never forgotten where he was or what he'd been doing. Concern for her filled him as he imagined what she was going through. The earl's hand on his shoulder had him setting his concern aside to address the most urgent problem—helping the lass was essential before getting to the bottom of what or whom she was running from.

"Where is here?"

The earl answered the softly asked question. "Lippincott

Manor."

She frowned. "Where is Lippincott Manor?"

"Sussex," the earl answered.

A commotion in the hall had Dermott glancing over his shoulder, relieved when the earl stepped into the hallway to greet the physician. "Thank you for coming so quickly."

"I was on my way back to the village when your stable hand intercepted me, your lordship." The doctor set his bag on the table by the wall, removed his coat, and rolled up his sleeves. While he washed, he asked, "How were you injured, Miss…?"

The physician paused, obviously waiting for the young woman to tell him her name. Her silence was telling, as was the way she reached for Dermott's free hand and held tight.

The doctor studied the lass while Dermott's gaze held hers. Amber eyes glistening with unshed tears had Dermott's gut roiling, but it was her reply to the physician that gutted him. "I… I'm afraid I do not remember."

He captured the first tear, and then the second, before a handkerchief appeared in front of his face. The earl was never without a spare one. "Thank ye, yer lordship." Handing it to the lass, he urged, "Dry yer tears now, and let the doctor have a look at yer wound. It needs to be closed."

She tightened her grip on his hand. "Is that why it aches?"

"Aye. 'Tisn't the size of it, but the depth. I'm leaving ye in competent hands. I must return to me duties." He thought to do just that, but the lass wouldn't let him go. "Ye need to let go, lass."

"Stay with her, O'Malley," the earl told him.

The physician added, "I will need someone to hold her still."

The doctor looked to the earl, who inclined his head and said, "Mrs. Wyatt, please remain with O'Malley."

"Of course, your lordship."

"Mrs. Jones, have one of the guest rooms prepared."

"Yes, your lordship. Her ladyship is bound to be waiting for you."

"No doubt waiting for my detailed explanation as to where I rushed off to. Please assure my wife that all is well, and that I shall speak with her shortly." The earl held the door open for his housekeeper, then closed it behind her to resume his place, halfway between the door and the young woman on the cot.

Dermott took note of the earl's protective stance, wondering if there was a specific reason for it, or if it was because of the young woman's injury. Knowing the earl would tell him when he was good and ready, Dermott turned his attention to the lass. He locked gazes with her and, for the life of him, couldn't think of anything to say. Sensing conversation might ease her worry over the cleansing and stitching of the wound in her head, he cast around for a topic that might distract her. Finally, his brain clicked into gear. "Well now, sure and ye picked a fine day for a stroll in the woods."

QUESTIONS SWIRLED IN her aching head, but no answers. Fighting to hold back her tears, she met the blond-haired giant's brilliant green gaze. Wondering what in the world she had been doing in the woods, she repeated her earlier question: "Why was I walking in the woods? Why Sussex?" She flinched as the doctor began to clean out the wound.

"Well now, there'll be plenty of time for those answers, lass. At the moment, ye're to be the guest of the earl and his countess. Ye have nothing to fear here at Lippincott Manor." Dermott nodded to the earl, who stood behind him.

Did Dermott hope that by answering her question, he would be able to distract her? He was mistaken—nothing would take her mind off the pain she would endure during the closing of the wound.

While she studied the earl, hoping to recognize him, she noted the concern in Dermott's green eyes. "Begging yer pardon for not properly introducing ye, lass. Earl Lippincott, please meet—" His eyes met hers, and he shook his head. "Forgive me, lass, but would ye mind if we called ye Miss Amber until ye recall yer name?"

She blinked, then frowned when she struggled to remember, but obviously could not recall her own name. "Er... No. May I ask, why Amber?"

"'Tis the color of yer eyes, lass."

"Oh." *Good Lord!* She hadn't even remembered the color of her own eyes! As shock filtered through her, the ache in her head trebled.

"Well now, I'm thinking Miss Amber is a lovely name, though Miss Brown would do in a pinch."

Brown? He stared at her head, and she realized it must be the color of her hair. She absorbed the fact that she had amber eyes and brown hair, immensely grateful to her rescuer for imparting those facts without questioning her. It would have only added to her frustration, confusion, and embarrassment.

Why couldn't she remember anything? Why was she in Sussex, and why on foot? Was there nothing she could recall?

Dermott leaned close, looked into her eyes, and said, "Hang on to me, lass. I won't be letting ye go."

Gratitude swept up from her toes. The kindness and strength of the gentle giant holding her hand pulled her to him. She studied the strong line of his jaw, the crooked line of his nose—he was handsome despite the slight flaw. Needing his reassurance, she asked, "Do you promise?"

"Aye, lass," his deep voice rumbled, soothing her, pulling her inexorably closer. "Ye have me word. Close yer eyes now, else they'll cross if ye try to watch while the physician closes yer wound."

His attempt at humor lifted one of the heavy weights holding her down. Though she did not laugh, she did as he bade her and was amazed to realize the strength evident in his callused hand holding hers did ease the worst of her fears—needles. She thoroughly disliked them, and though she tried not to, she flinched when she felt the sharp point pierce her skin.

"Easy, *mo ghrá*—hold tight to me hands now. Ye need to be still. 'Twill be over before ye know it."

Though the physician worked efficiently and quickly, her head swam as she felt each prick of the needle and tug of the boiled threads, pulling the wound closed. The image it conjured in her brain had her heart pounding and her breaths coming in short, sharp pants.

The last words she heard before giving in to the darkness were those of her rescuer. "Hang on, Amber-lass—'tis nearly finished."

CHAPTER TWO

Dermott kept his expression neutral as he knocked on the earl's sitting room door. The last thing he needed to do was tip off the earl that his mind was on the lass he'd rescued just past dawn that morning and not on the reasons he'd found her running for her life in the first place.

"Enter." The earl was standing in front of the window with his hands clasped behind his back when Dermott stepped into the room.

"Ye wanted to speak to me, yer lordship?"

Lippincott turned around. "Close the door."

Dermott ignored the frustration filling him at the lack of information he'd been able to obtain, and wondered if the lass's condition had worsened since he left her to patrol the perimeter of the estate. "Have ye received a missive from His Grace?"

The earl gave a slight shake of his head. "I received a message from an acquaintance of mine. Lord Eggerton has asked for my assistance."

The name was unfamiliar. Dermott didn't ask, though he silently wondered why the earl was speaking to him about Eggerton's request instead of his cousin Sean, who was head of the duke's guard at Lippincott Manor. He squared his shoulders. "Whatever the task is, ye know ye can count on me." Lippincott didn't respond at first, and a troubling thought occurred to

Dermott. "Does this have to do with the lass I rescued?"

The earl met his gaze. "I do not know yet. Moments ago, I received a missive from Gavin King. There was a duel this morning… Lord Eggerton is dead."

Dermott sensed the missive from the Bow Street runner and Eggerton were linked somehow. "Can ye still honor Lord Eggerton's request?"

"As it seems Eggerton's request was his last, I intend to. It's a tangled tale, and one I'll have to eventually share with my wife, but…"

Dermott knew without being told. "Lord Eggerton is an acquaintance from the time before ye met or married her ladyship."

Lippincott inclined his head. Clasping his hands behind his back again, he began to pace. The earl was troubled, and Dermott wanted to do whatever he could to help.

"I hold ye in the highest regard, yer lordship, as I do His Grace. Ye can trust that I won't speak of whatever is weighing ye down beyond this room…unless ye give me leave to."

The earl stopped in front of the fireplace. "Eggerton and I were part of a small group that used to spend our evenings in gaming hells. He is—*was*—nearly twenty years my senior. I knew he was a widower and had a daughter of marriageable age. I lost touch with Eggerton once my brother assumed the dukedom and helped me see the error of my ways. I left that life behind. I haven't heard from him since… Until today."

Dermott knew it was important to let the earl continue—he'd have a chance to ask questions later. He nodded, and the earl raked a hand through his hair.

"Apparently Eggerton's missive was delayed. He requested that I shelter his daughter Georgiana, should she arrive on my doorstep sometime this morning."

Dermott was about to ask what he meant by *should* she arrive, but the earl held up a hand and said, "That's not all. Eggerton implored me to refuse Viscount Trenchert entrance to the manor if he arrived looking for Georgiana."

"Do ye know the viscount?"

The earl nodded. "Aye. Before I get into that, there's more—and it's a bloody mess. Eggerton gambled away his fortune, London town house, Eggerton Hall here in Sussex, Georgiana's dowry, and promised her hand in marriage to Trenchert."

Dermott knew without asking that the earl was more than familiar with the viscount in question—and sensed none of it was good. "One of the footmen we've trained can assume me shift guarding the perimeter while I search for the lass. As ye haven't met her, do ye know what she looks like?"

Lippincott scrubbed a hand over his face, and Dermott's gut roiled as acid sluiced through it at the telling action. "Eggerton added a description so I would recognize her, knowing we had never met."

Dermott tamped down the unease snaking through him as the earl's gaze locked on his.

"Georgiana has light brown hair, amber eyes, and stands about five feet, four inches tall. She'd be wearing a dark blue gown, burgundy coat, and carrying a small leather portmanteau."

Dermott's jaw clenched as worry lanced through him. "Well now, at least now we know who the lass I rescued was running from…Viscount Trenchert! But where was her carriage, coachman, or footman? Why was she all alone?"

Lippincott frowned. "That's one of the things we need to find out, along with whether or not Trenchert has followed her. Trenchert Manor is in Sussex, as is the viscount's newly acquired estate—Eggerton Hall."

Dermott frowned. "What do ye think happened?"

"If I were her father, I would have had her leave London and avoid Trenchert at all costs. Eggerton is"—the earl paused to correct himself a second time—"er, *was* an excellent shot. He obviously hoped to return from the duel victorious, as he mentioned he would collect his daughter this afternoon."

"Will ye wait until she regains her memory before ye tell

her?"

"I'm not certain. I have already sent a missive to the doctor and plan to discuss it with Aurelia before I make my decision. We need to handle this situation with utmost caution and care. My wife's help will be invaluable, as she will be able to see this from Georgiana's point of view and help me wade through this disaster. If Trenchert finds out Eggerton's daughter is here and comes to collect her, he is well within his rights to demand that we turn her over to him."

Dermott disagreed. "Only if his lordship scribbled the wager on a bit of foolscap."

The earl's pained expression conveyed what Dermott feared. His next words confirmed it: "Knowing the viscount, he would insist he had the wager in writing before accepting it."

Dermott didn't give a bloody damn about the wager! He had never met a woman who grabbed hold of his heart with a look before, nor had he been asked to extract a lass whose very existence was tangled in such a web before. He'd made a vow to the duke and the earl—and he would die to uphold that vow. But he'd made another vow at dawn that he confessed to his cousins: he would protect the lass with his life. From all that the earl had confided, Dermott would never let the viscount near her. He did not give a bloody damn if her father had wagered her hand in marriage to the man. Trenchert would never lay a finger on her while Dermott had breath left in his body.

"Ye can count on me to protect the lass, yer lordship. Is there anything else ye need from me?"

The earl stared at the missives on his desk. "I'll speak to the others. As you were the one who found Lord Eggerton's daughter and brought her here, and she seems to trust you, I wanted you to understand the situation we are facing and be prepared to act accordingly. We will be able to hold off the viscount for a short time, on the outside chance he discovers Miss Eggerton is here."

"Do ye want me to switch with Flaherty? He's guarding the

interior."

Lippincott nodded. "Aye, and ask to take the next few shifts indoors. I want Miss Eggerton to remain as calm as possible as she heals. It is obvious that she trusts you."

"Ye're hoping her memory returns quickly."

"The physician said it could happen at any time. Mrs. Wyatt has been plying her with weak tea, broth, and calf's foot jelly. She and Mrs. Jones have been taking turns sitting with her."

"And her ladyship?"

The earl's expression lightened as he answered, "Aurelia has loaned her something to wear—the poor young woman's clothes were damp and bloodstained. Have we been able to recover her portmanteau?"

"Nay." The fact that it was not where she had dropped it was worrisome. Someone had collected it. Was that someone working for the viscount? "If that is all, I'll let Flaherty know of the shift change."

"Excellent."

Dermott was reaching for the door when Lippincott added, "Stop in and see how Miss Eggerton is doing. A brief visit from you may lift her spirits and jog her memory."

Dermott frowned. "What if she remembers scaling that wall and jumping but not the rest?"

"She may remember what happened to her father's coach…and mayhap what happened to his coachman and footman."

He nodded to the earl. "I'll speak to Flaherty first."

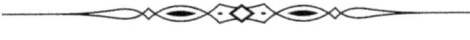

CHAPTER THREE

DERMOTT KNOCKED ON the doorframe and waited for Mrs. Jones to give him permission to enter. "Thank ye, Mrs. Jones. His lordship has given me leave to visit with ye, Amberlass, as I'll be switching with Flaherty and guarding the interior for the next few days."

The shadows in the lass's eyes lifted. Was it due to seeing him or the prospect of having him nearby?

"Do you switch shifts often?"

Her question did not surprise him. "Whenever the need arises. As it happens, his lordship thought ye'd feel more comfortable with meself than either of me cousins." A faint pink blush stained her pale cheeks, adding much-needed color to her lovely face. He planned to stop in often, mayhap prodding her memory to return. "Well now, Mrs. Jones, I'm thinking the lass isn't averse to spending a few minutes chatting with the likes of meself."

The housekeeper smiled. "Charmer. Why don't you have a seat next to Miss Amber, while I speak to the footman stationed in the hallway?" Addressing Miss Amber, the housekeeper added, "If you need me, I'll be right outside."

Dermott was more than pleased when the lass nodded without taking her gaze off him. Her undivided attention would make things all that much easier when he told her of his vow to the duke, the earl...and to her. But not yet. Not now. There was a battle to be waged with an unscrupulous viscount, and the matter of restoring her father's honor. It wasn't impossible—the difficulty would be with the lass suffering from her head wound and her loss of memory. They would have to use care, or the results could be disastrous.

"Thank you, Mrs. Jones."

The lass's voice reminded him of the dew-laden faery flowers in his ma's garden, and the sound they made as they swayed and danced when a whisper of an early morning breeze swept past them.

"Is something wrong, Mr. O'Malley?"

He sat on the chair beside the cot and studied her closely. "Ye have a bit more color in yer cheeks. Could it be that ye're happy to see me?" Her laughter reminded him of tiny bells tinkling. Entranced, he leaned closer. "Ye remind me of the *fae*, lass."

Her eyes widened and pleasure shone bright in their amber depths. "Surely not one of the *pookas*."

"Nay, large, scary beasts that they are," he agreed.

"Mayhap a wood sprite or dryad?"

"Well now, I had been thinking wood sprite when first I saw ye coming out of the forest, though ye were wearing a burgundy-colored coat—and not brown or green, which would have disguised ye," Dermott admitted. "But ye could not be one of the tree gods with yer angel's face and faery wings."

To his delight, she glanced over her shoulder. "Did I sprout wings when I hit my head?"

His laughter seemed to please the lass as she smiled up at him. "Yer smile adds to the beauty of yer laughter, Amber-lass." He caught himself before blurting one of the questions weighing heavy on his mind: how old was she? Why had no man offered for her hand before now? And why in the bloody hell had her da been compelled to wager his homes, his fortune, her dowry, and his daughter's hand on the turn of a card?

Her smile slipped. "I'm sorry. I did not mean my question to offend you, Mr. O'Malley."

"'Tis just O'Malley, lass. Forgive me, I was thinking deep thoughts just now."

She drew in a breath and slowly exhaled. "I would never want to give you reason to think badly of me, Mr....er...O'Malley."

He brushed a lock of pale brown silk out of her eyes and tucked it behind her ear. Every blessed thing about the lass reminded him of the faery folk. He didn't know whether to thank his ma for filling his head with tales handed down generation to generation...or to curse her for it.

"Is it something else then that has you frowning at me?"

Dermott immediately straightened, squared his shoulders, and reassured her, "Nay, lass, me mind took a quick journey back home just now. 'Tis half a decade or more since I've been able to visit."

Her eyes filled, and she blinked, causing a tear to cling to her lashes before slowly trickling along the curve of her cheek.

He captured it on the tip of his finger, staring at the moisture it left behind. "Don't feel sorry for the likes of me. Ma keeps me informed of the goings-on at home, and I do the same when I send me wages to her every month."

Another tear escaped. Unable to stop himself, he reached for her hand. "Why are ye crying, lass?"

Eyes that held a dozen secrets beseeched him to understand. "It's just a feeling I get every time you mention your mum." She rubbed her free hand over her heart.

He sensed her mind was struggling to clear itself. A deeper thought occurred. When she regained her memory, would she mourn the loss of her own ma all over again? He'd have to ask his lordship how long ago the lass's ma had passed on. That way, he might be able to offer words of comfort.

The stark realization that she had lost her da too hit him. He could not envision losing both of his parents—losing his da had gutted him. He hoped the lass's heart was strong enough to handle the double blow when her memory returned.

O'Malley needed to distract her. "Have ye had any other thoughts ye could not explain since last we spoke?"

An adorable frown line appeared between her wispy brows. "You'll think I've not only lost my memory, but my mind," she confessed.

"Ah, lass, I'd never be thinking that. Tell me what's troubling ye."

Her gaze collided with his, and unbidden, her worry seeped into him. Was she remembering bits and pieces of her last conversation with her da? "I'm either dreaming things or remembering them."

"What makes ye say that?"

She bit her plump bottom lip, and he had to call on his control to hide his reaction. God help him, the need to give in and sip from her lips was overwhelming. What flavor would he find when she allowed him to sample a taste?

The lass sighed, answering, "It had to be a dream."

"And why would that be?" She licked her lips, and he had to fight not to groan out loud. God, he wanted the lass in his arms and her lips on his...more than was wise. He reined in his wayward thoughts and dug deep for his ironclad control. With it back in place, his patience returned. "Amber-lass?"

Various emotions swept through her lovely eyes before one took hold...sadness. "Because my father promised Mum he'd never gamble again...the night she passed away." She paused. "I cannot recall when that was, but have a feeling in my heart that I cannot dismiss. I feel it could have happened and wasn't a dream."

Ah, she either remembered, or dreamed that her mum was gone. The hard hit to his gut at all the lass had endured, and yet still had to face all over again when she remembered her past, was unexpected. He cleared his throat to speak. "I wouldn't worry over it now, lass. Rest and more than an invalid's diet is what ye need."

She blinked, and the sadness abated. "The physician prescribed an invalid's diet for a sennight." She wrinkled her brow and confessed, "I know it is not allowed, but I would dearly love something sweet to eat." Her smile bloomed slowly as her cheeks pinkened again. "Do you think you might convince Mrs. Wyatt that I'm well enough to have just one tiny scone and a cup of strong tea?"

He was willing to give his life to protect her—and may yet be asked to do so. Her small request was well within his power to grant. "Well now, as it happens, Mrs. Wyatt owes me a favor. I'd be willing to trade it for a scone and tea for ye, if ye'd like."

Her radiant smile nearly blinded him as his heart burst from his chest and landed on the floor at her feet. He rubbed a hand over where his heart used to reside and dared a glance down to see if he was bleeding. *No blood.* 'Twas just his imagination.

"Are you all right, O'Malley? You've gone pale."

Her worry enabled him to set his fanciful thoughts aside, knowing what he envisioned could never happen...unless the *fae* were involved. He stood and straightened to his full height. "Just an empty stomach, reminding me 'tis time to eat. I'll see about procuring the tea and scones I promised ye, lass." He glanced over his shoulder and tilted his head to listen to the conversation still going on in the hallway. "Best not let Mrs. Jones know what we're up to."

She nodded, held her hand to her heart, and promised, "I won't say a word."

"There's a lass," he murmured, pressing a kiss to the top of her head. "Rest until I return."

He would later swear he felt her eyes following him from the room. He thought that mayhap the lass was a bit taken with him. Much to his delight, lasses had been falling at his feet the whole of his life...that was, until he signed on as one of the duke's guard. He had not had the time, nor inclination, to catch any of the lasses following him around since then. Mayhap 'twas time to let a lass catch him. But as he thought of the woman with the entrancing amber eyes, reality hit him like a blow to the gut. *She's* betrothed...though her hand in marriage was wagered, not promised.

Anger tore from his aching stomach to his throat. Curling his right hand into a fist, he pounded it against the wall. "That's for ye, Trenchert." He punched the wall again, punctuating each word: "Bloody. Buggering. Bastard!" The footman stationed in the middle of the hallway stared wide-eyed at Dermott, who paused in front of the man. "He'll will never touch one hair on the lass's head!"

The footman heartily agreed, "Never!"

Satisfied that he'd spoken the promise aloud, punctuated it with his fist, and had the footman's agreement, Dermott added, "Or me name isn't Dermott *fecking* O'Malley!"

The footman grinned. "I thought that was Flaherty's middle name."

Dermott snorted with laughter. "Nay, 'tis Seamus *flaming* Flaherty."

The footman was laughing when he asked, "What is your cousin Sean's middle name?"

Without missing a beat, as he strode down the hall to the kitchen doorway, Dermott called out, "Sean *bloody* O'Malley!" He stepped into the heat of the kitchen—and the glower on Mrs. Wyatt's face.

She wielded a huge serving spoon as if it were a blade, pointing it at Dermott's gut. "Language, Mr. O'Malley!"

He felt his face flush, as he could imagine it was his ma standing there ready to smack him upside the head with her favorite serving spoon. "Begging yer pardon, Mrs. Wyatt. 'Twas just—"

"I excused it earlier because of the prodigious amount of blood while you were keeping pressure on the wound in Miss Amber's forehead. But that danger has passed, and the gash in her head tended to by the physician. You have no reason to use foul language now, and I want none of your excuses. Be about your business."

Dermott felt like he was a lad again, being corrected by his ma. Mrs. Wyatt was right—he needed to take more care with his words when inside his lordship's household and near the ladies on his staff. "I begged yer pardon—what else to I have to do to receive yer forgiveness?"

"You could stop swearing, for one."

"I'll do me best," he promised with a hand to his heart, and immediately thought of the lass. She'd done the same just now.

The cook turned her back on him and stirred what he hoped was the filling for her hearty meat pies. He was partial to them, and was about to say as much when she looked over her shoulder and demanded, "What do you want?"

She'd never spoken to him that way before. Had his propensity to insert swear words bothered her that much? He never swore in front of his lordship or her ladyship. Not that that was an excuse for doing so in front of Mrs. Wyatt. He'd been in the hallway at the time—not in her domain—but well within her hearing range.

"Mrs. Wyatt, I'm devastated if I've injured yer sensibilities by cursing within yer hearing." She whirled around, anger in her eyes, and he added, "I beg ye to forgive me."

The cook lowered the spoon she had raised over her head. "Try to use some discretion. Her ladyship could have been in the kitchen. She has been known to do so a few times a week, you know."

Chastised, he bowed his head. "It is just as important that I remember yer tender ears are averse to hearing such, too. It won't happen again."

She placed the spoon on the table beside the stove and brushed her hands on her apron. "Well, aren't you going to ask me?"

He tilted his head, considering his words carefully. Finally, he said, "Ask ye what?"

Mrs. Wyatt blew a strand of hair out of her eyes and huffed. "Yes, I baked two batches of cream scones, and yes, I'll still save one or two for you."

Warmth filled him as he grinned at the cook. "Ye're an angel,

Mrs. Wyatt."

She shook her head and motioned for him to be on his way. When he didn't move, the cook asked, "Now what is it?"

He glanced around them before leaning close to conspiratorially whisper, "The lass, Miss Amber, is pining for a bite of one of yer delicious cream scones, and a wee drop of strong tea. She's famished."

Mrs. Wyatt crossed her arms and harumphed. "Scones?"

"Aye, and tea. The poor lass's stomach was rumbling by the time I left her."

"It's likely she has a concussion."

"Her eyes are clear, and she's alert."

"She was unconscious when you brought her to us, and cannot remember her name," the cook reminded him.

"Three-quarters of a scone," he bargained.

"And what, pray tell, would I do with the other quarter?"

"Ye have no worries. I can take care of that for ye."

She chuckled. "I just bet you will, but we cannot take the chance. Doctor's orders."

"All right, then. Half a scone, and tea the way ye like it, not too strong, not too weak. Though I do not believe the physician would approve of yer adding a splash of cream and spoon of sugar in her tea."

Her smiled bloomed. "You know how I like my tea?"

"Aye." He walked over to where she stood by the stove and returned her smile. "Thank ye for always taking care of meself and me cousins. Ye don't have to bake the extra scones ye leave on the sideboard for us to tuck into our pockets, or the cake ye hide in the wardrobe...but ye do. We're grateful. *I'm* grateful."

She flushed and patted him on the arm. "There is nothing like cooking for a hungry, appreciative man." She sighed. "Charmer. Half a scone with tea—not too weak and not too strong—but nothing else in her tea until the end of the week."

He bent down and brushed a kiss to her cheek. "Ye're an angel, Mrs. Wyatt."

She smiled as she made shooing motions. "Out of my kitchen. I have a tea tray to prepare for Miss Amber."

"Angel," he repeated as he retraced his steps to the room at the end of the hallway. The footman was waiting for him at his assigned post and asked, "How do you get Mrs. Wyatt to bake scones for you? She doesn't for the rest of us."

"Have any of ye stopped by the kitchen on yer way to yer posts and said a kind word or two, or complimented her on the meals she prepares for ye?"

The footman stared in the direction of the kitchen and shook his head.

"Start with greeting her when ye're on yer way to yer first shift of the day. Little by little, add in kind words and a smile or two. I wouldn't be surprised if she offers to save a scone or two for ye."

"Do you know, I never thought about complimenting her before, though Mrs. Wyatt is an excellent cook."

"Well, there ye have it. The next chance ye have to speak to her, I'd start with a compliment."

"Thank you, O'Malley."

"Me pleasure!" As Dermott approached the room where the lass was resting, he wondered what it would be like if he were married to a woman who could cook like Ma or Mrs. Wyatt. He was muttering about going down on one knee, winsome lasses, and marriage when he heard footsteps echoing in the servants' stairwell behind the closed door. He paused so he would not startle whoever was about to open the door into the hallway, and shook his head. *Marriage?* The thought was mind-boggling. Could he balance working for the duke and marriage like his brothers, Patrick and Finn, had? Should he speak to the earl first, or the lass?

I should wait until she has her memory back.

The housekeeper opened the door to the servants' staircase and smiled at him as the idea of wooing and wedding the lass filled him. The utter rightness of the feelings rioting inside of him—and the thought of marrying the courageous lass—had every drop of blood draining from his brain.

She hurried over to where he stood. "Is anything wrong, O'Malley?"

He met the housekeeper's questioning gaze. "Everything is fine, Mrs. Jones. I'm thinking the lass is starting to heal. Must be yer excellent care, and that of Mrs. Wyatt."

She smiled. "That is wonderful news. I did notice she seemed to become more focused on her surroundings the longer I sat with her. His lordship will be pleased."

"Aye, I was thinking the same meself. I'm going to have a quick word with the lass before I resume me post. If ye have need of me, or if the lass seems troubled for any reason, have one of the footmen find me. I'll be on the third floor for the next little while."

"Of course, O'Malley. Thank you."

As he watched the housekeeper make her way down the hallway, he wondered how quickly the lass's mind would snap into place. The physician had said it could happen any time. Could that be in a fortnight, two days, or two hours?

Resigned not to have the answer, he sighed and summoned up a smile for the woman who was as brave as his brothers or cousins. She just did not realize it, nor would he be telling her so until she had her memory back and remembered who she was.

He knocked on the doorframe and entered the room. "Ye're in luck, lass. Mrs. Wyatt has agreed to a smidge of one of her delicious cream scones."

The lass's smile was blinding, the look in her amber eyes hopeful. "And the tea?"

The poor woman had been through so much and had so much more to deal with when her mind cleared. He hoped she'd be strong enough to handle the double blow—her father was dead, and she was betrothed to Viscount Trenchert.

He clenched his hands into fists at his sides, and the lass immediately looked away. "It doesn't matter about the tea, O'Malley. You have already procured the promise of something sweet. I know the calf's foot jelly is good for me." She paused and cringed as a shudder racked her slender frame. "But the *taste!*"

Dermott was not immune to her reaction to the dreaded remedy the duke's cook and housekeeper favored. Nor was he immune to the entreaty in her soft voice and the way the hope faded when he did not answer right away. Needing to keep her hope alive, even if it was for such a trivial matter as the earl's cook agreeing to sneaking in a cup of stronger tea, he said, "Don't fret, lass—Mrs. Wyatt has agreed to a send in a stronger cup of tea to go with the bit of scone."

Pleasure shone from the depths of her whiskey-colored eyes and struck him dead center in his chest. He could feel her emotions as if they were his own. His brain struggled with the why of it, while his heart accepted what he should have known from the start. The lass was the other half of his heart.

Patience, his heart soothed. *Bollocks!* his mind countered.

His emotions tugging him in different directions, Dermott had no idea what else to say. He bowed to her, spun on his heel, and left the room. Before he reached the door to the servants' staircase, he heard his name being called.

Stifling a groan, he paused and glanced over his shoulder, and noticed the cook beckoning to him from the other end of the hallway. He retraced his steps, ignoring the powerful need to peek into the room and drink in the beauty of the lass resting there, and his long strides soon had him stepping over the threshold into the kitchen.

The scent of scones warm from the oven felt like one of his ma's hugs. "I have a confession to make, Mrs. Wyatt, but if ye breathe a word of what I'm about to tell ye, I'll deny it to me dying day."

She nodded. "You have my word, O'Malley. What do you want me to keep a secret?"

He glanced over one shoulder and then the other. Neither of the footmen were close enough to overhear what he was about to say. He leaned close and whispered, "Yer scones taste better than me ma's."

The cook's eyes widened as her smile brightened. "Thank you, O'Malley. That is high praise coming from you." She walked over to the cupboard on the wall opposite the oven and took a linen from the folded pile. Without saying a word, she placed it on the table, put two scones in the middle of the cloth, wrapped it up, and slipped it into her apron pocket. Patting it gently, she said, "When Mrs. Jones arrives to tell me it's my turn to sit with Miss Amber, I'll bring a tray with a cup of broth, a small bowl of calf's foot jelly, and a small pot of stronger tea."

O'Malley grinned. "Ye won't mention the scones in yer pocket?"

She leaned close and whispered, "Not if you don't."

He pressed a kiss to her cheek and bowed. "Ye have me eternal thanks."

"Oh, and what has Mrs. Wyatt done to deserve such?" the housekeeper asked as she entered the kitchen from the other doorway.

Without missing a beat, Dermott lifted his hands—each one holding a freshly baked scone.

Mrs. Jones chuckled. "Never mind, O'Malley. Everyone knows you have a fondness for scones."

"I have a tray of cream tarts and another batch of scones set aside for her ladyship," Mrs. Wyatt told the housekeeper. "Her ladyship is hopeful his lordship will be able to join her for tea this afternoon."

"Why don't I mention it to his lordship on me way to me post?" Dermott said. "Oh, and by the way, Miss Amber is waiting for ye."

The cook nodded. "Thank you, O'Malley."

With that, the women parted—Mrs. Jones to speak to the countess, and Mrs. Wyatt to speak to the lass…and slip her a scone or two. Satisfied all was as right as it could be—for the moment—Dermott stepped back into the hallway and headed for the door to the main part of the house.

He paused to deliver the message about afternoon tea to the earl. They spoke for a few moments before he bowed and walked to the main staircase. Taking the stairs two at a time, he reached his post on the third floor a second or two late. There was no urgent reason that he should worry over not arriving at the exact moment in time his shift began, but he would make sure it did not happen again. *I cannot let the lass distract me from me duties.* Shaking his head, he realized it would take a concerted effort on his part to keep his head on straight where the lovely lass was concerned.

"Lord, 'tis O'Malley again. I may need yer help with one more thing…"

Chapter Four

Viscount Trenchert crumpled the missive in his fist and stormed out of his study. He did not say a word to his butler, communicating his displeasure with a look. The servant was half the viscount's age, and well aware of his temper. He stepped back quickly, out of the line of fire.

"Where is the messenger?"

"Waiting in the anteroom by the rear entrance, your lordship. Shall I bring him to your study?"

The viscount stared at his servant, wondering yet again why he put up with the puffed up, self-important buffoon.

"Your lordship?"

Where in the bloody hell was his intended? "There is no time!" he barked. Somehow Eggerton had had a contingency plan. Had Eggerton had an epiphany, or a vision of his demise, that had him making arrangements, should he not survive their early morning meeting on the field of honor?

Honor! Ridiculous term for the field where two rivals met to solve disagreements, quell gossip, or protect a woman's reputation. Trenchert had fought and won every time he stepped through the morning mist onto the grassy field of judgment. It appealed to him, reminding him of the medieval ordeal of trial by combat—without the actual fighting. He used his brain and his ability to ensure ahead of time that no one would betray him, nor would anyone mention the fact that he always turned on the fifteenth count, shooting his challenger, or rival, in the back. All it took was the appropriate amount of coin. No one had dared in the past, and he did not see it as a problem now.

"Shall I send him on his way?" the butler helpfully asked.

"Nay, I want a word with him. I am expecting another missive to arrive shortly. See to it that I receive it the moment it arrives!"

The viscount stalked to the door to the servants' side of the house. He did not bother to greet the cook, or any of his staff, though he did cast a glance at the newest scullery maid. She looked ripe for the plucking. He leered at her before continuing along the hallway to the room by the rear entrance.

He entered the room and took the young man's measure with one glance and mentally found him wanting. *Lazy oaf.* After he found out where Miss Eggerton had disappeared, he would replace the messenger.

The lad scrambled to attention. "Is there a reply, your lordship?"

"Go back to your post, and report back to me when Eggerton's daughter returns." The young man hesitated, irritating the viscount. He sneered. "Is that too difficult to remember?"

"Nay."

He stared at the messenger, willing him to remember to show deference. The youth's Adam's apple bobbed up and down. Excellent—he hadn't lost his ability to silently intimidate.

"Er... Nay, your lordship."

The messenger hesitated for another moment, but the viscount refused to hand him a coin for delivering the missive that would force him to resort to his secondary plan. Trenchert would have to track down the chit himself. He spun on his heel and retraced his steps, slowing when he spied the scullery maid in the pantry with her back to the door. He slipped inside, locked the door, and stalked toward her. "I have been waiting for this moment, precious."

The maid spun around, hand to her throat, horror in her eyes.

He backed her up against the wall, clapped his hand over her mouth, and told her in detail what he planned to do to her. When she struggled, he rasped, "That's it, precious, fight me—the rougher the better."

>>><<<

A FEW HOURS later, the encounter in the pantry long forgotten, the second missive arrived. He didn't bother to have the messenger wait. The sender would not be waiting for a reply. He broke the wax seal and smiled. "Well, well, it appears as if my bride-to-be has not only run away…but disappeared. Plucky chit."

She must have left sometime after her father returned home, between midnight and one o'clock this morning. If the unlucky lord had planned for every contingency, he would have had a carriage ready and waiting to whisk his daughter to their country estate.

Did the fool forget Trenchert had an estate in Sussex not far from Eggerton Hall? He leaned on the mahogany desk, steepled his hands, and tapped his fingers together as he considered the time involved to reach the countryside. With two swift changes of horse, she could have reached her destination, but what of the servants? Would Eggerton have had time to warn them of the situation?

Damn the man's hide! Trenchert should have kicked the lord before leaving him to bleed out in the grass. But he would not have achieved his unblemished record on the dueling field if he had not taken every precaution to leave as quickly as he arrived—with the way made clear by the amount of coin that had changed hands to ensure his escape.

Leaning back in his chair, he contemplated his options. He could shell out more coin and send a man to Sussex with orders to drag his reluctant bride-to-be from the shelter of her family estate back to London. The other would be to order his carriage made ready and go after her himself.

He slowly smiled. It would be more cost effective, and guarantee that Eggerton's daughter would not give him the slip. He'd wasted enough time manipulating the deceased lord into the card game that cost him his homes, his fortune, his daughter, and her dowry...and ultimately his life.

His decision made, Trenchert rang for his butler. When the servant arrived, the viscount instructed him, "Have the carriage made ready and my valet pack my bag. I shall be leaving for Sussex in forty-five minutes."

"At once, your lordship."

He did not bother to reply—everyone in his employ knew he disliked conversing with his staff and that punctuality was essential to their continued employment.

A short while later, his carriage was on the road heading south to his country home in Sussex. Leaning back against the leather squabs, he could not relax as anger simmered inside of him. He thoroughly disliked having his plans thwarted. As he pondered the petite beauty with the entrancing amber eyes, his thoughts changed direction, and he imagined the pleasure that awaited when he finally got his hands on her.

Deflowering his enemy's daughter would be worth the wait.

CHAPTER FIVE

"Ah, O'Malley." Lippincott waved Dermott into the study. "I was about to send for you."

"Expected as much, yer lordship, as I've eyes and ears everywhere and heard a messenger arrived. Is it the missive ye've been expecting from Bow Street?"

The earl held it up. "Aye." He broke the wax seal and read the short note. "Apparently, Trenchert has never lost a duel." Lippincott frowned. "Though, rumor has it, not because he is an excellent shot."

Dermott blew out the breath he'd drawn in. "There's another possibility—one neither of us would ever consider. He either had someone lying in wait for his opponent to arrive and ambush him, or the viscount never waited for the full count to turn and fire."

Lippincott nodded. "Given the urgency of the matter, King and the duke's London man-of-affairs Captain Coventry rallied and have culled the information we need." His gaze met Dermott's. "They have pieced together what appears to be Trenchert's murderous past. No one has ever uttered a word about the outcome of a duel involving him before. Once they dug into the particulars of the viscount's past dawn appointments, it has come to light that the same seconds and physician have always been in attendance."

"Well now, yer lordship, wouldn't ye want to have a physician well known to you on hand if ye were the one meeting an opponent over a brace of pistols? One experienced in dealing with the damage a lead ball can do. I would prefer if the physician had served as a surgeon in His Majesty's military."

"I would too—however, it is not only the number of duels he has fought, but also the fact that the viscount has been the one to challenge his opponents. Every time."

"For a variety of offenses or slurs?"

"Nay," the earl replied. "Every man accused the viscount of cheating...at cards."

O'Malley's anger surged dangerously close to the surface. "The man has no honor, and the lass is caught in a web of lies and deceit by her own father's weakness—gambling!"

The earl walked over to the window overlooking the gardens and clasped his hands behind his back, staring without seeing the beauty beyond the window. "I wonder if she knew about her father's part in this whole affair."

"I cannot say for certain, yer lordship, but if it was me ma, she'd have known Da was involved in wagering. Then again, me da was smart enough not to. Ma would have skinned him alive."

The dark look on the earl's face disappeared as he turned around and walked over to his desk. He lifted the missive and handed it to Dermott to read.

He scanned the note and handed it back. "Will ye be sending a reply to Captain Coventry advising that ye'll be sending a missive to King to find out if he was called to investigate any of the deaths resulting from the viscount's duels?"

"I was about to," Lippincott replied. "However, I did not want to arouse any suspicion that someone I was acquainted with challenged, or was challenged to, a duel. It *is* illegal, you know."

Dermott agreed, "Aye, that it is, but that won't stop a man from protecting his wife's honor." His gut roiled as another possibility occurred to him. "Nor an innocent young woman he has vowed to protect."

Lippincott was silent for long moments. "Aurelia would have my head on a platter if she found out."

Dermott met Lippincott's steady gaze. "I was referring to meself, yer lordship. Ye'd best be knowing that I made a vow when the lass was in me arms, blood seeping from the wound on her forehead. I vowed to protect her with me life. If I have to challenge the viscount to a duel, ye can be certain that I will!"

The earl inclined his head. "It seems to be an occupational hazard. All of the men in my brother's guard have rescued women in their darkest hours, saving them from ignoble ends. And each and every one have vowed to protect the women, adding them to the long list of those already under their protection before marrying them. How many women at last count?"

Dermott frowned as he started counting in his head, but the image of the lass he rescued distracted him. *"Bollocks!* I lost count when I forgot to add those of the duke's staff in Cornwall. I have to start over."

Lippincott chuckled. "Don't bother. I know it's not just my wife, our son, and myself that are under your protection here at Lippincott Manor, O'Malley. It's the staff and tenant farmers, and as of your dawn rescue, the daughter of a former friend from my checkered past. Eggerton was well liked and generous with others whenever fortune smiled upon him. I was floundering trying to find my way when I followed my eldest brother Oliver into the gaming hells. Thought I had found my path. In the aftermath of Oliver's death—his *murder*—it was Jared's immediate acceptance of the responsibility assuming the title that had me questioning my choices. He never wanted to be the duke—he preferred country life and working with his hands."

The earl raked a hand through his hair, and Dermott sensed the man still blamed himself for not stepping up and offering to help restore the fortune the fifth duke had gambled away.

Lippincott's next words confirmed it: "I should have done more to aid Jared when he spent hours poring over the accounts from all of the ducal properties, looking for ways to restore what had been a sizeable fortune."

"Ye cannot shoulder the blame for what was not yer doing, yer lordship. Though I'd never met the fifth duke, I knew of him by reputation. Ye're nothing like him, and more like His Grace than ye know."

"But I did not roll up my sleeves and spend every waking moment consulting with our solicitors, stewards…or tenant farmers. Jared did."

The bleak expression in the earl's eyes reminded Dermott of his ma the day he and Emmett announced their plans to follow their older brothers Finn and Patrick to England. The wages they sent home helped, as did the three men he heartily approved of who'd married their sisters and moved onto the farm. He and Emmett were able to board the boat with the faith that their wages would tip the scale so Ma wouldn't have to go to sleep each night worrying that she'd lose their great-grandda's legacy—their farm.

"Aye," Dermott agreed. "But I heard from me brother Patrick that His Grace was not only handling the duties of his new title, but the prospect of navigating Lady Phoebe's first Season. Thank goodness he met and married Her Grace when he did."

"Persephone has been a godsend to this family," Lippincott replied.

"Aye, yer lordship, but do not forget yer part in bringing the family name back to where it had been. Ye stepped in at a crucial time, and were there to save Lady Phoebe when that madman had a blade to her throat." Their eyes met, and understanding flowed between the men. "I may not have been in the same position as yerself, yer lordship, but when it became obvious to me that our failing farm needed more than me brothers' wages, Emmett and I made the difficult decision to follow in their footsteps."

"I never asked," the earl said, "but who replaced you working on the farm?"

"Ye may remember that we have three sisters." The earl

inclined his head, and Dermott continued, "Their husbands, good men that they are, moved in with Ma to work the farm. With the wages the four of us have sent home, our brothers-in-law have been able to add rooms onto the cottage and build two more. When help is needed at harvest time, they call on our Mulcahy cousins, who have a farm nearby."

"In times of crisis, families need to be able to count on one another. I realized that I had a skill Jared could benefit from—my ability to move about in Society and rub elbows with some of the more influential members of the *ton*. My brother spent as little time as possible in London. He had no use for it...until he inherited the title."

Dermott could not resist asking, "And who was it that broke His Grace's nose at Gentleman Jackson's?"

Lippincott's jaw dropped, and for a moment not a sound emerged, until he snorted with laughter. "It was an accident, as you well know."

"Oh aye, yer lordship. 'Tis a tale well known among the *ton*...and His Grace's guard."

The earl shook his head. "I'm not certain how we ended up discussing my brother's broken nose, when what I intended to do was to thank you for being the one to rescue Eggerton's daughter. I'm grateful, O'Malley. Although we will be facing accusations, most of them false, I know I can count on you, Sean, and Flaherty to guard Eggerton's daughter."

"Is there anything else you think we need to know about Viscount Trenchert?"

The intensity in Lippincott's gaze drilled into Dermott's. "He has no honor and is not to be trusted under any circumstances."

Dermott digested the information, then asked, "Have ye considered adding to the guard? Ye know their ladyships would be more than happy to spend time under one roof, while at the same time add to our number by two more: me cousins Michael O'Malley and James Garahan."

"I have been trying to decide how to approach the conversation with my wife, but am not sure I am ready for the discussions between Aurelia and Calliope discussing whose roof will continue to shelter Miss Eggerton," the earl said.

"Faith, but ye have the right of it. I'll be leaving that up to yerself and Viscount Chattsworth to handle. Their ladyships are a delight when they are trying to convince one another—and yerselves—to agree with them. I'm thinking it might be best not to move the lass. She has enough to deal with at the moment."

"Excellent point. Healing physically and worrying when her memory will return may delay her healing," Lippincott murmured.

"Aye." Dermott knew he should speak up about the vow he'd made carrying the lass to safety. He shifted from foot to foot and cleared his throat. "About that vow I confessed to ye…"

The earl raised one brow in silent question.

"I'll do me best not to kill the viscount." When the earl stared at him without speaking, Dermott added, "I made a decision as well when I was wrapping the makeshift bandage around Miss Amber's head." Uncertain how the earl would react, he waited for the man to speak.

Lippincott stared for a few moments before reminding him, "I understand, and before you bring up the subject, your cousin Sean has not had any difficulty protecting my family *and* his." A bit of the acid eating away at Dermott's gut calmed when the earl added, "I do not expect it to be an issue for you either. But keep in mind that she has lost her memory and may not remember who is friend or foe. I am not certain if she has any other family now that her father is dead."

Dermott nodded, and the earl continued, "She doesn't know who she is, who is chasing her, or why. Beyond that is that bloody scrap of foolscap where Eggerton agreed to turn over his home, his fortune, Georgiana's dowry, and his promise that she would wed Trenchert."

"I will keep all that in mind." Dermott paused, and although he had never asked the earl a personal question before, his heart and head were still trying to settle the matter of the instinctive need to protect the lass and not let her out of his sight. "I'm a bit flummoxed, and was wondering if I could ask ye a question."

"Of course," the earl replied.

"It has to do with matters of the...er...heart."

"After the number of bones you have broken, times you have been clubbed, stabbed, or shot protecting our family, you have more than earned the right to ask me anything."

"Thank ye, yer lordship." He rubbed a hand over his heart. "Before I ask, I need ye to understand, 'tis me heart that has me head muddled."

Lippincott nodded. "Having suffered the same not that long ago, I have a feeling it has to do with a woman."

Dermott sighed. "Forgive me for speaking of such, but do ye remember how ye felt the first time ye saw her ladyship?"

Lippincott slowly smiled. "Aye, as a matter of fact, it is a night I will never forget—for more than one reason. It was the night I met the love of my life—and the night that nearly cost my sister and me ours."

Neither spoke of the shared memory of the madman who'd burst into the duke's town house. Neither of them would ever forget that night and the chaos that followed.

Dermott cleared his throat. "'Tis plain to all who see ye together that ye've a deep and abiding affection for one another."

"Aurelia is not just my wife and mother of our son...she is my life."

Encouraged, O'Malley continued, "Ye can see from the way the lass is thinking deep thoughts that bits and pieces of her memory are coming back to her. Earlier, when I was sharing a story about me ma, she started to cry." His gut ached as he remembered her silent tears. "When I asked her what was wrong, she said she couldn't put it into words other than to say 'twas something she felt inside every time I mentioned me ma. Then the lass rubbed her hand over her heart. I'm thinking bits and pieces of her memory are closer to the surface, waiting for her to recall them."

Lippincott did not argue—a good sign that the earl accepted the latest addition to those Dermott would protect. His heart chose that moment to whisper of forever with the lass, but he could not afford to think about that now. He had a duty to do and a mystery to uncover—unless the lass remembered whom she was running from.

Dermott's gut told him it was Trenchert—or if not the viscount himself, one of his lackeys. It wasn't enough to think it... He would need proof before making any accusations.

"I know you won't pressure Miss Eggerton into remembering, but keep it in mind in your bid to get to the bottom of whom she was running from, and what led her to the desperate moment she jumped off that wall."

"Ye have me word, yer lordship, but I have a bad feeling in the pit of me stomach."

Lippincott nodded. "Aye. Trouble's coming."

Chapter Six

She woke with a start, chilled to the bone as the nightmare that woke her replayed in her mind. Brushing a lock of hair out of her eyes, she scooted until she was leaning against the lavender-scented pillows, trying to calm her racing heart. Was it truly a dream, or had she remembered something? For the life of her, she did not know.

Drawing in a deep breath and slowly exhaling, she looked around the bedchamber, starting in the corner by the door, asking herself if any of the furniture sparked a memory. The mahogany wardrobe and washstand were of the finest quality and highly polished. The lovely pink and white ceramic pitcher and bowl on top of the washstand were faintly familiar, but not quite right—

Blue and white flowers! Yes, that was it! The shape and floral pattern were familiar—it was the color that was different.

Nearly giddy at the fact that she recalled something from her shadowy past, she drew her knees up to her chest and hugged them. Putting her mind to it, ignoring the dull throb in her forehead, she closed her eyes. The memory of washing her face and hands before slipping into the borrowed nightrail filled her and felt very familiar. It was obviously a nighttime routine for her. She was grateful to have even these two tidbits of information, bringing hope that she would slowly but surely recall who she was, where she lived, and why she had traveled all the way to Sussex from London.

London! "Yes," she whispered. "I traveled from London." Letting her mind go back to her nighttime routine, she was grateful the countess had been beyond generous and welcoming, unlike a few of the other members of the *ton* she'd been introduced to.

Hands covering her mouth to keep her squeal of surprise contained, she repeated what she'd just thought aloud. "Members of the *ton*." A platinum-blonde beauty with the tongue of a viper flashed before her eyes…and the pain that accompanied it had her hands dropping to her sides as she closed her eyes again and leaned against the down-filled pillows. The physician had warned her to expect a headache that would come and go as the swelling went down and her brain began to recover. What he could not tell her was when her memory would fully return. She refused to accept that it would not eventually do so.

Lady Agnes. Her eyes popped open, and she pressed the tips of her fingers to her lips. The name that popped into her head belonged to the haughty daughter of a peer whose name or title she could not recall. But she definitely remembered the way Lady Agnes had stared at her hair first, and gown second, before dismissing her as if she were not worthy of the lady's regard. Receiving the cut direct without a word had sliced her to the bone and had her struggling to retain her composure. At least in that, she'd succeeded.

A flash of a conversation with an older woman kneading bread on a floured surface soothed her. The room was warm and welcoming, filled with a combination of scents that had her stomach rumbling. Savory stew and berry tarts had her mouth watering and her heart racing. It had to be a memory, because she had not been in the earl's kitchen.

Frowning, she racked her brain trying to recall if she worked in the large kitchen with the kindly woman. It did nothing but increase the pounding in her head. "Am I a servant on the run from a harsh master who turned me out without a reference?"

She glanced at the mauve velvet lady's chair in the corner by the washstand before noticing the door to the wardrobe stood open. Her eyes locked on the familiar clothing—a well-made gown the color of twilight hung beside a burgundy coat. A flash of pain and a wisp of a memory of being fitted for both garments—and being stuck by a pin—had her gasping.

"I remember that fitting!" It was in a bedchamber with pretty yellow walls that glowed when the early morning sunlight shone through the windows overlooking a walled garden.

The knock on the door startled her. She pulled the covers up to her chin before saying, "Come in." The door opened, and the housekeeper entered, followed by a maid who carried a small tray. "Mrs. Jones, isn't it?"

The housekeeper smiled. "I'm so pleased that you remember me. How did you sleep last night, now that we moved you to one of the guest rooms? The beds are quite comfortable."

"I slept deeply." She decided to wait before mentioning the nightmare/memory.

"Excellent. How do you feel this morning, Miss Amber? Has your headache lessened?"

Amber... The handsome guard who rescued her had given her that name when she was struggling to recall her name and kept drawing a blank.

Mrs. Jones directed the maid to place the tray with a small teapot, teacup and saucer, and small bowl on the table beneath the window. "Are you hungry?"

"I, uh, believe so." The flash of a nightmarish face, twisted with anger, glared at her. She shivered.

The housekeeper shooed the maid out of the room and retrieved the cream-colored shawl draped over the arm of the lady's chair.

She sighed as the warmth cut through the chill, and thanked the older woman as she tucked the shawl around her.

"There now, that should help you warm up from the outside." Walking over to the table, the housekeeper poured what appeared to be very weak tea—judging by the pale color—into the teacup. Well, at least she'd had a stronger cup yesterday. Mayhap she could ask the kindly cook for another a bit later.

"Mrs. Wyatt's broth will give you a bit of energy, but you should drink the tea first."

She was tempted to wrinkle her nose, but refrained, obeying when the housekeeper told her to have a sip. It wasn't as unpalatable as she feared, though she did wish for a stronger cup of tea that would warm her belly and give her the boost she needed upon rising. She bobbled the cup, splashing hot tea on the saucer and her wrist, then sucked in a breath and bit her bottom lip.

Mrs. Jones retrieved the cup and blotted her wrist before rushing over to the washstand. The housekeeper poured water into the bowl, dampened a cloth in it, and hurried back to her side. "Place this on your wrist—the water is tepid, but will cool your skin. I sent the maid downstairs to bring more hot water for you to wash with. You slept longer than we anticipated."

"Thank you, Mrs. Jones. I'm not normally so clumsy, nor do I think it my custom to sleep well into the morning."

"Can you tell me what you were thinking when you splashed hot tea on yourself?"

She nodded as the worst of the pain receded. "I like strong tea in the morning."

The housekeeper smiled at her. "That is wonderful news! Their lordships—and O'Malley—will be so pleased. You can have a strong cup in a few days' time. At the moment, the doctor has prescribed weak tea along with an invalid's diet of broth and bread. Mrs. Wyatt insisted that she add a bit of butter to your bread."

"Please thank her for me."

"And," the housekeeper continued, "she asked me to gain your promise not to mention it to the physician when he arrives this afternoon to see how you are progressing."

She smiled. "I wouldn't dream of it." Already planning to ask

Dermott to sneak two more scones for her, and to ask the cook for another pot of strong tea, she felt better having been able to make a few decisions. For now, she would keep that to herself and ignore the temptation to speak of the delicious scones. She would not want the handsome-as-sin Irishman, nor the kindly cook, to get into trouble for going against the physician's orders. It was entirely her doing that Dermott asked the cook about the scones and the tea. She'd never forget his thoughtfulness, or the cook's willingness to bend the strict dietary rules the doctor put in place.

The housekeeper shook her head. "If I know O'Malley, that rascal probably wheedled an extra scone or two from Mrs. Wyatt and shared them with you."

She felt her cheeks flush and looked away.

"Don't worry, Miss Amber—I won't give either of you away." Mrs. Jones removed the cloth, dipped it in the cool water, and wrung it out before placing it back on her wrist.

The woman's kindness was a balm to her aching heart. "Do you think you could drop the 'miss' and just call me Amber?" She congratulated herself on taking the initiative and making the decision. Until she remembered her name, she'd go by the name Dermott had given her.

It was a boon to be able to retain what happened from the moment she opened her eyes and stared up into the brilliant green eyes of the handsome Irishman who rescued her. Well, at least, that was what everyone had told her. She wished she could recall more of what happened, but her mind was blank.

The housekeeper smiled. "Of course, Amber. Now tell me," she said, handing her the teacup. "What did you remember?"

"I did remember something else...a name...but not *my* name."

Mrs. Jones waited patiently.

"Lady Agnes."

"A friend of yours?"

Amber snorted, and promptly felt her face heat with mortification. "Forgive me. That was an unladylike response." The words she uttered echoed in her head, but instead of hearing her own voice, she heard a deep, familiar one that brought tears to her eyes.

"Mayhap it would be best to speak of Lady Agnes another time. I'll take your empty cup. Do you think you can drink the broth and eat the bread?" Her stomach rumbled in reply, and the housekeeper's smile returned. "I will take that as a yes."

Grateful that the intensity of the burn on her wrist was fading, Amber was able to hold the bowl and finish every last drop. "That was delicious."

"Mrs. Wyatt has a way of making the ordinary taste divine." The housekeeper handed Amber the plate with the buttered bread. "Slowly now—the last thing we need is to upset your stomach. Though you did not exhibit signs of it yesterday, you could have a slight concussion."

"Thank you for caring. You remind me of my mother."

Amber's eyes widened as she and Mrs. Jones stared at one another. Finally, the housekeeper spoke. "I am no doctor, but, I daresay, your memory seems to be returning. Now you can cease fretting over the possibility that you won't remember your name or how you came to be near Lippincott Manor."

The name of the earl and countess's home seemed to trigger a memory, but it was hazy and not clear. Amber confided, "I had what I thought was a nightmare, but maybe it wasn't."

The housekeeper took the empty plate, then smoothed Amber's covers before asking, "Would you like to tell me about it?"

Amber frowned. "I think I should tell O'Malley, too. Do you know when he might have time to speak with me?"

"I know he will have the time, but first, you need to rest a bit and digest," Mrs. Jones replied. "When I return, we'll see how you feel. If I think you are up to a visit, we'll make you presentable."

Amber's hands flew to her cheeks. "Oh dear! Am I that disheveled?"

"Not at all, but now that you are not in the same dire straits as you were yesterday," the housekeeper said, "it would not be seemly for O'Malley, or the earl, for that matter, to visit with you in your bedchamber wearing a shawl over your nightrail."

"Borrowed from her ladyship. I have yet had the opportunity to thank her," Amber said.

"Lady Aurelia will most likely pay you a visit after she tends to Master Edward in the nursery," Mrs. Jones told her.

"I would like that, very much," Amber replied.

She pushed the covers aside and started to swing her legs to the side of the bed, but the housekeeper stopped her. "Do you need to use the chamber pot?"

Amber flushed with embarrassment. "Er...I may have to shortly, but was going to wait until I was alone. I've never needed assistance like that before—and wouldn't want to trouble you."

"Would you rather risk becoming lightheaded and falling on your face?" Mrs. Jones asked. "The risk that you would tear the stitches the doctor already used to close your wound is a possibility. Not only would the earl and countess call me to the carpet, but O'Malley..." The housekeeper shook her head. "That doesn't even bear thinking about." Mrs. Jones helped her to stand, and with her matter-of-fact attitude convinced Amber to accept her assistance with the chamber pot.

Amber felt steadier as she washed her hands, prompting her to ask the housekeeper, "Would it be all right if I washed my face, too?"

"As long as you do not get the threads wet, dip your head too low, or move too quickly. We don't want you to become dizzy and faint. Steady and slow, now," the housekeeper cautioned.

Amber felt infinitely better having washed the sleep from her eyes, wishing the round of soap was heather-scented instead of lavender.

Her gasp had Mrs. Jones placing an arm around her back. "Lean on me—"

"Heather!"

"Heather?" Mrs. Jones echoed.

Amber's eyes filled with tears. "My mother's family was from Scotland and preferred rounds of heather-scented soap. She said the heather reminded her of her grandparents' home in the Highlands." Lost in memories that were beginning to bombard her, she leaned heavily on the housekeeper and let herself be led back to the bed. Mayhap she should close her eyes for a bit. She could dress later.

Sinking onto the mattress, she met the housekeeper's questioning gaze. "No names yet, but if I close my eyes I can see my mother's face, though not clearly. She was beautiful, with auburn hair and amber eyes. Papa likes to remind me that I look like her, though my hair is not the same color at all." More tears filled her eyes, and this time slipped free. "She's been gone such a long time."

"You have made great strides in the short time I have been with you this morning," Mrs. Jones said. "I believe it is time to give your weary head a rest. Don't overtax yourself. I'm going to step outside and speak to one of the footmen. Try to close your eyes and sleep. You need it after remembering so many things this morning." She smoothed the covers up to Amber's chin and promised, "I'll be right back."

Amber closed her eyes and let the memory of her mother's loving embrace surround her as a hint of heather lulled her to sleep.

CHAPTER SEVEN

"SHE ASKED WHAT?" Lady Aurelia covered her mouth with her hands, realizing she'd raised her voice in her excitement. "There, there, love," she crooned, leaning over the cradle. Knowing what her babe needed, she gently rubbed her son's back until he quieted again.

In a voice just barely above a whisper, Mrs. Jones apologized, "I'm so sorry for waking Master Edward, your ladyship." She repeated what she had just said: "Miss Amber asked if everyone could just call her Amber until she remembers her name."

Aurelia nodded. "I cannot imagine how difficult this is for her to navigate. Injured, alone, and no idea who she is or why she is in Sussex."

The housekeeper agreed, then said, "She remembers a few other things."

"Oh?" The countess turned to meet the other woman's gaze. "What else did she recall?"

"Her mother is from Scotland, loved heather-scented soap. She passed away some time ago, and her father likes to remind Amber that she resembles her mother." Mrs. Jones paused, then added, "Though they do not share the same auburn locks."

"The poor thing—to be able to recall bits and pieces of her life, but not enough to tell us who she is and why she was alone when O'Malley found her." Staring down at her babe, fussing and wiggling, trying to find a comfortable position, Aurelia whispered, "I know what it feels like...to be without a mother...and a father." She drew in a breath and let it out. "Anything else that might help us discover who she is?"

"She mentioned a Lady Agnes, and from the expression on her face, I take it the memory was not a welcome one."

The countess searched her memory, sorting through the plethora of names of the ladies of the *ton* she had been introduced to. For reasons she could not explain, she concentrated on those who had been eager to spread the horrible rumors that had been fabricated about herself and Edward...before and after they wed. "Lady Agnes Sullins."

"That name sounds familiar, your ladyship. Is she a friend of yours?"

Aurelia huffed. "Not even an acquaintance, though we met on one or two occasions before it was discovered that she was among those spreading those lies about Edward and me."

"Now that you mention it, I do recall her name along with a handful of others added to the list..."

Aurelia stared pointedly at her housekeeper. "What list?"

Mrs. Jones closed her eyes and shook her head. "I beg your pardon, your ladyship, but I was not to mention it. Forgive me for doing so—it is because of this frightful situation."

The countess put her hands on her hips and tapped her foot. She wanted to raise her voice, but did not dare. Her darling babe had finally quieted down. "You'd best tell me. I shall insist to his lordship that I forced the information out of you."

The housekeeper placed her hands to her waist as if to steady herself before answering, "The duke's men have a list of names that are the first individuals they suspect whenever a new rumor, wager, or threat arises."

"I see." And Aurelia did, though she did not appreciate being left in the dark regarding such matters. "Thank you for telling me."

Her babe started fussing again, and Mrs. Jones asked, "Is his tummy upset?"

The countess nodded. "This happened the last time I ate some of Mrs. Wyatt's delicious mutton stew a few hours before feeding him."

Mrs. Jones walked over to stand beside her. "Are you certain?"

"It was the first time he woke screaming and drawing up his little legs to his bottom as if he were in pain." Aurelia sighed. "It has not happened again until today. While I've been trying to coax him back to sleep, I've been trying to think of what could have possibly been the cause."

"Do you think his stomach upsets are related to what you eat?" Mrs. Jones could not hide the skepticism in her voice.

"I had not given it much thought before Persephone gifted me with a copy of the journal her nanny Gwendolyn has been keeping. Patrick O'Malley's wife is a marvel. Do you know she has been recording bits of information gathered over her years working as a nanny?"

"As all people are not the same, it would stand to reason, all infants are not either," the housekeeper remarked. "I would imagine it has come in handy on more than one occasion."

"From the innate way Gwendolyn has understood our niece and nephew from the beginning, I would venture to say it has." Aurelia felt the twinge that twisted into a definite kink in her lower back. Ignoring it, she continued to lean over her son's cradle. Her arm was tiring, but her little one was quieting, so she kept up the circular motions that seemed to soothe him. Her darling babe need to sleep... *She* needed him to sleep!

"Gwendolyn was the one who solved Persephone's teething woes with her twins. I never would have thought of soothing sore gums with whiskey, nor did I believe a babe's jaw could be so strong." She lifted her right hand and flexed her fingers. "My knuckles were sore from him biting down on them." Worry filled her as exhaustion threatened again, but, pushing it aside to care for her son, she whispered, "It's a very good thing babes cannot remember the pain of stomach upsets and teething."

The housekeeper agreed. "Shall I send one of the footmen to fetch his lordship?"

The babe chose that moment to lift his head and wail pitifully. Aurelia scooped him up to soothe him, but he kept screaming. "Please, though I do hate to interrupt Edward's meeting with the men."

Aurelia tried to remember exactly how her husband had held their babe, which seemed to calm him the last time. It had been the only thing that worked. She shifted him further up to her shoulder, but he still screamed. Poor little darling—this was one of those times that only his father could soothe him.

Mrs. Jones came back into the nursery. "He's getting a bit louder, isn't he?"

Aurelia jiggled and crooned, paced from the window to the door and back again. Tears filled her eyes at the thought that she was such an incompetent mother, she was unable to soothe her babe. She refused to let them fall, rationalizing that all she needed was five minutes to gather her composure.

The knock on the door had relief flowing through the countess. She was closer to the door and yanked it open, only to stop short and stare at Dermott O'Malley.

"I heard the screams, yer ladyship. Can I be of help?" the guard asked.

When she shook her head, Dermott started to speak softly to her babe in what she now recognized as Gaelic. All the men serving in the duke's guard spoke in the musical Irish tongue—though more often than not, it was to curse. There were a few times they'd murmured endearments. She remembered the first time she met Sean O'Malley's wife Mignonette. She had heard him murmur tender words to her when he thought no one was listening.

Watching Dermott closely, she marveled that little Edward's hair-curling screams had turned to whimpers as her son leaned back to stare at the huge man. She braced herself, anticipating that, at any moment, her babe would throw back his head and let go of another spine-tingling scream. Instead, her son did quite the opposite—he reached for the big Irishman.

Dermott softly chuckled. "Well now, lad, mayhap ye should wait until yer da...er...his lordship arrives."

Edward's little face scrunched up, but before he could cry, Aurelia handed her son to Dermott. "I'm a desperate woman." Her babe stared at him. In the relative quiet after the storm, she heard a heavy footfall in the hallway that had her sighing in relief.

The earl stepped over the threshold and stopped in his tracks. "O'Malley?"

"Begging yer pardon, yer lordship, but—"

"I gave him no choice, darling. Our babe was screaming and only paused when he heard Dermott speaking. The musical sound of the words calmed our son until he quieted down."

"'Twas just something ma used to say to us when we were young: *mo ghrá, mo chroí*. Meaning: *me love, me heart*."

Lippincott watched the youngest member of his guard sway from side to side, speaking in a low, lilting voice to the heir to the earldom. "How is it that you are proficient with all manner of weapons—including your fists—and yet our son seems to trust you, when recently he will only let Aurelia or me hold him to console him?"

Dermott flashed a grin at the earl. "Da and me older brothers, Patrick and Finn, would line up to kiss Ma on their way out to the fields, leaving meself, Emmett, and Eamon to help her with our three younger sisters. The lot of them had powerful lungs. More often than not, Ma would hand Grainne, Maeve, or Roisin off to meself or Emmett."

The earl nodded. "What about Eamon?"

Dermott grinned. "The bug—er, little devil would make himself scarce until our sisters quieted."

"Is there anything else about your family that would surprise me, O'Malley?"

Dermott didn't lift his head to answer—he was too busy

tracing the tip of his forefinger along the babe's one eyebrow and then the other. "Not that I can think of at the moment, yer lordship. If I do, I'll let ye know."

Aurelia smiled. "Persephone mentioned Gwendolyn taught her to do what you're doing right now, Dermott. Tracing your fingertip over the curve of one eyebrow and then the other. It always soothes Richard and Abigail to sleep. Did your mother teach you that?"

"She taught us to sway side to side. I watched me sister-in-law crooning to Their Graces' twins once or twice. Gwendolyn has a way with babes. 'Tis not just her excellent reputation that she brought with her to Wyndmere Hall. The first time I met me niece, she was screaming her wee little head off, but Gwendolyn just smiled and made soothing sounds, as she used her fingertip to stroke the babe's brows, mesmerizing little Deidre into a deep sleep."

"I haven't had a chance to read the next section of the journal yet. Persephone slipped a piece of paper between certain pages for me to read," Aurelia murmured. "When I have five minutes, I'll have to see if there are a few hints about what foods to stay away from—"

She glanced at her husband and O'Malley, biting her bottom lip before she blurted out the rest of what she was going to say. It was one thing to speak of nursing your babe to another woman or your husband—but to a man who was not her husband? Unthinkable!

"Thank you for calming him, Dermott," she said instead.

"Me pleasure. If it's tummy troubles he's having, Ma used to have us hold our sisters up against our shoulder bone—the angle used to ease some of their distress. Though I have no idea why."

Aurelia placed her hand on her husband's forearm. "Darling, why don't you see if that works—your shoulders are far broader than mine." She watched him shift their babe onto his shoulder, and a wave of love swept up from her toes. Aurelia touched his forearm and mouthed, *I love you*. The intensity in his brilliant blue eyes warmed her heart.

Before she lost her train of thought entirely, she told him, "I'm late visiting Miss Amber." She pressed a kiss to her husband's cheek and one to the top of their babe's head. "I shall return shortly."

"Seeing as how you have everything in hand, your lordship," Mrs. Jones said, "I was overseeing the household inventory when her ladyship rang for me. I'd best get back to it. Anderson will be anxious if I do not have the information for his quarterly reports."

Undaunted at the prospect of soothing his son, the earl nodded. "I believe our solicitors are due to visit in a few weeks' time. I'd best let you get back to the task, Mrs. Jones. I wouldn't want to annoy my brother by being late supplying the information he needs regarding Lippincott Manor and our tenant farmers."

When she swept past him, his son opened his eyes and gave him a gap-toothed, drooling smile. A heartbeat later, his face scrunched up and he began to cry. The earl swore beneath his breath and locked gazes with Dermott. "Do you think whiskey would work on a stomach upset, too?"

Dermott scratched his head. "I wouldn't be knowing about that, but I firmly believe a sip of the Irish can cure all ills."

The earl shifted his son slightly, hoping it would quiet him down. "Do you have your flask on you, O'Malley?"

Dermott reached into his waistcoat pocket, and was about to hand it over when the babe wailed.

"Use the glass on the table by the wardrobe," the earl instructed him.

Dermott found the glass and poured enough for the earl to dip his finger in and offer to his babe with enough left over for the earl. A glance at the worry lines between the earl's eyes, and Dermott topped off the short glass and nodded to it.

While Edward hiccupped and chewed on his father's whiskey-soaked forefinger, the earl reached for the glass with his free hand.

O'Malley lifted his flask. *"Sláinte!"*

The earl lifted his glass. *"Sláinte,* O'Malley!"

CHAPTER EIGHT

Finding Miss Amber sleeping peacefully, Aurelia returned to the nursery to find her husband and Dermott quietly speaking. Their son was in his cradle—praise the Lord—sleeping. She smiled at them and walked into the room.

"That was fast," the earl remarked.

"Is everything all right?" Dermott asked.

"Miss Amber was asleep. I did not want to wake her—she has had precious little rest since you brought her here."

"'Tis her worry that keeps her awake," Dermott said. "Though we've told her we'll protect her, I'm thinking 'tis the unknown and who she is running from that has kept her awake."

The earl nodded. "It would keep me wide awake."

"That would be my guess, too," Lady Aurelia agreed. "The poor thing could not hold off the sleep she desperately needs to recover from her injury any longer."

※※※

"Thank ye," Dermott said. "Thank ye both, for allowing me to bring Miss Amber here to be tended to and recover."

"Given the missive I received from Lord—" The earl stopped speaking at the quiet gasp from his wife.

The sound told Dermott all he needed to know. The earl had not informed her ladyship of the missive from a former acquaintance and a time his lordship had put behind him...the deceased Lord Eggerton. A quick glance was all Dermott needed to take two steps back...out of the proverbial line of fire. "I'd best be getting to me post."

"Do not take one more step out of this room!" Lady Aurelia hissed.

Dermott looked at the earl. The lack of emotion showing on his lordship's face had him wondering how the earl would extract himself from what would be a tricky situation and discussion with his wife.

"Pray, forgive my wife for speaking out of turn." Lippincott pinned his wife to the spot with his gaze. "I am certain when her temper cools, she will realize that as one of the men who have willingly put their lives on the line to protect us time after time, you have duties that eclipse her demand that you remain."

Dermott's gaze swung to that of the countess. Her hand trembled as she brushed a lock of hair that had slipped from its pins out of her left eye. Understanding filled him as hurt flashed in the depths of her eyes. "Nothing to forgive, yer lordship. Her ladyship is a bit like me ma, wanting—nay needing—to know what is happening around her that will affect how she can protect her babe."

The earl's brilliant blue eyes flashed with anger that he quickly banked. "I see to the protection of our babe and my wife."

Dermott hesitated to say more, but their lordships had unknowingly placed him in the middle of their quarrel. "Aye, and ye have done a fine a job doing so, yer lordship." He waited a beat before adding, "Her ladyship has done the same, protecting and nurturing yer babe, as me ma would say."

When neither of them spoke, just continued to stare at one another, Dermott decided it would be best if he deflected their anger at one another toward himself. He could more than handle whatever barbs they tossed at him. He'd grown up dodging his ma's temper.

He bit back a smile, remembering Da used to call it the "bloody Flynn temper," then cleared his throat to speak. "What I meant to say, yer ladyship, is that if ye're wanting to ring a peal over me head, I'm ready when ye are." Her snort of laughter, quickly silenced, relieved his worry that his lordship would be angry with him for speaking so familiarly with her ladyship. One look at the furious expression on Lady Aurelia's face had him bracing to duck—her hand was close enough to the journal on the table to lob it at his head.

"My wife is above such an explosion of temper, O'Malley. Moreover," the earl drawled, "she would never stoop so low as to hurl the journal in her hand at one of my men."

Dermott watched the normally even-tempered countess turn her frosty glare on the earl, noting that she did not set the journal on the table. "Your *brother's* men."

"When they are stationed at Lippincott Manor, my dear, they are my men and report to me."

Dermott swallowed his laughter. It would not do to add to the argument taking place in furious whispers. In spite of the tension between the earl and his wife, neither one wanted to wake their babe. A good sign.

"What missive?"

The earl frowned at his wife. "As your husband—"

She raised a hand up in front of her, and her expression turned to one of bleak despair. "I thought you trusted me, Edward." The earl reached for her hand, but she tugged it from his grasp. "I am certain you and O'Malley are needed elsewhere." She turned her back on her husband and rasped, "Please leave. You are bound to wake our babe, and I am too tired to repeat the last few hours trying to get him to fall asleep."

She glanced over her shoulder at Dermott, and his gut clenched. The sadness in her blue eyes dimmed until they were a washed-out gray. He could not speak of missives sent or received unless given leave to. It was his duty, and that of his cousins, to protect the earl and his family to the best of his abilities. If a part of his duty meant they would withhold pertinent information from Lady Aurelia, so be it. They'd vowed to protect the duke and his family, and extended family, with their lives. 'Twas a well-known fact that anyone blessed enough to be a member of the O'Malley/Garahan/Flaherty clan would never forsake a vow. Generations of O'Malleys, Garahans, and Flahertys had pledged an oath...and many had died to uphold it. If he was called to do so, he would without question.

"Thank you for soothing our son, Dermott. He was in desperate need of sleep."

He bowed to Lady Aurelia. "'Twas me pleasure, yer ladyship. If ye have need of me, ye've but to ask." He turned to the earl. "With yer permission, yer lordship." He waited for the earl to nod before leaving the nursery. His long strides ate up the distance between the nursery and the door to the servants' staircase. Ascending, he nodded to the footman stationed on the third floor, relieving him.

The earl expected trouble to arrive at any hour, and had asked his men to train a few of the footmen to stand guard while waiting for reinforcements to arrive: Michael O'Malley and James Garahan. The only wrinkle in the plan was that Dermott's cousins were not the only ones to arrive—though it only be a few miles between Lippincott Manor and Chattsworth, the viscount's family would be accompanying him for the duration. Dermott silently added his cousins' wives to the list—they would stay with Sean's wife. Safety in numbers. He knew he would not be able to leave his wife—or babe—behind if summoned to act as reinforcements at any of the duke's, or the duke's family's, homes.

Alone in the corridor, he made his hourly sweep of the floor, opening doors, checking rooms, and pausing by the windows to scan the perimeter. All was quiet...but for how long?

Heavy footfalls had him retracing his steps to the servants' staircase, expecting either Sean or Flaherty to appear.

The door opened and Sean stepped into the hallway. "We're

to expect Michael and James to arrive within the hour."

Dermott sighed. "And the viscount and his family."

Sean tried to cover his snort of laughter but did not succeed.

"'Tisn't a laughing matter having to add the viscountess and their babe to our list of those under our protection."

His cousin studied him closely before asking, "Are ye saying ye aren't up to the job?"

"*Bugger* it, Sean. Ye know as well as I do that whenever the countess and viscountess get together, we are running to keep up with the trouble they stir up."

Sean grinned. "'Tis mischief, not trouble."

Dermott shook his head. It wouldn't make any difference if he disagreed; all of the O'Malleys—brothers and cousins—were known for their stubbornness. "All is quiet on this floor. I'll head down to the second floor and send one of the footmen to fill me post."

Sean followed him down to the lower level. "Did I mention another missive from Coventry arrived right after the viscount's?"

Dermott opened the door and looked over his shoulder. "If it wasn't to tell his lordship that he was sending two of his men to add to our guard, ye can fill me in later."

Sean's grip bit into Dermott's arm. He spun around and elbowed his cousin. "What in the bleeding hell do ye want from me, Sean? I'm doing me duty to His Grace and his lordship, and have the added worry of Trenchert and God knows how many of his cohorts searching the area for the lass!"

His cousin dropped his hand to his side. "If ye think for one moment that I do not understand the position ye're in, ye've *bollocks* for brains! I have been in yer boots and know exactly what ye're facing. 'Tis the only reason I haven't knocked ye on yer *arse* for dereliction of duty. Captain Coventry is sending three of the men recently hired at His Grace's insistence that he needed more men based in London to relay firsthand information regarding threats, rumors, and bloody wagers against the family. The lot of us worked in London before we were hired by the duke, and some of the men were suggested by yerself and me when Coventry asked for recommendations."

The slash to Dermott's pride was nothing compared to the guilt slashing his guts to pieces. *"Shite."* He raked a hand through his hair and stared at his cousin, who was a mirror image of himself. Chiseled features, bright green eyes, and light hair. Taller than their Garahan and Flaherty cousins, and just a bit broader through the chest and shoulders. Dermott knew from the glint in his cousin's eye that he was anticipating a bare-knuckle bout with him, which had the potential to go on for hours. They were equally matched, and beating the bloody hell out of one another would not solve anything.

As if Sean knew what Dermott was thinking, he nodded. "I'd give me eye teeth to go a few rounds with ye, but we've plans to put in place before our cousins arrive. Hopefully, they'll bring Michael's stepson Bart with them. The lad's been practicing with his fists as well as weapons."

"Aye, he more than proved himself when those blackguards tried to destroy the crops he and his ma had planted the night Michael came to their rescue." Dermott frowned. "You don't think our cousins will bring MacReady along with them, do ye?" Sean's snicker had Dermott's frustration easing. He admitted, "I suppose we'll have to make an allowance for the crusty Scot, given that his head's as hard as granite and he never listens to reason. MacReady has proven himself time after time protecting the viscount, Lady Calliope, and their son. I'm thinking he'll be called upon to add to the protection of our cousin's wives, as well as the viscountess."

"Aye," Sean agreed. "He still serves as the viscount's valet and sometimes footman. Oh, and don't discount that, in a pinch, he's been known to ram his hard head into more than one intruder's gut."

"Thought he was going to do that to us, more than once." Dermott couldn't keep his snort of laughter contained. "Thank ye for helping me remember what's important, Sean. I cannot let meself get distracted."

"By the lass's pretty face or the trouble we know will soon find its way to the earl's door," Sean murmured, "ye won't. Ye're an O'Malley, boy-o."

Dermott shoved Sean out of the way with his shoulder. "If ye understand how I'm feeling, then ye'll know I'll do whatever it takes to protect her. I vowed to the moment she opened her eyes and looked up at me with trust so deep and true, nothing could shatter it."

"Ah, well, in that case, ye'll have no choice in the matter," Sean predicted.

"What matter?"

"Marriage."

"I didn't ask the lass to marry me…" *Yet*, Dermott's heart prodded him.

"Yet," Sean mumbled.

Dermott's heart echoed the word a second time, but he stood firm in his conviction that he could not afford to marry the lass. She already had his head in a muddle! "I don't think—"

"Well now, that isn't anything knew. Patrick and I have discussed yer propensity not to think in the past. Remember the time on the docks when that behemoth came at ye with a knife in one hand and a cudgel in the other?"

"I'll not likely be forgetting, and before ye say anything else, that was when Emmett and I first stepped off the boat from Ireland. We've learned how to navigate our way on the docks and through the stews since that day. If ye're done spouting, we've work before our cousins—and their charges—arrive."

"Don't forget to stop in and ask how Miss Amber is feeling."

Dermott jolted to a stop. "Is something wrong? Has something happened?"

Sean didn't bother to answer—he was already halfway down the stairs to the first floor.

"Bloody buggering knot head." Dermott put his cousin's taunting out of his mind. He had a shift to finish, plans to go over with Flaherty and Sean when he was through…after he paid a visit to the lass. Hopefully, he could get it all accomplished before their cousins arrived from Chattsworth Manor.

Heading to the lass's bedchamber, he prayed aloud, "Lord willing."

CHAPTER NINE

AMBER WOKE WITH a start. She had only closed her eyes for a moment. How long had she been sleeping? The knock on her door had her pulling the covers up to her chin before answering, "Come in."

Mrs. Jones seemed pleased when she bustled into the room. "Your color is much better. The physician is here to see you."

"Oh, but I'm not dressed."

The housekeeper tutted while she helped Amber to sit up and then fluffed the pillows behind her. "There is no need to don more than your dressing gown. Let me fetch it for you."

Amber was about to protest that she did not have a dressing gown, but fell silent when remembering she had arrived with only the clothing on her back. Everything she had been wearing since she regained consciousness was courtesy of Lady Aurelia. She needed to speak with the countess to thank her again for not only her hospitality, but lending her garments to wear. It was unheard of, and would be frowned upon among the ladies of the *ton*. Mayhap her friends—even though she could not remember a single one—had not been true friends.

Mrs. Jones slipped the pale blue velvet dressing gown with the deep ecru lace at the collar and cuffs around her. Amber dutifully slid her arms into the sleeves. A flash of a similar dressing gown in a lovely shade of deep green startled her.

"Green."

"Green?" the housekeeper echoed.

"Er...yes. I remember a dressing gown in deep green velvet. Papa gave it to me on my birthday."

Mrs. Jones seemed pleased with yet another piece of the puzzle that was Amber's past surfacing. "We'll be certain to mention it to the doctor. I'll ask the footman to send him up."

Amber wished she could recall more than snippets of her life...specifically her name. Then mayhap the mystery of why she was in Sussex on foot could be solved, and she could be on her way to her intended destination.

A thought struck her, filling her with sadness. When she left, she would never see Dermott O'Malley again.

The knock on the doorframe had her turning her attention to the doctor standing on the threshold with Mrs. Jones right behind him. He smiled. "Mrs. Jones said you were looking much better. I concur. Now then, let's remove the bandage and have a look at my stitches."

She submitted to the physician's ministrations, and although the cleansing of her wound was not comfortable, she bore it as it needed to be done. "Just a few more days, and we can leave the bandage off," the physician said.

Amber had not asked for a looking glass to see the damage the fall had done to her forehead, but was thinking it was past time she did. It was unnerving not being able to summon up an image of her own face! Seeing her reflection might spark more memories. "What about the threads? When will you be able to remove them?"

The doctor closed his bag and studied her closely before answering, "The lack of fever is an excellent sign that infection did not set in. Your color and appetite returning is also a good sign."

She opened her mouth to speak, but he held up a hand, and she fell silent. "There are more important signs of your recovery than the moment I remove the threads. Try to be patient," the physician urged. "I shall return in a few days, unless his lordship sends for me before then. At the most, a fortnight, at the very least, ten days more. We do not want to rush the healing, as the wound is close to the brain, Miss Amber."

"Yes, of course. I was just curious. Thank you for taking such excellent care of me."

He nodded and bade her goodbye, following behind Mrs. Jones, who showed him out. When the housekeeper returned, she was smiling. "That went very well. Since you did not ask, and since I suspect O'Malley and Mrs. Wyatt have been sneaking scones and strong tea to you behind my back—"

"Oh, but I—" Amber fell silent at the expression on Mrs. Jones's face.

"As I was saying, as your appetite seems to be improving rapidly, I asked if you could resume a regular diet a few days early."

Hope filled Amber as her stomach rumbled loudly. She placed her hand over it. "And?"

The housekeeper laughed. "I sent word down to Mrs. Wyatt. She's baking one of her currant cakes to serve at teatime. It is delicious and absolutely melts in your mouth."

"Thank you, Mrs. Jones. I cannot believe I forgot to ask. My mind seems to be distracted."

"Understandable," the older woman said before turning to answer the knock on the door. "Ah, Jenny—wonderful, we can use your assistance. Miss Amber, meet Jenny, Lady Aurelia's personal maid. She'll help you get dressed. We are expecting company for the next few days."

"Oh, I beg your pardon. Of course I shall be happy to return to the room by the pantry."

Mrs. Jones shook her head. "That will not be necessary. Lippincott Manor has more than enough guest rooms."

"I see. I shall keep to my room, then, so that I do not interfere with the earl and countess's guests."

"You will do no such thing, Miss Amber. His lordship and

ladyship were in full agreement that as soon as the physician released you from bed rest you would be welcome to join them for meals. Her ladyship is looking forward to visiting with you, and introducing you to Master Edward."

She had heard the servants speaking of the heir to the earldom with fondness. "I would like that above all things."

"Now then, her ladyship has sent over a gown in a lovely shade of rose—although not similar in color to the dressing gown you mentioned earlier, it will complement your coloring. Jenny placed it in the wardrobe while you were resting."

With the help of the two women chattering while helping her dress, Amber was ready in no time. Brushing her hands against the soft fabric, she smiled. "I am not certain when I will see her ladyship—would you please thank her for me? She has been so generous with her wardrobe."

"Lady Aurelia is known for her kindness and generosity," Jenny said, as the housekeeper instructed another maid to straighten the room. "Please have a seat while I tend to your hair. I promise to be mindful of your injury."

"Oh, I had not planned on doing much more than re-braiding it."

"If you'll allow me, I can fashion a lovely coil at the nape of your neck. It won't take long at all. Let me get the looking glass for you."

"I confess, I haven't actually seen one—or asked for one—since O'Malley brought me here," Amber admitted.

"Will it disturb you to see your injury?" the maid asked.

"Of course not. I'm so very grateful to O'Malley for rescuing me and for the care and concern of the earl, the countess, and everyone who has been so kind to me."

"Let me fetch the looking glass I left on the washstand when I arrived."

Amber had to still her trembling hands. What would she see? A nameless face or one she recognized? Would she also remember how she came to be in the countryside? She noticed the frown on the housekeeper's face as Jenny carried the ornate silver-backed looking glass over to where she sat.

The maid did not seem to notice, explaining, "Miss Amber is going to watch while I fashion her hair into a loose coil. I have a lovely sweep in mind that will not brush against her forehead or injury."

Amber drew in a breath and exhaled, bracing herself for whatever the glass would reveal. Jenny handed her the mirror. "Thank you, Jenny. I confess to being curious as to how long the scar will be. I'll just take a quick look—" Her gasp of horror echoed in the room as her memory came crashing back. *"NO!"* Her keening cry had the door bursting open and O'Malley racing to her side.

<hr />

"What's happened? Lass, are ye in pain?"

Tear-drenched eyes turned to him as she placed the back of her hand over her mouth and shook her head.

"What is it, then? The scar? Ye can hide it with the sweep of yer hair."

She shook her head and dropped her hand to her lap. "He'll find me. He'll never give up."

"Who, lass? Who is after ye?" She stifled an anguished sob that cut through to his heart. He went down on one knee by her side. "I'll stop whoever it is." He handed her his handkerchief, waiting while she wiped her eyes and blew her nose before adding, "No one will get past me, lass. Ye're safe here."

"You don't understand. There is nothing you can do," she said between sobs. "Papa gambled away our home and his fortune, along with my dowry and my hand in marriage. Nothing will stop the viscount from finding me and forcing me to marry him."

Dermott's heart nearly stopped at the thought of the vile man the earl had described earlier. He would die before letting the lass marry that bloody bastard! "There's where ye'd be wrong, lass. Reinforcements are on their way to guard ye."

She started to shake her head again, but he grabbed hold of her upper arms. "Look at me, lass." When she lifted her chin and stared at him, he vowed, "Know that I speak the truth when I tell ye that ye won't be forced into marriage—"

Amber did not let him finish. "Papa told me I had to leave for Sussex immediately—to hide from the viscount. Can we get word to my father in London? I... I need to speak with him."

God in Heaven! How could he tell the lass that her father was dead? "I'll speak to his lordship about it. Ye said ye trusted me, lass. Are ye going back on your word?"

She blinked. "No. I do trust you."

"Then ye have nothing to fear. Ye have meself and the rest of the duke's guard stationed in Sussex to protect ye."

"But the viscount..." She fell silent and looked into his eyes. Though hers were still damp with tears, the trust she spoke of shone bright as a beacon light in their amber depths. "Forgive me," she whispered. "I trust you with all my heart, O'Malley."

He loosened his grip on her upper arms and slowly slid his hands down past her elbows to her hands. As if he sensed she needed reassurance, he gently squeezed her hands and looked deep into her eyes. Her tear-spiked dark lashes reminded him that the return of her memory did not relieve her fears. It doubled them. Lifting one hand to his lips, he brushed a kiss to the back of it. "I vow that I'll protect ye with me life, lass."

Releasing her hand, he rose to his feet, nodded to the housekeeper and maid, and strode from the bedchamber without a backward glance. Dermott knew if he stayed a moment longer, he would have swept the lass into his arms and kissed the breath out of her.

Shaking his head as he returned to his post at the far end of the hallway, he knew the lass was forever firmly embedded in his brain. Even if he closed his eyes, her image would appear. The curve of her cheek, the softness of her skin, the fullness of her bottom lip that taunted him to press his mouth to hers.

The last image of the lass gazing up at him in wonder had him envisioning the lass in bed—*his*—with the same look in her eyes as he covered her with his body and—

O'Malley stifled a groan, refusing to let his mind think such thoughts of the innocent lass.

An hour later, he was still fighting not to think about her. Relieved that it was time for the change in shifts, he made one last round on the second floor. He reminded himself that he had no business thinking of the lass that way—or at all. They were not betrothed! She was promised to another man, though with God as his witness, he would find a way to sever the betrothal... Nay, not betrothal—wager!

His mind made up, he strode toward the main staircase, marveling that her amber eyes were filled not only with trust and admiration, but the flicker of something infinitely more precious... Love.

Lord, he silently prayed, *I could use another favor.*

Chapter Ten

Lady Aurelia paused in the open doorway and smiled before entering. "Oh, how well that gown suits you." She walked over to where Amber stood by the window. "You look beautiful."

Amber turned to greet the countess as she tamped down the worry lancing through her. She had placed her trust in the handsome Irishman who had rescued her. Before he left, Dermott had given his word to protect her with his life. *His life!* The very thought of him doing so had her shivering as a chill raced up her spine.

"Are you all right, Miss Amber?"

"Yes, thank you. I was woolgathering."

Countess Lippincott studied her until Amber began to feel uncomfortable. As she was about to speak, Lady Aurelia smiled. "I came to invite you to join me for a cup of tea in my upstairs sitting room. It is quiet and has a lovely view of the gardens."

Amber gathered her composure. "Thank you, your ladyship. I would enjoy that."

"Excellent. I rang for tea before coming to collect you. My very dear friend Lady Calliope is on her way for an extended visit. You will have a chance to meet her and her darling babe William. He is a week younger than our Edward." She slipped her arm through Amber's and whispered, "Of course, her husband will be accompanying them as well—he is as cranky as mine when they believe trouble is on its way."

"Oh?" Fear slashed through Amber's belly. She slid her arm free. "Have I brought trouble to your door?" Before Lady Aurelia could answer, Amber rushed on to say, "If so, I shall leave at once! There must be an inn nearby where I can find accommodations. I could not in good conscience allow harm to come to you or your family, your ladyship. You have been so kind to me."

The countess grabbed hold of Amber's hand and tugged on it. "You may have lost your memory, but I'm beginning to wonder if you have lost your mind! O'Malley could have dropped you off at the physician's home in the village, but he brought you here—to *us*—to protect and tend to your injuries." She opened the door to a lovely room at the opposite end of the long hallway and all but dragged Amber inside. Spinning around, Lady Aurelia placed her hands on her hips. "You. Are. Staying. Put!"

For the life of her, Amber could not imagine why the countess would care whether or not she stayed or left. "I…er… Well, as I have no conveyance at my disposal, and did not arrive on horseback—"

Lady Aurelia slowly smiled. "As a matter of fact, you did. O'Malley was cradling you in tight to his chest as he galloped toward our stables."

Amber's mouth hung slack. She couldn't seem to find adequate words to respond. She had never asked how she came to be at Lippincott Manor.

As if satisfied with her reaction, the countess continued, "The poor man's worry was evident, given the loud conversation I chanced to overhear."

"Loud?"

"Have a seat. Please?" Amber complied, and the countess continued, "I was trying to dislodge a bubble… Our darling babe eats so fast, he creates them. Poor thing."

Amber smiled. "I am an only child—" She covered her mouth with her hands as tears welled in her eyes. Blinking them away, she lowered her hands. "That thought just popped into my head.

Do you think it's true?"

"From the emotions on your face, I would venture to say it is. I did not have any brothers or sisters. Uncle Phineas took me in after…" The earl's wife paused, as if reliving that time in her life was difficult.

Understanding filled Amber. The time after her mother passed away had been a nightmare. One she prayed she'd wake up from. She needed to ease the other woman's sorrow. "I lost my mum, too. It has been Papa and me for the last few years." She sighed. "For the life of me, I cannot understand why I cannot recall my name." She frowned, thinking of what she'd confessed to Dermott. "Though what I have remembered is unnerving…frightening."

"When did this happen?"

"Jenny was fixing my hair—and thank you again for letting me borrow another of your gowns and your maid. I have a vague memory of someone helping me dress, but she was older than Jenny."

"Pinning your hair reminded you of something distasteful?" the countess queried.

"It was the first time I'd seen my reflection since arriving," Amber whispered, fighting to hold back the emotions battering her. "O'Malley has probably already told the earl. He will no doubt bundle me into a carriage and send me back to London."

"You do not know my darling Edward well enough to make that judgment. He is a born protector, as is his brother the duke."

"But surely, as O'Malley is one of the duke's guard, he will be expected to share what I told him with your husband and the duke."

The knock on the door interrupted their conversation. "Come in," the countess called.

The door opened, and Mrs. Jones stepped aside for one of the footmen to precede her. The tea tray he carried was laden with the accoutrements for tea, along with an assortment of delectable treats—cream tarts, berry tarts, and scones.

"Thank you, Mrs. Jones. I am more than ready to for a strong cup of tea and something sweet. Please thank Mrs. Wyatt for me."

The housekeeper asked, "Shall I stay and pour?"

"No, thank you. But please do let me know as soon as our guests arrive."

"Of course, your ladyship. Just ring if you need anything else."

"I will. Thank you."

Amber was pleased to note the way the countess treated her housekeeper and the footman. It reminded her of her mum.

Lady Aurelia poured tea and filled a plate, passing it to Amber. "Have something to eat before we continue our conversation. I always feel better able to face difficult situations with food in my stomach."

Amber sipped and nibbled, feeling a bit more relaxed with each bite of the delectable sweets the cook had prepared for them. Blotting her mouth with a soft linen napkin, she met the steady gaze of the countess. "Thank you, your ladyship."

"My pleasure. Now what was it that you told O'Malley?"

"My father gambles." When the countess did not say anything, Amber continued, "He lost our home and his fortune."

"I am sorry to hear that."

Though it pained her to do so, she confessed the worst of it: "Papa gambled away my dowry...and my hand in marriage."

She had not realized she was crying until the lace-edged handkerchief appeared in front of her.

"Wipe your eyes, Amber."

She did as Lady Aurelia bade her, wringing the damp handkerchief in her hands. "Aren't you going to ask me to leave?"

"Whyever would I do that? If your father gambled away your home, where will you go?"

She had not thought of that. "I... I have no idea."

"Well then, you shall remain here with us indefinitely."

"I could not impose upon you—"

"I insist."

Lady Aurelia's voice was firm enough to have Amber biting back her refusal. "What will the earl say? Won't he disagree with you?"

"First, let me remind you that none of this is your fault. I am certain you did not goad your father into wagering over a hand of cards."

"Well, no, but—"

"Nor would you have suggested he wager your home or his fortune."

"Of course not."

"As to your dowry," Lady Aurelia continued, "do you recall if there was a gentleman courting you that you were enamored of?"

Amber sighed. "No. I have no idea why I can recall that, without remembering my name."

"Your name will come," Aurelia said, reaching over to pat the back of Amber's hand. "Now then, what was O'Malley's reaction to your conversation?"

Amber's eyes met Lady Aurelia's. "He told me I would not be forced into a marriage."

"Is that all?"

Amber blinked back the tears that seemed to be her constant companion today. After drawing in a deep breath and slowly exhaling, she answered, "He vowed to protect me with his life."

The countess beamed. "Well, I believe that is the answer to your situation and should put your mind at rest."

"It isn't an answer. When the man comes to collect his wager, the earl will have no choice but to turn me over to him."

"That, my dear young woman, is something I refuse to do."

The countess suddenly pushed to her feet. "Edward!" She rushed over to her husband's side, leaning into him when he placed his arm around her. "I am so happy to see you."

"Are you?" He stared down at his wife, and Amber noticed the look that passed between the couple. They obviously shared a deep affection. "And what of your declaration from half an hour ago?"

She pushed away from him and returned to her seat. "You know that I spoke in haste."

"Do I?"

"Stop tormenting me over my loss of temper, Edward, and join us for a cup of tea."

He smiled. "Although I would enjoy nothing more, I have come to advise that Calliope, William, and their babe have arrived." When she started to rise from her seat for the second time, the earl motioned for her to remain seated. "I sent word to Mrs. Wyatt to prepare another tea tray and send it to you here—or would you prefer the downstairs sitting room?"

"Will you and William be joining us?"

"Not until this afternoon's tea…after luncheon."

"Then here will be lovely, Edward. Thank you."

The earl turned to leave, then abruptly spun on his heel. He stalked over to where Lady Aurelia sat, pulled her to her feet, and kissed the breath out of her.

Amber could not take her eyes off the passionate display. She sighed when, just as abruptly, the earl did an about-face and strode through the door.

"Oh my," she whispered.

Lady Aurelia had her hand to her heart. When she finally tore her gaze from the empty doorway, she blew out a shaky breath. "Lord, that man vexes me."

Amber thought it best not to speak, but could not hold back the giggle.

The countess frowned at her for a moment before dissolving into giggles herself. "And then he kisses every thought from my head just to irritate me further."

Unable to remain silent, Amber commented, "It was most obvious that you were quite vexed with his lordship."

Aurelia's eyes were filled with merriment as she fanned a hand in front of her face. "I love him quite desperately, you know."

Amber wondered if, one day, she too would find a man to love desperately. One who would vex her in the extreme.

A blond-haired giant of a man filled her mind's eye.

Mayhap she had already found him.

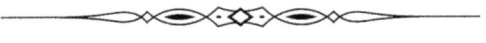

CHAPTER ELEVEN

"How could she have escaped?" Viscount Trenchert roared.

The underling delivering the message took a step backward. "I have no idea, your lordship."

The viscount glared at the footman. If he were to cash in on his wager before the authorities caught wind of his early morning meeting at Chalk Farm—and the lifeless body of the unfortunate Lord Eggerton—he needed to find the chit, and fast! He stalked over to his desk to pen a reply and thought better of it. "Give the messenger my verbal reply: 'FIND HER!'"

"Ye...yes, your lordship." The servant backed out of the viscount's study and closed the door. The sound of footsteps running down the hallway only irritated Trenchert further. It was time to replace the bumbling idiot.

Pouring a glass of brandy, he ruminated over the fact that Eggerton had surprised him. He had misjudged the man, and that had never happened before. Trenchert had never been caught unaware. Eggerton had had a plan all along. Proof of that was the fact that his daughter was not in London at all! Bloody inconvenient, to have to hie after the chit.

He sipped and savored the French contraband. "I believe I shall enjoy the taming of my betrothed." The image of her naked, spread-eagle on his bed—wrists and ankles bound to the bedposts—had him hard as stone. He could almost hear her pleading, begging him to release her. Anticipation surged through him, and he slowly smiled. "I haven't deflowered a virgin in quite some time."

After tossing back the remainder of his brandy, he set the glass on the sideboard and stalked from the room. He had to speak to his contact within the Bow Street Runners to ensure there would be no backlash with this latest lord who'd challenged him to a duel…and lost.

Chapter Twelve

Dermott rushed down the servants' staircase, having been summoned by Sean. He was pleased that the viscount and the earl had not pushed back against the suggestion that they send an outrider in advance of their arrival when traveling between their estates.

The distance was not all that great, but given the continued rash of threats and rumors, it was better to be overcautious than to be lax in their protection of the duke's extended family.

Standing alongside Sean and Flaherty, he waited for the man dressed in the forest-green livery of Viscount Chattsworth's household to rein in his horse in front of the stables and dismount. "His lordship and ladyship will be arriving in three-quarters of an hour," the man said.

Sean motioned for one of the stable lads to come forward and see to the servant's horse, then asked, "Any message from me brother, Michael, or cousin, James?"

"None."

When Sean frowned, Dermott elbowed him. "I'm thinking our cousins will be expecting to go a few rounds with us. We can squeeze in some time to sharpen our bare-knuckle skills a bit later tonight, after things have settled down. I'll take the first shift standing guard."

Sean agreed, "We cannot let our hand-to-hand skills get

rusty."

Satisfaction filled Dermott—he needed to release some of the pressure and worry building inside of him. "Do ye think James will have gone soft now that he's a married man?"

Sean snorted. "If anything, he'll be ready to take on all comers. He has added a wife to his list of those he's protecting, same as meself and Michael have."

Dermott knew his cousin had the right of it, especially after he'd told his cousins he'd added the lass to *his* list. But now wasn't the time to remind Sean or Flaherty. They had increased the necessary shifts and manpower surrounding Lippincott Manor—and added three more lives to protect.

"Finch is waiting to speak with ye," Sean told the footman who'd delivered the message from Chattsworth Manor. "While ye're here, ye may be on double duty, as footman and, if needed, guarding the perimeter."

The younger man squared his shoulders. "I've been training with Michael and James."

"Have ye now?" Flaherty nodded. "Sharpening yer observational skills as well as weaponry?"

The footman grinned. "You can count on me!"

"Best go and see Finch now, lad," Sean said, then watched the way the younger man sprinted to the rear entrance. "Were we ever that young and eager?"

Dermott waited a beat before answering, "Aye, but that was before me da and yers were tossed in that cell." Meeting his cousin's gaze, he murmured, "Me life is divided into three separate and distinct parts: growing up on the farm, me da's passing, and arriving in London."

Flaherty, who had been silent, spoke up. "There's not a one of us in the family who will ever forget what happened to yer da, Dermott."

Dermott grunted. "Nor what happened hours before they were released."

Sean added, "Nor the fact me da and yers were exonerated…

Bloody bastards were hours too late releasing them."

Dermott's gut iced over as he remembered the day clearly, and his eldest brother's and Sean's reactions when they shared the news. His gaze met Sean's, and he knew now wasn't the time to speak of that atrocity—or his da's death. "We'd best be ready for the onslaught once their ladyships get together..." He let his voice trail off, as if not wanting to say what they three of were already thinking...and bracing for.

Dermott shoved the ache of his da's passing deep, concentrating on protecting their lordships and their families. "With the five of us guarding them—"

"Don't be forgetting me nephew-in-law Bart and the captain's men," Sean said. "Coventry is sending three of the new London guards."

Flaherty grunted. "Michael's stepson is a good lad to have at yer back in a fight. I'm pleased Captain Coventry took our suggestion of hiring on some of our contacts from the docks."

"And the stews," Dermott added.

Sean nodded. "He appreciated the fact that our contacts are cut from a similar cloth to ourselves. Honest, fiercely loyal, and highly skilled in hand-to-hand combat and weaponry."

"When will they be arriving?" Flaherty asked.

"Midday at the earliest," Sean answered.

⁂

THE CACOPHONY OF voices—feminine and masculine—drifted up the stairwell from the entryway. Amber had left her door open a crack, hoping to hear Dermott's footsteps approaching, or see his handsome face when he paused in her doorway. She cocked her head to one side to better hear. Smiling, she realized the viscount and his family must have arrived. Was it a bit earlier than they were expected? From the way Lady Aurelia spoke of her dear friend, Lady Calliope, Amber had the impression it would not matter.

She was anxious to meet the viscountess, hoping that the other woman would remember meeting her in London—even though Lady Aurelia had not. The sounds grew louder, and the cry of a babe reached her. *The viscount's heir,* she thought with a smile. She paused as a feeling of warmth filled her. Was *she* fond of children?

Dropping her forehead into her hands, she wished there was some way to extract more memories from those still tangled in her injured brain. She desperately wanted to at least be able to introduce herself with her real name. Lady Aurelia had invited Amber to join her and Lady Calliope in her private upstairs sitting room when the viscount and viscountess arrived. It was quieter there, the countess had informed her, so they would be able to chat about anything and everything they desired without interruption. She was looking forward to joining them.

As the bright, bubbly, feminine voices filled the air, she wondered how long it had been since the two women had had a chance to visit. She waited a few moments, hoping that the memory of visiting with friends would break through the edges of the fog in her brain. When it did not, her thoughts drifted back to the handsome Irishman who was never far from her thoughts. She sighed deeply. The man had her dreaming of rainbows and reaching for the stars. All it took was one of his intensely dark and desperate looks. She could not quite decide what he was thinking. Pulling her into his embrace and kissing her...or something far more intimate that she could only speculate about.

Papa had been too embarrassed to speak of what went on in the marriage bed. But he had enlisted the aid of their housekeeper and cook once she was of an age to marry.

A gasp escaped before she covered her mouth with her hands. Stunned, she slowly let them drop to her sides. Relief speared through her—she had to be at least eight and ten, possibly older. Amber recalled Papa creating a list of gentlemen he deemed worthy enough to ask for her hand. She was elated by what had just popped into her mind, and at the same time frustrated. She could not even remember the servants' names! Despair swirled inside of her. What would become of her? Would she be sent off to a hospital, or worse, an asylum where people who had lost their minds were cared for?

"I have not lost my mind," she reasoned aloud. "I am fully capable of thinking, as I had been before whatever happened to me happened. The names will come to me in time—mine and Papa's—then all will be well, and I can return home."

The futility of trying clung to her thoughts like a vine, dragging her spirits down. Unable to give up, she tried to remember all that Dermott had told her when she came to. *I must have liked to climb trees in my youth,* she thought. After all, Dermott had said she was standing atop a stone wall when he first saw her. She'd never struck her head, so far as she could recall.

The sudden flash of memory had her stiffening her spine and sitting up straight. "I used to climb fences—to walk along the top rail!" Another flash, this time of fluffy white clouds and a bright blue sky, had her smiling—until the memory of sharp pain spearing through her shoulder filled her. "I wasn't supposed to be on the top of the fence rail. Hadn't Papa warned me?" The memory of how proud she'd been balancing there was short-lived, followed by her windmilling her arms to steady herself before she fell. Her shoulder had taken the brunt of the impact when she'd landed inside one of the corrals at their country home—

"We have a country home!"

She had to tell Dermott! Shooting to her feet, Amber rushed to her bedchamber door, flung it open, and plowed into a solid wall of muscle.

"Whoa there, lass. Where are ye off to in such a hurry?"

She blinked and stared up at the dark-haired, dark-eyed man who steadied her. He was dressed in black and had the same emblem Dermott had over his heart, an embroidered golden Celtic harp, and the word *Eire* in Kelly green. Was he part of the same guard as Dermott? "I, uh... Who are you?"

The man smiled, and the resemblance to Dermott was uncanny. "Name's Garahan. I'm one of the Duke of Wyndmere's guard stationed at Chattsworth Manor. Ye must be the lass me cousin, Dermott, rescued."

"Yes, my name—well, at least my temporary name—is Amber."

His measured look as he studied her caught her off guard, as did his question: "Temporary—and why would that be? Are ye hiding from someone?"

She frowned. "I do not think so, but, you see, I'm having a bit of trouble recalling what happened before I opened my eyes and looked into eyes of the clearest green."

His eyes were alight with amusement. "Green, were they?"

"Er...yes. He introduced himself as Dermott O'Malley—he works for the duke here at Lippincott Manor. Although I'm not quite certain I believe him, he informed me that he rescued me when I fell off the top of a stone wall."

Garahan's lips twitched. "What were ye doing up there?"

She shrugged. "I don't remember, and that is the other part of my problem. I do not recall my name or what I am doing here." Deciding to trust Garahan, she asked, "Is Dermott busy at the moment? Do you think you could find him for me? I have remembered something important."

He locked his gaze with hers as if considering her request. "Well now, was it yer name that ye remembered?"

She shook her head and schooled her features to appear confident. "Not yet, but I'm hopeful."

"In that case, I'll let me cousin know that you need to speak to him. Was there anything else I can do for ye, Miss Amber?"

"No, thank you. I'm grateful that you'll relay my message to Dermott. I need him."

The guard bowed to her, studying her for a moment before continuing on his way down the length of the hall to the door to the servants' staircase. Dermott must still be manning his shift.

The voices had moved from the entryway and were quieter. It would be best if she waited in her bedchamber for the summons from Lady Aurelia, as she was unsure of who would arrive first—a servant to announce that the countess was waiting for her in her private sitting room, or the man who filled her mind and heart completely…Dermott O'Malley.

Settling into the green velvet lady's chair by the window, she let her mind wander. Mayhap resting it would be a better idea than continually struggling to remember what she desperately needed to know.

The knock on the door startled her. She turned toward the door, thinking it would be the summons to meet with the countess and the viscountess. "Come in."

The man who had captured her attention from the moment she'd opened her eyes to a world washed with uncertainty—and not a wisp of memory—stepped over the threshold and walked over to where she sat. "Is something troubling ye, lass? Ye're pale as flour. What's happened?"

She closed her eyes for a moment to thank the Lord for sending Dermott to rescue her. "We have a home—here—in Sussex!"

He nodded. "Sure and that's good news. Is it nearby? Do ye remember the earl and the countess now that ye remember having a home in the country?"

"Er…no. I'm afraid I do not."

"I did not mean to belittle what ye remembered, lass. 'Tis a wonderful thing that bits and pieces are starting to fill in the blanks. I cannot imagine being in yer place. 'Twould drive me bloody insane."

Her eyes widened at the expression. Surely he had not meant to use such coarse language in front of her.

He tilted his head back and stared up at the ceiling. Was he counting?

"Forgive me, lass. 'Tis me mouth moving before me brain tells it to again. I should not use such language in front a lady like yerself."

She bit her bottom lip, and was about to tell him he was forgiven, but got lost in the brilliance of his emerald eyes...eyes that were locked on her lips. A tingling sensation had her pressing her lips together to quell thoughts of fitting her mouth to his. Hers would not be the first lips he kissed, though the thought did not bother her overmuch. She wondered—was he as distracted by thoughts of kissing her as she was of kissing him? Staring at his beautifully sculpted lips, she could well imagine how masterful his kiss would be. Passionate, demanding a response from her.

Had she been kissed before, or was her knowledge culled from reading romantic tales?

Dermott cleared his throat. "I'm powerful sorry to have insulted ye with me words, lass. 'Twasn't me intention."

He had been worried that she was upset, when all the while she'd been wondering what it would be like when he finally kissed her! "You are forgiven. I have been known to speak without thinking on occasion..."

"Something else ye recalled. At this rate, the pieces ye're struggling to fit into the puzzle of yer life will be falling into place so fast, ye'll not be able to keep up with it."

"Why can I remember that I was trying to escape someone, but not his name?"

He reached for her hands and held them securely in his. Warmth radiated from his callused palms to hers. "Never fear, lass. I'll protect ye until ye remember everything, and we're able to sort things out."

"Oh. Dermott. I did not know you were in here." Lady Aurelia stood in the doorway, watching them intently.

"I remembered something, your ladyship," Amber said. "I thought it would be best to tell Dermott."

"Garahan found me. As ye and Lady Calliope were visiting, I thought it best to speak to the lass first."

"I see." The thoughtful expression on the countess's face worried Amber. Was Lady Aurelia vexed with her, or was it something else entirely?

"I don't know why I immediately thought to tell Dermott. It's just... Well, I—"

Lady Aurelia smiled. "I completely understand. Our Dermott was the one to rescue you and deliver you into our safekeeping. You trust him implicitly. I felt the same the first time I danced with Edward."

"Thank ye for understanding, yer ladyship," Dermott replied. "I need to speak with his lordship."

"I believe he is in the library."

"Thank ye." Dermott bowed to the ladies and left.

The countess walked over, slipped her arm though Amber's, and confided, "If I had not already fallen head over heels in love with Edward, my head might have been turned by one of my brother-in-law's guards."

"They are a handsome group," Amber admitted.

"You have no idea what a heart-stopping tableau the sixteen of them standing broad shoulder to broad shoulder make." Lady Aurelia waved a hand in front of her face. "Positively numbed my brain and stole my breath."

They were laughing as they walked toward the countess's sitting room. "Mrs. Jones should be arriving momentarily with our tea," she said. "I just came from the nursery. Calliope is settling little William in for a much-needed nap. He was awake the entire ride over. Our maids will be watching over them while we have our tea. You'll meet Calliope's maid, Mary Kate, later."

Amber wondered why the countess—and apparently the viscountess too—did not have a nanny. Wasn't it too much to ask their lady's maids to take on that chore? Besides that, wasn't it unusual?

Unsure if it would be too gauche to ask, she thought maybe she should forgo tea with their ladyships. "I would certainly understand if now is not a good time to visit. I'd be happy to wait to meet Lady Calliope another time."

"Not necessary. Our darling babe is still asleep, but Edward won't stay that way for long. I have learned to make good use of the time in between feedings and naptime."

Neither feeding nor naptime sparked a memory. She must not be accustomed to being around or used to caring for babes. "I'm looking forward to meeting Viscountess Calliope and sharing a cup of tea with you both. Thank you for including me."

"My pleasure. Sitting in seclusion waiting for your memory to return is pointless, don't you think? Something as simple as chatting over tea is far more enjoyable, and just might prod your memory. I cannot think your sitting in silence trying to force yourself to remember would engender your brain to suddenly do so."

"I never thought of it that way," Amber said as they entered the sitting room. "Thank you for your kindness and thoughtfulness. I'm beyond grateful."

Tea arrived as they settled across from one another on matching pale green and cream striped settees.

"Shall I pour?" the earl's housekeeper asked.

"No, thank you, Mrs. Jones," the countess replied. "I do believe it's Calliope's turn to pour. She should be here any minute."

The housekeeper smiled. "Just ring if you need anything else."

A glance at the large tea tray the footman had carried in had Amber wondering what else they could possibly need. Before she opened her mouth and asked, which would not have been well done of her, a slim woman with hair the color of sun-warmed honey swept into the room.

"Ah, here's Calliope now. Come join us for a much-needed spot of tea and something sweet."

"You always know just what I need, Aurelia, thank you," the viscountess replied.

Lady Aurelia beamed. "Calliope, I'd like you to meet Miss Amber. Miss Amber, Viscountess Chattsworth."

"It's a pleasure to meet you, Amber."

"I confess I was listening to your happy voices," Amber said, "as they twined with the deeper voices coming from the entryway. You are very lucky to share such a close friendship with someone your age." *Why can I not remember having friends?*

"We have been through a lifetime together in such a short amount of time. It draws one closer to one another," Aurelia said. With a smile for her friend, she nodded to the small tray with the covered dish. "If you'll remover the cover, Calliope, you'll find something that you and Uncle Phineas enjoy."

Calliope whipped off the lid and started to laugh. "Kippers! Oh, I do love them, though William is not as fond of them as your uncle and me. How is dear Uncle Phineas? Does he plan on visiting soon?"

Amber watched the two women chatting and laughing and felt a deep sadness as a wisp of a memory of sharing tea—not with any young women her age, but with her mum—slipped in and out of her mind. Before she could grab hold of it, the memory evaporated.

"More tea, Amber?"

"Er…yes. Thank you." A feeling of gloom and doom seemed to weigh her down. Did it have to do with her mum, or something more ominous? She would have to wait and see. Promising herself to enjoy the short time spent over tea, she joined in the lively conversation, knowing Dermott would protect her when trouble came looking for her.

CHAPTER THIRTEEN

DERMOTT NODDED TO his cousins and Bart—Michael O'Malley's stepson. "Ye've grown more than an inch since the last time I was at Chattsworth Manor."

The cheeky grin was proof that Bart was happy and adjusting well to his new father.

"I hear me cousin has been teaching ye the fine art of bare-knuckle fighting."

The boy squared his shoulders and curled his hands into fists to demonstrate the series of punches he'd learned so far.

"Impressive, lad. Care to go a few rounds later? Since ye're family, I'll go easy on ye."

Michael shot him a look of warning. For a moment, Dermott wondered if his cousin needed permission from his wife. He could not imagine that was the case. Harriet—or Harry, as she was known to family and friends—was a formidable, but admirable, woman. Dermott admired the way she'd dug in and kept the family farm running after the death of her first husband.

Unable to decipher the look, he backtracked. "But we'll need to be holding off until after things have settled down here at the manor, won't we?"

"I'm sure we could squeeze in the time..." Bart looked at Michael for confirmation, and when he did not receive it, he shrugged. "Duty first."

"Aye, Bart. Ye've been listening to yer da...er, Michael." Dermott couldn't recall hearing Bart refer to his stepfather as Da. Best to keep it simple, as they had far more to worry about. He had to keep his mind where it belonged and not where it tended to wander...to the amber-eyed lass. The problem for Dermott was how in the world to disengage his heart now that it was firmly in the lass's grasp?

Garahan was late joining the others. "I was just on the roof. Our reinforcements are headed this way."

"They should be expecting one of us—or a few of us—to meet with them," Dermott said.

"Aye," Sean agreed. "Coventry explained the situation to the men when he hired them. The captain was in agreement with us that, for His Grace's sake, the duke should not be introduced to the men recently hired as eyes and ears in and around London."

"The men will need to meet all of us," Garahan said. "Not just Sean and Dermott. I'm certain I speak for everyone when I say that we've no wish to meet with the wrong end of a pistol or knife."

The chorus of "ayes" had Sean nodding. "'Twas me intention to meet with them, as we'll be working together when on patrol."

Flaherty nodded to Michael and Bart. "We've all given our vow to protect the duke and his family. It shouldn't take long to make the introductions and divide up our duties, specifically the longer patrols—the perimeter patrol, and the longest patrol, to the village and back."

Dermott was glad Garahan spoke up. It would be detrimental not to have the newest London recruits unfamiliar with the duke's guard. A glance at his cousins had a sliver of worry settling at the base of his skull, causing a dull throb. It was imperative that the men Captain Coventry had sent them knew the faces of each and every man protecting the earl, the viscount, and their families—especially at night. He rubbed a hand absently on his forearm. He'd been on the receiving end of a lead ball from a situation all too similar to what they now faced. *Shoot first; ask questions later.*

He met Garahan's gaze and knew the moment his cousin remembered that night. "Flaherty is right," Garahan said. "Have ye forgotten the night Dermott was mistaken for an intruder and shot?"

Bart's eyes widened. "You've been shot like Michael? Where? Did they have to dig the lead ball out of you?"

Michael chuckled as he lightly cuffed his stepson on the shoulder. "Ye've a bloodthirsty mind, Bart. Dermott can tell ye all about it later." He turned to stare at three riders on horseback approaching. "We've got company."

Dermott was not surprised that the men in question nodded to them, but continued on the path that would lead behind the stables to the outbuilding where Dermott and Flaherty were housed. As the only married member of the duke's guard stationed at Lippincott Manor, Sean, with his wife and infant son, lived in a newly constructed cottage—a gift from the earl and countess—not far from one of the tenant farmers.

Garahan grinned. "Stratford, 'tis been some time since we've run into one another."

The bull of a man grinned. "You're still alive, Garahan?"

They were laughing as Sean said, "I see that ye two seem to know one another, Garahan. Stratford, me name's Sean O'Malley. Who have ye brought with ye?"

"Varley and Tarleton."

The men were not among Dermott's London contacts, but he did not bother to ask his cousins if they knew the men. The cousins and brothers in the duke's guard trusted one another's instincts implicitly. In their line of work, it was essential to their survival and that of those under their protection.

Garahan crossed his arms in front of him and relaxed his stance. "Men, I'd like ye to meet me cousins. Michael and Dermott O'Malley, and Seamus Flaherty. Sean is the head of the duke's guard stationed at Lippincott Manor. Michael's in charge at Chattsworth Manor."

Stratford stared at Garahan long enough to have him asking, "What?"

"Where do you fit in, Garahan?"

"I work with Michael."

"Ah, so he's in charge of you." The other man slowly smiled. "I would have thought it would take at least two men to keep you in line."

The look on Garahan's face was comical, but Dermott swallowed his laughter. He'd earned the moniker of peacemaker among his brothers and cousins when they were young. Dermott had not had to step in between either since they'd left their homes back in Ireland. Though he had stood between the duke and his family more than he had anticipated would be necessary. Going after Hollingford during the viscount's attack on Wyndmere Hall had earned him another moniker—the duke's mercenary. The duke was well protected, as Dermott was in good company with his brothers: Patrick, Finn, and Emmett, as the duke's sword, dragoon, and man-at-arms. His O'Malley cousins: the duke's protector, shield, rapier, and lance. His Garahan cousins: the duke's hammer, defender, saber, and enforcer, and his Flaherty cousins: the duke's champion, sharpshooter, cavalier, and blade.

It was agreed that for their first shift, Stratford and Varley would guard the perimeter, while Tarleton would be their eyes and ears in the village. The men stowed their gear in the outbuilding and then set off to man their first shifts.

Extra manpower notwithstanding, Dermott's uneasy gut sensed Trenchert would be making his first move in the next twenty-four hours. His greatest worry was that word would somehow reach the viscount that the physician had been to Lippincott Manor to tend to a young woman rescued by one of the duke's guard.

He knew the doctor would not openly speak of his patient or the care given. On the other hand, there could be a conversation regarding the physician and why he had not been available for one of the villagers in need while he tended to an injured lass at Lippincott Manor.

An itch between his shoulder blades had him asking to switch shift locations in order to remain closer to the lass. She was *his* responsibility, his mind insisted, while a deep sense that she was the other half of his heart filled him. Time would tell.

"Dermott?"

He paused with his hand on the door to the servants' staircase, surprised to find Bart rushing toward him. "Is there trouble, lad?"

"No, but Michael and Uncle Sean decided that since you switched shifts, now would be a good time for me to learn from you."

"Learn?"

"As it's an interior shift, if we split the duties, you will have time to explain what you do and what things would possibly indicate trouble is brewing."

He frowned at the youth. "I see. Whose idea was it, Sean's or Michael's?"

Bart shrugged. "I didn't ask—this is the first time they have included me in guard duty outside of Chattsworth Manor."

Dermott nodded. "Well then, we'd best get to it, lad. Where would ye prefer to start, on the attic level or down here?"

He noticed the lad glance down the hallway toward the kitchen and could not help but smile, sensing the lad was like he and his brothers and cousins had been at the same age—hungry from the moment they opened their eyes in the morning until they closed them at night. The earl's cook seemed to know when someone was in need of a good meal—or just a quick bite of a scone or two.

"Why don't ye start down here? I'll begin me shift on the attic level. We'll switch in two hours."

Bart grinned. "Thanks, Dermott!" He turned around and rushed off to the kitchen.

"Ye aren't guarding the scones or defending the berry tarts, boy-o!"

The lad laughed. "I just wanted to introduce myself to the cook, in case she's heard about me and wanted to meet me."

"Ye're a terrible liar, Bartholomew Mayfield O'Malley!" Dermott didn't expect a reply, and was surprised when Bart turned around to face him.

Walking backward toward the kitchen, the lad said, "Garahan's been teaching me that there are times when a lie is necessary to save someone's neck."

Dermott sighed. "Best not be lying to yer ma or Michael."

"I won't."

"Or their lordships, or any of us in the duke's guard," Dermott cautioned.

"I won't. I promise."

"Good lad. I expect to see ye on the third floor in two hours."

"I'll be there!" Bart called out as he disappeared into the kitchen.

As Dermott ascended the stairs, he murmured, "I'd best be asking Mrs. Wyatt not to give all of the scones she normally saves for meself to that likeable lad."

He was smiling as he reached the third floor to begin his shift.

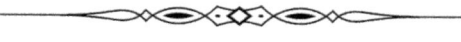

CHAPTER FOURTEEN

THE FEELING OF impending disaster continued to weigh heavy on Amber. She felt a sense of urgency to remember...but what? It was obviously something of extreme importance. By the time the teapot was empty and all that remained on the plate piled high with teacakes, scones, and tarts were crumbs, she was exhausted. Despite the wonderful company, and feeling as if she had found two new friends, her head began to throb. The more she tried to hide the turmoil inside of her, the more intense her feelings of urgency, magnified by the ache in her head.

"Thank you for an enjoyable visit. I'm honored, your ladyships. Though, if you do not mind," Amber said, "I would like to lie down for a little while."

Lady Aurelia studied her intently before answering, "Are you feeling poorly? You should have mentioned that your head was bothering you. We never would have gone on and on talking about our sons, the wives of the men in the duke's guard, and the goings-on at Lippincott and Chattsworth."

"I thought it would eventually go away," Amber confessed. "But it hasn't, even though I am almost back to feeling like myself... Almost."

"I do hope you rest for as long as you need," Lady Calliope said.

Amber thought to tell them that she felt fine, just tired, but from the looks the other women were giving her, she knew the only person she would be fooling was herself. "Thank you both—I enjoyed myself. I cannot recall the last time I had the opportunity to sit down and chat over tea."

"Although we have not known one another long," Aurelia said, "I feel as if we are kindred spirits. I have enjoyed our tea immensely."

"I have too," Calliope added. "I hope you don't mind a bit of advice, but please do rest now and whenever else you can." The two shared a telling look before Aurelia nodded, and Calliope continued, "You are safe here."

"Dermott and the others will see to it that no harm will come to you while you are staying with us," Aurelia reiterated.

An ache in the pit of Amber's stomach had her automatically pressing her hand against it to relieve the pain. "I cannot stay here indefinitely," she reasoned. "At some point, I will have to return to my family's town home, as..." Her voice trailed off as she searched her brain for a clue as to where that home might be. Finally, she had no choice but to say, "That is, as soon as I remember what part of London that might be...and my name."

"I am certain you shall remember in no time," Calliope replied.

"Out of the blue," Aurelia added.

Amber was about to remind them of the possibility she might never regain her full memory, but the knock on the door interrupted her.

"Come in," the countess called.

The door opened, and Lady Aurelia's maid entered the room. "Someone's hungry a bit earlier today, your ladyship."

Aurelia's smile was radiant. "Is he? Well now, I shall not keep my darling babe waiting."

Calliope was quick to follow her. "Did Mary Kate ask for me to come as well? Was my little William starting to stir?"

Jenny nodded. "Yes, but do not worry, as Mary Kate has matters well in hand. But they will soon be—" The distinct sound of a babe crying could be heard. "We'd best hurry!"

"Calliope and I will come at once," Lady Aurelia said. "Please accompany Amber to her bedchamber. She is going to rest for a bit."

"Of course, your ladyship."

Amber fell silent as she followed Lady Aurelia's maid, wondering what it would feel like to have a babe of her own to love and cherish. Shocked at the turn of her thoughts, she nearly laughed out loud, but managed to rein in her reaction and not embarrass herself. She chided herself for putting the cart before the horse. She needed to marry before she began to even *think* about having a babe.

Dermott O'Malley's handsome face and muscular frame filled her mind before she was able to dismiss the idea. A beautiful babe with bright green eyes, soft blond hair, and a cunning smile filled her mind. No matter how hard she tried to set the image aside, it was well and truly stuck there. She sighed, knowing he had an important job to do: protect the duke and his family. Amber would never want to interfere. It was bad enough she had taken him away from his duties. Now that she was feeling a little better, and able to recall more of her past and herself, she expected to see less of the handsome Irishman.

Pausing in front of the door to Amber's bedchamber, Jenny held it open for her. "Is there anything I can get for you before I leave, Miss Amber?"

"Not a thing, thank you," Amber answered. "I just need to close my eyes and rest."

"Someone will be by to check on how you are feeling in a little while."

"Oh, but that will not be necessary," Amber told the maid.

"Doctor's orders."

"I see." And she did—the earl and countess were being cautious as well as solicitous because of the wound to her head and resultant memory loss. Her guardian angel must have intervened for her to have ended up in the care of such generous people.

"Thank you for letting me know, and please thank her ladyship and his lordship for me."

"I would be happy to." Jenny followed her into the room and turned down the covers. "Do you need help getting into bed?"

Feeling as if she needed to return the kindness of her host and hostess, Amber asked, "Is there anything I can do to help, since the viscount and his family are now staying here? I have been known to sew a fine seam and have mended more than one of Papa's cambric shirts..." She trailed off as the memory of his face filled her—warm gray eyes, a ruggedly handsome face, and a shock of dark hair streaked with gray.

With the vision of her father filling her mind's eye, she staggered toward the bed and sat on the edge of it.

"Are you all right, Miss Amber? You've gone pale." Jenny stepped out into the hallway to speak to the footman stationed there.

Amber was still reeling at how clear Papa's image was—and how it came on so suddenly that she could do no more than sit and let her mind absorb it. She struggled, but could not recall his name...nor hers.

"I've sent the footman to ask Mrs. Jones to come up. She'll be here in a few moments." Jenny paused and gave a hesitant smile before asking, "Would you like me to sit here with you, or would you rather be alone? I can wait outside."

"Would you mind terribly if I'd rather be alone for a few moments?"

"Not at all, Miss Amber, I'll be right outside. Call out if you need me." With a brief nod, Jenny closed the door behind her.

Alone, Amber settled on the bed and closed her eyes. Her mind called up moments in time with a younger version of her father. Not wanting to force her brain to work harder, as it always left her feeling drained and with an aching head, she let it wander at will. Before she could order herself not to, her thoughts returned to the broad-shouldered, green-eyed, captivating man who'd rescued her. Did he have any idea that he'd stolen her heart?

Her belly began to ache again. What if he had someone special in his life? What if he was *married*? That thought had an uncomfortable roil rumbling in her stomach. She'd never experienced such an emotional upheaval before. Had she never been in love? Searching her feelings, she could not recall ever feeling one-quarter of what filled her to bursting whenever Dermott was near. If he did have a sweetheart or intended, she would have to accept it.

What would be hard to accept was the fact that her heart was no longer her own. Dermott O'Malley held it in the palm of his strong, calloused hands. Thoughts of being held in his arms—against his broad chest, leaning her head against the steady beat of his heart—kept her company while she closed her eyes. The Irishman's face comforted her as she drifted off to sleep.

THE SOUND OF a deep voice broke through her slumber, prodding her to wake. She rubbed her eyes and sat up in bed. The rumbling continued, and she wondered who was standing just outside her bedchamber door. Reaching up to tuck in a few stray hairpins, she scooted to the edge of the bed and rose. Still a bit sleepy, but no longer as wobbly, she walked over to the washstand, intending to splash her face with cool water.

The heavy knock startled her. She turned to stare at the door. "Who is there?"

"Lass? 'Tis me, Dermott. May I have a word with ye?"

"Dermott?"

"Aye. I need to speak to you about something important, lass."

"Just a moment, please." She quickly washed her face and hands, then dried them on a soft linen cloth before smoothing them over her skirts. It was no use—she was a rumpled mess. But she dared not keep the man waiting after all he had done, and continued to do, for her. She walked to the door and opened it.

"Ye're still pale."

It sounded like an accusation, and she immediately defended herself. "I am always a bit pale on rising."

Dermott frowned, but did not argue with her. How could he, when he hardly knew her? "His lordship wishes to speak to ye, if ye're up to it."

She clasped her hands to her waist. Had something happened? Has someone come looking for her? Amber wanted to ask if her ladyship would be in attendance, but recalled she was tending to their infant son. "Of course. In his study?"

"Aye. If ye'll come with me." He stepped back so that she could precede him.

"I heard voices a few moments ago."

"Forgive me. I did not wish to wake ye, lass."

"I had not intended to fall asleep. I was only going to rest my eyes."

"Ye obviously needed the rest. 'Tisn't a problem—we only want ye to rest and recover, Amber-lass."

Butterflies fluttered inside of her when he rumbled he name he'd given her, and she could feel herself blushing. Thankfully, Dermott was behind her and could not see her face flaming with embarrassment at her body's reaction to him calling her *Amberlass*. Relishing the feeling close to her heart, she asked whom he had been speaking with.

"One of the other guards."

Amber wondered why he did not mention the man's name, then decided that, in his role of protector, Dermott would be cautious about speaking out of hand. Feeling uneasy at the prospect of this meeting, she asked, "Should I be concerned that the earl wishes to speak to me?"

He shot her a lethal grin that had her heart skipping a beat. "Not at all. His lordship takes his responsibility seriously. I brought ye here so yer injuries could be tended to...and for yer protection, lass. He will go to any lengths, as will I, to protect ye. Earl Lippincott is a fair and impartial man. 'Tis an honor to be guarding himself and his family."

She paused, and as she hoped, he moved to stand beside her. When he did, she placed her hand on his forearm. He swept his gaze from the hasty bun she'd fashioned, to her lips, before returning to look deeply into her eyes. Her body responded as warmth swept up from her toes, and the dratted flush returned to her cheeks... She could feel the heat in them.

His green eyes darkened, but still sparkled. "Well now, the color's returning to yer pretty face, lass. I'm glad."

Amber knew she had better get a hold of herself before she fell completely under his spell. She had to find out if there was a woman in his life. Did she dare ask?

Longing gripped her heart at the thought that there may be someone else. Though she had only just met him, she felt such a strong pull toward him. Dare she ask? It wouldn't be right to let herself continue to hope for more if his heart was already engaged, bound to another. She *had* to ask, otherwise she would have fallen in love with a man who was beyond her reach.

She trembled as her heart picked up the beat—did she truly love him? Had she ever loved another? Then a strong sense of rightness filled her. She had never felt this way before. She was in over her head, in love with one of the duke's guard!

"May I ask you a question?"

"I don't think the earl will mind waiting a few moments more. What would ye like to know?"

Before her courage deserted her, she blurted out, "Are you married?"

He snorted with what she suspected was laughter before he cleared his throat to speak. "Nay, lass. I'm not married. Is there anything else ye wanted to ask?"

"Er...yes. Since I have already asked you such a personal question, I do have one more. Is your *heart* engaged?"

He slowly smiled, and she could not help but sigh at the sight. Lord, he was sinfully handsome.

"Aye."

Amber felt as if every ounce of air was being squeezed out of her lungs, and she struggled to draw in a breath. Of *course* he had already given his heart—he must have had dozens of women throwing their hearts at his feet. How could he not?

She felt the tears forming and willed them away. Hadn't she already embarrassed herself enough for one day? Belatedly, she realized her hand was still holding his arm. Releasing her grip, she apologized, "Please forgive me. I do not know what came over me."

When he did not speak, merely studied her closely, she hastily added, "Thank you for all you have done for me, Dermott. I will never forget your kindness, or how you saved me."

He frowned. "I would have done the same for anyone in need, lass."

"Of course," she whispered.

"Ye don't have to worry—the earl isn't planning to boot ye out of his home, lass. He just wants to speak with ye, but he has been tied up with other matters."

Relief twined with sorrow that the man who filled her thoughts and mind from sunup till sundown would never be able to return her feelings. Shoving her feelings deep, she managed to respond, "Well, that is wonderful news, isn't it?"

"Aye. I'm not certain what ye've been thinking, lass, to lose the roses in yer cheeks that quickly. But whatever it is, try to set it aside. I don't want his lordship to think I've been treating ye badly."

"Oh, you would never do that."

"What makes ye say that, lass?"

"I...er... Well, that is..." What could she say that would not make her sound any more of a bacon-brained female than she already had? Asking Dermott if he was married or had given his heart away?

His gaze locked on hers. "Looking at ye is like a glass of water to a man dying of thirst. Essential."

She felt the warmth in her cheeks again and wished she was not so fair that her blushes were so easily seen. Turning from his sharp gaze, Amber was surprised when the tip of his finger beneath her chin urged her to look back at him. Their eyes met, and she was nearly swept away by the power of her attraction to him. Dermott O'Malley was quickly becoming far more important to her than she was to him. How could she be, when his heart was already taken?

"We'd best be going," he murmured. "His lordship does not like to be kept waiting long."

She practically ran to keep up with Dermott. When they reached the study, he paused, holding her gaze for long moments without speaking. Tracing the curve of her cheek with the tip of his finger, he rasped, "Don't worry so, lass. As I told ye, the earl is a fair man. Trust him... Trust us."

"I do trust you, Dermott," she whispered, unable to tear her gaze away from his beautifully sculpted lips. Would they be firm or soft? Did she dare ruin the man's opinion of her, more than she already had, by acting the complete hoyden and giving in to the urge to touch him again? What would he do if she reached up and touched the tips of her fingertips to his full bottom lip?

Could he read her mind? The emotions in his eyes were ones she had never seen before. From her limited experience, she guessed it could be passion. Passion and love were entwined, were they not? But lust, if she remembered their housekeeper's warnings...lust was not tied to any emotions at all. It was an animalistic urge. Nothing more.

His eyes changed to a deeper, intense green, and she wondered if he felt something too. But how could he feel anything toward her so quickly if his heart was already taken? Was he that free with his feelings? Did he have more than one sweetheart? Given how utterly beautiful he was, she sensed it was a distinct possibility. No. It would go against his strict code of conduct and the deep-rooted honor that she sensed within him.

What had come over her? Her uneasiness told her that this behavior was not normal for her. It had only been a few days since she had wakened staring into the depths of his brilliant emerald eyes. She wished she were still in London so that she could ask their housekeeper or cook about the feelings tangling into a series of tight knots in her belly.

Resolved that she would have to navigate the situation and her feelings without advice, she looked into the depths of his eyes. This would be her only chance, and though she knew his heart was taken, she accepted responsibility for her soul being stuck in Purgatory—but more, accepted the fact that she would be damned for eternity as she gave in to temptation and traced the fullness of his bottom lip with the tip of her finger.

His strangled groan surprised her. She dropped her hand and stepped back. "Forgive me—you did say your heart was engaged. I know that I will be leaving soon, and will never see you again. I could not help myself, though I should not have been so bold as to touch you. I have no idea what came over me."

His gaze locked on hers. "There's nothing to forgive, as I know exactly what came over ye, lass. For the same feelings have been driving me to the brink of sanity." He bent his head, and she lifted onto her toes, meeting him halfway. The anticipation of feeling his lips pressed firmly to hers had her knees wobbling, her body trembling, and her heart racing.

The door opened, and they jolted apart. The earl stood in the doorway looking from Dermott to her and then back again. Finally, he said, "Excellent. You're here. I thought I was going to have to ask one of the footmen to find you. Come in."

Dermott placed his hand to her small of her back, gently urging her into the earl's study.

"Won't you have a seat?" the earl inquired.

"Thank you, your lordship." She settled in one of the brown leather chairs by the fireplace. A glance at Dermott, and she knew he was uncomfortable. Was he concerned that the earl had seen them about to kiss? Should she be? Had he truly just told her that he felt the same way toward her, or had she imagined it?

Lord, what a bumblebroth this was turning out to be.

CHAPTER FIFTEEN

"I TRUST YOU are feeling better, Miss Amber." The earl's confident tone eased some of the tension in the room.

"Much better, your lordship. I cannot thank you enough for your kindness in allowing me to recuperate here."

"It is our pleasure. I would never turn away anyone in need of help when it was within my power to give it." He glanced at Dermott and said, "Besides, our Dermott was the one who galloped to your rescue, even though you did not heed his warning not to jump off the wall."

"I... I'm afraid I do not remember climbing that wall, let alone how I came to be on top of it." Worry that she would never know was slowly eroding the calm she had been working so hard to embrace. The very atmosphere at Lippincott Manor was soothing, serene.

The heavy knock on the door had the earl calling out, "Enter!"

Sean O'Malley opened the door and filled the entryway. "There's trouble." He glanced at his cousin, and, without speaking, must have conveyed a silent message to Dermott.

"I'm right behind ye." Dermott bowed to her. "Amber-lass, I need ye to stay with their ladyships."

"Yes, of course."

"They are in the nursery," Lippincott told her. "I shall escort you. Sean, I expect a full report when I join you in your quarters."

Sean shook his head. "Behind the stables, yer lordship."

"Very well. I shall be there as soon as I deliver Miss Amber to the nursery. Send one of the footmen—better yet, send Bart to stand guard outside their door."

"Aye." Sean and Dermott shared another telling glance, and strode from the room without another word.

Amber's worry trebled, but she buried it deep, keeping it to herself. The earl was silent as he accompanied her to the nursery. He knocked on the door before opening it. "Ah, my love, there you are. Miss Amber will be joining you and Calliope for the duration."

Lady Aurelia narrowed her gaze at her husband. Lifting her chin to a defiant angle, she demanded, "What are you not telling me, Edward?"

He lifted her hand to his lips, brushed a kiss to the back of it, and nodded. "I shall tell you all I know as soon as the men fill me in." When the countess opened her mouth to speak, the earl frowned. "Time is of the essence." Nodding to the viscountess, he said, "Under no circumstances are you or my wife to leave this room." Turning to Amber, he added, "I am counting on you to be the voice of reason, Miss Amber. My wife and Calliope have been known to race off thinking to lend their aid, but manage to end up in the midst of yet another near disaster."

Amber had no notion what to say in response to the earl's claim but, "You have my word, your lordship."

"Excellent." He strode to the door and paused on the threshold. "Bartholomew will be standing guard. Do not under any circumstances attempt to distract him or extract information from him."

When neither Lady Aurelia nor Lady Calliope responded, the earl demanded, "Have I made myself clear?"

The viscountess agreed immediately. "Yes, of course, Edward." The earl crossed his arms and stared at his wife. After a few tense moments, she inclined her head regally. *"Abundantly."*

Amber could feel the tension crackling between the earl and his countess. Though the earl had not said or done anything to cause her concern, she worried for the sake of the countess nonetheless. Thank goodness the babes were still asleep, obviously used to people carrying on conversations while they did.

Finally, the countess threw her hands up in the air. "Fine! Calliope, Amber, and I promise not to overpower Bart, tie him to a chair, and make him tell us what is going on."

Lippincott's lips twitched, and Amber sensed he was fighting the urge to smile. Satisfied, the earl gave a brief nod, stepped into the hallway, and closed the door behind him.

"The nerve of that man!" Lady Aurelia fumed. "Does he think we do not know trouble is headed our way? How are we to prepare ourselves or the staff for injuries if they keep us in the dark?"

"I agree, Aurelia. Surely your husband and mine must realize they need us to stand at the ready to care for the wounded. Why else would William have brought us—and our guard—here to stay with you?" Calliope murmured.

"Wounded?" Amber asked.

"Er...yes," Aurelia answered.

"I see. Mayhap the viscount brought you here with your guard as a precautionary measure," Amber suggested.

Aurelia slowly smiled. "I take it you are accustomed to being the peacekeeper in your home."

Amber nodded, pleased that she had, in fact, regained another piece of her life.

"We tend to think the worst," Calliope confided. "To be honest, we have been through one difficult situation after another since marrying into the duke's family."

"Edward has been stabbed, and William shot protecting the family," Aurelia said. "How can they not understand that we do not want them to wade into whatever danger is coming our way?"

"How were you able to cope with your husband's injuries? I would have been frantic with worry...although I have never been married," Amber added, "nor have I been engaged, that I can recall."

"Do not try to second-guess yourself," Aurelia advised. "When one speaks so decisively, it is most often because of their instinctive knowledge of facts."

"I could not have said it better," Calliope added. "You are able to remember more each day. Your memory shall return fully, soon."

One of their babes chose that moment to fuss. Soon, the tension in the room evaporated as the women changed and cooed to their babes. Amber waited for them to tug on the bellpull to summon their wet nurses. Not that she had any intimate knowledge on the subject, but didn't all ladies of the *ton* use them?

When they settled in the twin rocking chairs, she asked, "Would you like me to ring for...er...assistance?"

Aurelia shook her head. "No, thank you—Calliope and I prefer a quiet atmosphere when feeding our sons. It is possibly the most soothing part of our days, wouldn't you agree?"

Calliope smiled as she traced the tip of her finger on her son's cheek, settling him in her arms. "I do agree."

"I'm sorry not to have thought that it would make you uncomfortable, Amber," Calliope apologized. "Why don't you step into the hallway and introduce yourself to Bart?"

Aurelia smiled. "What a wonderful idea. My darling earl did not ask *you* to give your word not to speak to Bart. Find out everything he knows!"

Amber hesitated, then asked, "But won't the earl be angry with me?"

Aurelia's light laughter was echoed by Calliope's. "No. However, I am quite sure he will be angry with himself for not thinking to ask for your promise before leaving."

Amber was awed by the beautiful sight of two babes suckling

at their mothers' breasts, and awed at how quickly the two little ones settled down once they began to nurse. She wanted to tell the ladies that they should listen to the earl, but couldn't when she was in full agreement with them. Pitching her voice low, she promised, "I shall see what I can find out for you."

"Do try not to be too obvious," Aurelia cautioned.

"I shall report back shortly," Amber replied. She quietly opened the door and slipped into the hallway.

"Something wrong?" The tension radiating off the young man guarding the door surprised her.

"Not at all. Their ladyships are feeding their sons, and I wanted to give them a bit of privacy."

Bart stared at her for a few moments with a look she could not quite define. Taking a moment to study the young man, she noted he was close in height to Dermott. Though he was broad through the shoulders, he did not have the same heavy musculature as Dermott or the other guards. The flush on Bart's face had her wondering if he was much younger than he appeared. Taking pity on him, she asked, "Are you new to the duke's guard?"

He blinked, then smiled. "I wish I *was* one of His Grace's private guard! My mum's married Michael O'Malley—he's head of the duke's guard for Viscount Chattsworth. My father passed away a few years ago."

"I am so sorry for your loss, Bart. My mum's been gone a very long time. Papa never remarried, though I suspect he and Lady Grey will come to an understanding soon. He has been escorting her to various entertainments for the last two years."

As soon as the words were out of her mouth, she knew them to be fact. Relieved, rather than shocked, she absorbed the words and held them to her heart.

"Mum was trying to do it all," Bart told her. "Taking care of the household chores—and the farm. She's strong, and stubborn as an ox." He met her gaze and lowered his voice. "Please don't tell Mum I said so."

Their shared loss had her immediately responding, "I

wouldn't dream of it."

He relaxed at Amber's ready agreement, and continued, "We didn't realize how difficult it had become to work the land without my father and his strength until the night our farm was under attack."

Shock reverberated through her. "Attack? Who would do that, and why?"

His frown was fierce, and he suddenly appeared very much a man capable of protecting his mother and their farm. "You would be surprised what a person will do for money…or revenge."

"Actually, I have a very good idea," she whispered. "My father gambled away his fortune, our home, my dowry, and…" The words stuck in her throat at the realization that she clearly remembered the conversation the night her father confessed what he had done. Papa had ordered her to Eggerton Hall. When a trio of thugs attacked her coachman and footman at the inn near the village, she'd done as her father had bidden her—she had escaped and made her way to Lippincott Manor!

A wave of dizziness had her swaying until a strong arm wrapped around her waist.

"Easy, Miss Amber," Bart murmured. "Dermott told me your returning memory might surprise you—shock you, even. Are you all right?"

His concern, and the way he steadied her, enabled her to regain her equilibrium. "I will be, thank you. I've been struggling to regain my memory… Now I almost wish I hadn't. When Mum was alive, she kept my father away from the one vice he could not seem to control."

Bart slowly eased his arm from around her waist, watching to make sure she was once again steady on her feet. "That must have been difficult for your mum and for you."

"When my mother died, it was up to me to remind my father, the way Mum had. It worked for the longest time, then recently, I noticed he was spending more evenings away—although he was not escorting Lady Grey to the evening's round of entertainments. That's when I knew he was gambling again. But that is not what I remembered... I must speak to Dermott. He has to know that nothing will stop the man coming to claim me as his bride." A tear escaped. She fought to control the need to give in to the tears, and won.

Bart seemed uncomfortable with her emotions, and concerned at what she had divulged. "Would you like me to get word to Dermott? The meeting should be concluding soon."

"What meeting?" she asked, as if she had little interest and was merely making conversation.

"The men are meeting with one of the new London guards. Captain Coventry sent three of them to help with the situation."

She murmured a vague sound of agreement. Obviously, *she* was the situation he referred to. What else could it be?

The door behind her opened, and Aurelia put a finger to her lips. "William and Edward have fallen back to sleep. Won't you come back inside? I've rung for tea."

Amber nodded. "Bart, you won't mention what I've said to you about my father, will you? I'd like to speak with Dermott before we tell anyone else."

"I won't say anything. Dermott will likely be the one to relieve me. He's been very concerned—and protective of you, Miss Amber."

The younger man's words went right to her heart and felt like a warm hug. "Thank you, Bart."

He nodded and resumed his protective stance outside the door. Amber entered the nursery, closing the door behind her.

Aurelia and Calliope were positively vibrating with excitement. "We heard the two of you speaking," Aurelia admitted.

"What did he tell you?" Calliope asked.

"Not very much," Amber replied. "Only that there is a meeting and one of the new London guards will be in attendance—three men arrived a short while ago. He also said the meeting would soon be over and Dermott would be relieving him."

Aurelia turned to Calliope. "I heard Persephone speaking

about new guards after Jared returned from London a few months ago."

"Who are Jared and Persephone?" Amber asked.

"Edward's brother, and my sister-in-law—the Duke and Duchess of Wyndmere."

Amber digested the information, then said, "Ah, so this must have to do with the duke's guard...and me, doesn't it?"

"Yes. I'm quite certain that it does."

Aurelia's honesty eased some of Amber's frustration at the vital bits of information still hovering just out of her grasp.

"I hope you will not think less of me," Amber said to the women, "but I have a confession to make."

"We would never think any less of you," Calliope assured her. "If Aurelia remained my friend after hearing the details of my circumstances after the death of my parents, you have nothing to worry about."

"Tell us what you remembered," Aurelia urged. "You have my word we shall never abandon you."

Amber dug deep for the courage and told them of her father's vice and what he had gambled away.

"Is that why you are in Sussex and not in London?" Calliope asked.

A sharp pain sliced through Amber's head as her memory returned with a vengeance. "Oh my Lord!" she whispered. "Viscount Trenchert!"

When she turned to rush out of the door and wavered on her feet, Aurelia and Calliope steadied her. "I have heard his name," Aurelia admitted. "Vile man."

"You have no idea," Amber rasped. "Papa came home a few nights ago and confessed that he'd gambled away everything—including my hand in marriage."

"No one would ever expect you to honor a wager such as that," the countess declared, then lowered her voice when Calliope motioned to their sleeping sons and shushed her. "It wasn't a written note, was it?"

Fear curled inside of Amber. "It was. That is why my father insisted that I pack my portmanteau—I don't know what happened to it. I had it when I climbed the wall."

"Did you travel in your father's carriage?"

"Yes, with our coachman and one of the footmen…" She fell silent as the pieces slipped into place. "The viscount's men were waiting for us when we stopped at the inn near the village."

"But you must have escaped if you made it to within a mile or so from here," Aurelia said.

"We had to leave the footman behind, because he had been clubbed over the head. I thought we were going to escape, but they were right on our heels… Our coachman told me to run and turned to fight. I need to tell Papa—" Bile rushed up her throat as fear such as she'd never known assailed her. "He told me to go to Lippincott Manor, insisting that the earl was an honorable man, and would protect me if anything happened. Do you know my father? Have you heard from him?" She waited for a moment before asking, "Where is he?"

When neither woman answered right away, her sense that something was terribly wrong was too much to bear. She yanked the door open. "I've got to find him and warn him!" She slipped around Bart and ran toward the servants' staircase. The door burst open just as she grabbed the doorknob, and she landed on her backside.

"Lass! What in the bloody hell are you doing out here?" Dermott helped her to her feet. "If I had any idea ye wouldn't listen to the earl's orders to stay put, I would have been more cautious opening the door."

Her face was flushed, and her eyes were bright with tears. "Where is my father? I need to find him." When he reached for her, she tried to wriggle out of his grasp, but he held her upper arms firmly. She struggled against his hold. "Please, let me go! Don't you see? Viscount Trenchert is behind everything! I must warn my father."

God help him, Dermott did not know how to tell her to soften the blow. "Where are their ladyships?"

She frowned at him. "In the nursery. I think they know where Papa is, but wouldn't tell me. I was coming to find you. If you know where he is, you would have told me, wouldn't you?"

He pulled her roughly into his arms and wished anyone else had the duty of telling her. Finally she stopped squirming. Had she guessed? It was best to just say it. Prolonging her agony would only make it worse, but he had to explain why he did not tell her.

"I gave me word, lass." He felt the first sob of anguish rip through her. *"Mo chroí,"* he rasped, cradling the back of her head in his hand, while she trembled against him as agony tore through her. *"Mo ghrá*, don't weep. I have never broken me word and was sworn to secrecy for yer safety, lass."

She cried harder. He lifted his head when he heard footfalls approaching. Digging deep to find the wherewithal to ease her out of his arms and into those of Lady Aurelia, he eased his hold on her. "I am more sorry than ye can imagine, lass. Forgive me."

Her tear-drenched eyes met his. "You knew."

Her accusation was a direct hit. "Aye."

"I was struggling to remember who I was, what had happened, and yet when I remembered my father, you gave no hint that you knew of him. Tell me what happened to him! He would be here otherwise. He promised me."

"There was a duel," Dermott told her. She bravely held his gaze, and he sensed that it cost her to do so. He owed her the rest of the truth, now that she'd guessed it. "He called out Trenchert for cheating."

Lady Aurelia rubbed a hand up and down Amber's arm, but Amber did not seem to notice as she shook her head. "No! I refuse to believe it. Papa would never fight a duel! There must be another explanation."

"I'm not at liberty to say any more, lass, without the earl's permission. Ye will have to trust that we will continue to protect ye... I will protect ye from the vile viscount! He'll never get his hands on ye as long as there is breath left in me body."

Lady Aurelia handed her a handkerchief. She blinked and managed to thank her before she dried her eyes and blew her nose. "Will you take me to the earl, Dermott?"

"Aye, lass." He held out his arm, waiting for her to take it. "He's in his study. We've received news that the viscount has arrived in Sussex. The earl has asked that I allow him to fill ye in on the rest."

She stared straight ahead, pausing only to reach for the curved railing on the main staircase. As they descended, she kept her head high, but never once looked at him. His gut clenched at the realization that it would take more than understanding that he would never break his vow to the duke and the earl. The lass had to grieve first before she'd be able to listen to reason.

Lord, let the lass understand how I feel...and believe me when I explain that she is in even more danger now!

Chapter Sixteen

"Amber-lass, I know your memory is coming back, but—"

"My name is Georgiana Hyacinth Eggerton," she interrupted. "Not Amber."

"Aye, lass, that it is. Since ye've remembered your name, ye need to speak to his lordship immediately, but there is something ye need to know." Stepping onto the marbled floor in the entryway, Dermott lengthened his stride, hurrying toward the earl's study.

"Is there a reason to hurry?"

"More than ye realize. The earl will have information ye need, but above all things, he does not want to upset ye, lass. But I must caution ye to hear him out no matter how painful what he has to tell ye might be."

She stared at him, but did not respond. He urged, "Can ye do that, lass?"

"Yes, Dermott, but I do not think…"

"'Tis best if ye don't until ye hear what the earl has to say." He nodded to the footman stationed outside of the study, who stepped aside to allow them entrance. Dermott knocked and waited for the earl to respond.

"Enter." The earl stood up as Dermott escorted the lass into the room. Lippincott nodded to Dermott before studying the lass's face. "I take it you have remembered more, Miss Amber?"

"Yes, your lordship, my name: Georgiana Hyacinth Eggerton. Dermott said you would be able to answer my questions."

"I shall do my best to answer any questions you have, Miss Eggerton. Won't you be seated?"

"Do you mind if I stand? I'm too anxious to sit for more than a moment or two."

"As you wish, Miss Eggerton."

"I understand you know where my father is. There is something of great import that I must ask him."

"I'm afraid that I do not know where Lord Eggerton is at this very moment. I can tell you he sent a missive, but it had been delayed. He asked that if you arrived at Lippincott Manor, I would do all in my power to protect you."

"From Viscount Trenchert?" The earl's surprise was evident, but she expected it. After all, he did not know her at all, and therefore would try to keep pertinent facts from her. It was what Papa used to do until he realized she would badger him until he told her everything. "Before you ask, yes, I do know of the viscount and have seen him from a distance one time. From what Papa has told me of his dealings with the man, he is not to be trusted."

"There is more that you need to know, but I must insist that you take a seat before we continue our discussion, Miss Eggerton."

Dermott cleared his throat loudly, reminding her of her promise to hear the earl out. She immediately replied, "Thank you for your concern, your lordship. Please forgive me for being difficult."

"In your place, I do not know that I would have been as agreeable as you have been while you struggled to remember who you are and what you are doing in Sussex."

"Thank you." She sat on one of the chairs in front of the earl's massive mahogany desk.

From the way the earl seemed to be searching for how to begin, her earlier apprehension returned tenfold. Georgiana did not want to think the worst, but how could she do otherwise? "Whatever you need to tell me must be dire indeed. Has my father been gravely injured?"

The earl's gaze bored into hers. "I'm afraid it is more than that, Miss Eggerton. Your father—"

"There's been an accident," she interrupted. "Was it his carriage?"

"It was not. If you'll allow me—"

"Virulent fever?" she asked.

The earl nodded to Dermott, who walked over to where she sat and reached for her hand, drawing her to her feet.

"He's gone, Dermott, isn't he?"

"If we could spare ye the pain, we would. I'm sorry, lass."

Her belly clenched and her throat tightened as fear chilled her to the bone. She lifted her gaze to meet the man who'd rescued her, protected her, and the compassion in the depths of his brilliant green eyes loosened the tight hold she had on her emotions. Once the first tear slipped past her guard, more quickly followed. When he gently pulled her into his embrace, she went willingly, needing the comfort of his quiet strength.

Though she was tempted to hide forever in his protective embrace, she knew her father would frown upon her ignoring the danger Trenchert posed. She shifted, and Dermott eased his hold on her. She moved to stand beside him as someone knocked on the door.

The earl answered, "Enter."

"Sorry to be late, Lippincott," Chattsworth said, entering the study. "I was conferring with the men. Apparently another missive arrived from King." He handed the note to the earl, who broke the wax seal and began reading.

The earl's frown was fierce as he read. Finished, he locked gazes with Dermott before she watched him turn to look at the viscount. "King advises that we are to continue to protect Miss Eggerton at all costs, and he reiterates Lord Eggerton's plea not to admit Trenchert to Lippincott Manor."

At the mention of the viscount who'd fleeced her father over a hand of cards, Georgiana started to tremble uncontrollably. She prayed for the strength to obey her father's last wishes. "Did Mr. King say anything else?"

Dermott rubbed her arms, soothing her until the shakes subsided. "Is there anything else ye recalled about the viscount?"

She nodded and shared the last conversation she had with her father, adding, "I overheard Papa speak of the man more than once, and none of what he said was good. Papa did not like the viscount, and had steered clear of him for the last few years. I…" She didn't want to speak ill of her father, but now was not the time to be missish and hold something back because it would paint her father in a bad light. "I still cannot credit that my father would sit down and wager at cards with the viscount. Papa did not trust the man, nor did he discount the rumors of the man's penchant for…" She gathered her courage, knowing she must tell them what she knew. "My father tried to protect me from those who would…er…take advantage or force their attentions on innocent young women."

"Say no more, Miss Eggerton," the earl said. "I know of Trenchert's vile reputation, which is the reason the man will not be allowed entrance to my home. Between William, myself, and my brother's guard, he will not be able to do more than make demands that none of us will accede to."

Gratitude filled her. "Thank you, your lordship." She bit her bottom lip, wondering if she should ask the question burning inside of her. Knowing she would not get any rest until she had the answer, she asked, "Would you tell me what happened to my father?"

She watched his blue eyes darken with emotion—a mix of sorrow and regret—although she had no idea what the earl could possibly regret regarding her father. Before she could repeat the question to him, the earl said, "He was involved in a duel."

Her gaze sought Dermott's. He nodded, and she whispered, "I did not want to believe it was true, even though you have only been truthful with me." Her heart ached as she accepted their words. "He did fight a duel...and perished."

"Aye, lass," Dermott answered. "I'm sorry for yer loss, and know what it feels like."

"How could you? Did your father perish in a duel?"

Dermott's gaze never wavered. "Nay, the circumstances of his death were far different. Da and me Uncle Sean were wrongly imprisoned. Me da fell ill and died in me uncle's arms hours before they were to be released."

Razor-sharp guilt sliced through her as Dermott's words brought her sharply back to the present and the thoughtless way she'd lashed out at him. Tears welled in her eyes. She tried to hold them back with a will of iron, but did not succeed. "Please forgive me. I should never have spoken to you so harshly. I am so sorry for your loss."

He inclined his head and handed her his handkerchief. As she wiped her tears, he murmured, "Ye're forgiven. Disbelief and anger are the first part of grieving, lass. Don't try to hold it in—ye'll be the worse for it."

"Thank you, Dermott." Self-disgust ripped through her. She'd struck out at the huge man verbally, as if he had no heart when he had protected her and tried to soften the blow as bits and pieces of her memory returned. Just because of his size and musculature, she had thought him impervious to the tone of her cutting words, never considering he too had suffered at some point in his life. His father's untimely death was still fresh. How long ago had it been? Knowing better than to ask, she fell silent.

From the tension surrounding her, she surmised that there was more to the story of her own father's death. She knew him to be quite capable with a pistol. Was he shot through the heart? Was that how his opponent killed him? "Were there seconds involved and a physician in attendance?"

Dermott answered her question with a question. "How do ye know so much about duels?"

She shrugged in answer, then asked again if there were seconds and a physician in attendance.

The earl nodded. "As is customary, seconds attended both men upon arrival and checked their weapons," he informed her. "Though the duel did not commence until the physician arrived."

"Papa is an excellent shot. In order for him to have been defeated, his opponent must have been a crack shot...or he cheated!"

Dermott had not moved from her side. He reached for her hand and gently squeezed hers. "I wasn't there, lass. Ye'll have to be patient while King and his men uncover what happened. Until then, 'tis just conjecture on our part...not fact. Not helpful."

She bit back her cry of anguish. The need to know had pain throbbing at the base of her skull. Georgiana was thankful for the pain in her head—it distracted her from what was left of her bleeding heart.

"Dermott, would you escort Miss Eggerton to the safety of Aurelia's upstairs sitting room? I'll have Mrs. Jones bring a tea tray for the ladies." Turning to her, the earl added, "Please let me fulfill your father's last wish and protect you, Miss Eggerton."

She wished she could do something other than hide inside Lippincott Manor, but the earl was only trying to do as her father had asked him to. "Of course, your lordship. Thank you for wanting to do as Papa asked. Shall I tell their ladyships what has happened?"

"I believe it best if we tell our wives ourselves," Lippincott answered.

"Aye," Chattsworth agreed. "We'd best see to it before they catch wind of it."

She inclined her head. "I'll let you handle the matter. But if they ask me what I know about a missive?"

"Do not repeat what we discussed," the earl replied.

"You have my word, your lordship."

Dermott chose that moment to speak up. "Once the lass gives her word, ye can count on it her to keep it."

"Excellent." Lippincott nodded to Georgiana. "Thank you. I

know this cannot be easy for you. Once we have convinced Trenchert that his attempts to get to you are fruitless, we will reevaluate the situation."

"Yes, your lordship. Thank you for understanding and for your continued protection."

"Dermott, stay with Miss Eggerton and our wives."

"Aye, yer lordship. Will that be all?"

"For now, but that may change at any time."

"Understood." Dermott ushered her from the room and toward the door to the servants' side of the house. "We'll stop in the kitchen—Mrs. Wyatt usually keeps a supply of scones handy. Ye look a bit pale. Are ye hungry?"

She put a hand to her stomach and shook her head. "No, but I would not turn down a cup of tea."

"The earl already requested a tea tray for their ladyships and yourself, so no doubt they are preparing it right now."

A weakness crept up from her toes, as sadness engulfed her entire being. It must be the shock of what happened to her father settling in.

"Lean on me, lass. We'll bypass the kitchen and head straight for Lady Aurelia's upstairs sitting room."

His strength was evident, and held in check, every time he touched her. His compassion shimmered in the warmth of the brilliant green eyes that met hers, silently asking how she felt. "Thank you, Dermott. I do not think I could face this without you."

He opened the door to the servants' staircase and stepped back so she could precede him. "Me pleasure, lass."

As she ascended, she wondered what would become of her if the viscount got his hands on her. By the time she reached the top and opened the door, she asked herself what she would do if he caught her unawares and abducted her. No one would search for her… She had no family. No home. No fortune.

Setting her worry aside as self-serving, she said a silent prayer for her father's soul, hoping her mother was waiting to greet him at the gates of Heaven.

CHAPTER SEVENTEEN

"FROM YOUR EXPRESSION, Lippincott," Chattsworth drawled, "you held back a part of King's missive...an important part. What didn't you want Miss Eggerton to hear?"

"And here I thought my indifferent look conveyed what I was thinking."

Chattsworth stared at him for a few moments before saying, "You and I have been through hell and back from the day we met our wives-to-be, battling rumor and inuendo, and outright physical threats to our families."

The earl agreed. "Do not forget the well-intentioned, but poorly thought out, decisions our wives have made trying to help. Instead they exacerbated the situations they poked their pert little noses in."

Chattsworth sighed deeply. "If they hold true to form, we'll have to assign two guards to Calliope...and two to Aurelia."

"They will invent a new way to try to slip past their guard to follow their instincts," Lippincott grumbled. "Thankfully, the men in the duke's guard allowed our wives to *believe* they slipped past them without being seen, instead following a discreet distance behind them. I never thought my lovely, petite wife would willfully go against my orders."

"Their bravery, when our families were under attack, knows no bounds, and is another facet that I admire about them,"

Chattsworth added. "Admit it—as do you."

Lippincott snorted. "I do, but wish they were not so headstrong."

"Is there a specific reason King did not want her to know Eggerton had been shot in the back?"

"Not that he mentioned. Given how Miss Eggerton managed to escape from those trying to abduct her, and what King knows of the women under the protection of the duke's personal guard, he may suspect Miss Eggerton will act as boldly as our wives." The earl paused, then said, "Lord help us—or Her Grace and my sister!"

Chattsworth's worry was evident as he said, "Persephone and Phoebe have caused their fair share of upheaval and hindrance in their bid to help Jared and Marcus."

"To be fair," Lippincott said, "all four of these brave ladies deserve our thanks for their interference. Without it, things may not have turned around for us when the *ton* was bandying about those despicable rumors concerning our families. I believe it was Persephone who thought to enlist the help of the staff and villagers near Wyndmere Hall the first time we were faced with public censure."

"Aye, and then again in London and here in Sussex," Chattsworth said. "Servants talk to other servants. Word spreads quickly along North Road from inn to inn and along the roads south, leading here."

"I need to decide how long to put off telling Miss Eggerton the truth, because I have no doubt the rumors will stem from Eggerton Hall and reach Lippincott Manor whether we like it or not."

"Why not enlist the aid of our guards' wives?" Chattsworth asked. "Sean and Michael O'Malley's wives, and James Garahan's wife, have become an integral part of the lives of those we employ to keep our homes running smoothly."

"Aye," the earl agreed. "And they have made friends among our tenant farmers' wives and those who live in the village."

Lippincott's troubled gaze met Chattsworth's. "We'd best speak to our wives and tell Miss Eggerton the whole of it before she finds out over a cup of tea."

※

AURELIA AND CALLIOPE were sitting on either side of Georgiana on the rose and cream striped settee in Aurelia's upstairs sitting room. "Are you quite certain your father would have more than held his own on the dueling field?" Aurelia asked.

"Absolutely. Papa taught me how to fire a pistol years ago," Georgiana said. "At first I thought it was because he had no son and heir, then I realized he wanted me to learn to protect myself. Though I couldn't imagine why until later when I overheard him and Mum arguing about his gambling."

"William does not know it," Calliope said, "but I am becoming quite proficient with Michael O'Malley's rifle. Aurelia is a crack shot with a pistol and therefore didn't need much more than for Michael to teach her how to clean and load the rifle."

Aurelia beamed. "Thank you for the high praise, Calliope. I must say Michael's rifle is quite cumbersome. Calliope and I suffered sore shoulders after our practice session," she confessed. "I did not expect the rifle to have such a strong kick."

"Calliope, do you think Michael would teach me how to load and fire his rifle?" Georgiana asked.

"I knew it!" the earl grumbled from where he stood in the doorway. "Well, Chattsworth, here's proof that it is *your* wife who gets mine into trouble."

"I believe it was *your* wife, Lippincott, who drove mine to Chalk Farm before dawn thinking to prevent me from keeping my dawn appointment with Chellenham."

"She should not have bothered," the earl reminded him. "No one expected Chellenham would be physically able to fight another duel immediately after facing Aurelia's uncle across the field of honor."

"Did you intend to join us for tea, husband, or to merely interrupt ours?" Aurelia asked.

Calliope reached for Georgiana's hand to give it a brief squeeze of reassurance. "William, the two of your arguing is upsetting Georgiana."

"We beg your pardon, Miss Eggerton." The earl strode toward where they sat, pausing to look over his shoulder at Chattsworth.

The viscount slowly walked over to stand beside him. "Please forgive us, Miss Eggerton."

Georgiana sighed and set her teacup and saucer on the table between the settees. Without being told, she surmised, "You held something back from me about my father. Something you thought would shock me."

The viscount inclined his head, and the earl answered, "Yes, for your protection. But after discussing every aspect of your situation, and ours with Chattsworth and the duke's guard, I have changed my mind."

"You need to be warned," Chattsworth said.

"If you think I would swoon with whatever news you have to impart, you are mistaken. My sensibilities have already been shocked beyond comprehension when I remembered what my father confided the night he sent me away from London." When no one asked what had shocked her, Georgiana continued, "My hand in marriage was used to sweeten the pot to ensure Viscount Trenchert would accept Papa's wager of our home, our fortune, and my dowry."

"Miss Eggerton—"

"Do be quiet, Edward," Aurelia told him. "Can you not see that Georgiana is holding up far better than either Calliope or I would have had we been the one to escape from the clutches of a despoiler of innocents, then suffered a grievous wound to the head and loss of memory? You and William should be praising Georgiana for her patience, acceptance of her situation, and courage in trusting that we are not in league with the dastard!"

The earl's expression changed from serious to what Georgiana recognized as deep affection. His words confirmed her supposition when he said, "Do you know how very much I love you, Aurelia?"

Lady Aurelia shot to her feet, put her hands on her hips, and glared at her husband. "Now is not the time—"

He closed the distance between them and reached for her hand, pulling her into his arms. "Now is the perfect time to remind you how grateful I am that you love me. I shall never forget the night I looked across the crowded ballroom and saw a petite vision of golden loveliness staring at me. You stole my heart that night, my love. I have trusted you to keep it safe ever since. As I will continue to keep yours safe. I shall never forget our first waltz—or how grateful I am that you were long gone before that madman held a knife to my sister's throat."

Georgiana stifled her gasp of shock at the image that brought to mind.

When the earl bent his head to kiss his wife, Chattsworth grumbled, "Kiss your wife later, Lippincott. We need to meet with the men!"

"Do you not remember the night you saved my life?" Calliope asked her husband. Chattsworth held out his hand. She placed hers in his and let him help her to her feet and into his arms. "I shall never forget the fear that sliced through my gut and my heart simultaneously. I had no idea you were one step away from the top of the stairs when I burst through the door...forcing you backward off the top step." Calliope cupped her husband's face in her hand. "You caught me midair and dragged me into your arms, holding me so tightly I could hardly breathe."

"My fault for barreling into you. I should never have argued with the duke, nor stormed out of his private study."

Calliope sighed. "Do you still not believe in destiny, my darling?"

Georgiana watched the tender way the earl and the viscount

held and kissed their wives. Hope speared through her at hearing that both their ladyships had met their husbands under unusual circumstances. Circumstances that had the couples seeing past the surface to the very heart and soul of one another. Desperate times called on a person to show their true selves. She sighed. Would she ever be so lucky?

Haven't you? her mind prodded her.

That thought struck a chord deep inside of her. How could she have forgotten what she was told when she regained consciousness? The first face she saw was the handsome Irishman, who, she was told, rendered immediate aid to her on the side of the road, then brought her to the safety of Lippincott Manor. Dermott O'Malley's first words to her were *"Ye're safe, lass."*

Hands shaking, she reached for the teapot, brushing against her teacup in the process, rattling it. The couples eased apart at the sound. In a bid to cover her embarrassment, she asked the earl, "Wasn't there something you wanted to tell me, your lordship?"

He met her direct gaze. "There is no polite way of saying what needs to be said. I apologize ahead of time for causing you more pain and distress."

His words soothed the edge off her worry. "Thank you, your lordship. Are you ready to tell me the rest of what you know about my father's death?"

"Trenchert turned and shot before his second finished counting the full twenty paces."

She jolted as if she'd been struck, spilling tea down the front of her borrowed gown. With trembling hands, she set her teacup and saucer on the table and absently wiped at the spill with a napkin. Her heart ached, and her throat felt tight, but she managed to hold back the anguish scraping her insides raw—she could fall apart later. Her composure back in place, she whispered what the earl had not said. "The viscount did not just cheat. He never planned to adhere to the *Code Duello*. I overheard my mum and father discussing it ages ago when she finally convinced my father never to sit across a table from the viscount or wager at cards against him again. Has Trenchert fought other duels? Has he ever anticipated the count before and turned, killing any of his opponents?"

When neither the earl nor the viscount answered immediately, a sob tore from her very soul before she stifled it. "Your silence confirms my suspicions." Her voice sounded hollow to her ears. It mirrored how she felt inside. "Viscount Trenchert murdered my father." Unable to control her tears at the news, she rasped, "Only a coward shoots another man in the back!"

"Aye, lass," Dermott said from where he stood in the open doorway. "Trenchert is the worst of cowards and deserves to pay for his crime."

If Georgiana could string two words together, she would have agreed with Dermott. As it was, all she could do was stare at the warrior standing in the doorway—his broad shoulders brushing against the doorframe, a tightly controlled rage burning in the depths of his emerald eyes, as righteous anger radiated off him in waves.

Lippincott held up a hand. "We'll discuss this later, Dermott. Right now we need to meet with the others to reinforce our web of protection around our wives and families."

Dermott's gaze never left Georgiana's. "Ye have me word, lass—he will pay for taking yer da's life."

Her throat was taut with the emotion. His promise seared through to the heart of the matter. If the viscount were made to pay for his crime, her father would not have died in vain. She looked at the man she trusted. Would he understand her silent message, or would he need her to tell him that she felt more than gratitude toward him? She struggled past the tautness in her throat to speak. "I count on it, Dermott, though I am afraid I will never be able to repay you."

"There's where ye'd be wrong, lass."

"Wrong?"

"Aye, ye can repay me by accepting me offer of marriage."

Georgiana gaped at him. "*Marry* you?"

"Aye, lass. Marry me."

"Did you hear that, Calliope?" Aurelia demanded. "Dermott just asked Georgiana to marry him."

Calliope smiled. "Twice, but she has yet to answer him."

"There is only one answer," the viscount said. "Unless we have been wrong about the sparks that fill the room whenever you two are in it."

"An answer William and I anticipated," the earl added. "The special license arrived today."

"Did it now?" Dermott asked. "Well, that simplifies things, though first, I'll need to know if the lass will have me." He turned to Georgiana. "I need to hear yer answer, lass."

Georgiana blinked. When she opened her eyes, Dermott was reaching for her hand as he went down on one knee.

"Will ye marry me, lass?" Hand to her throat, she nodded, and he smiled. "Ye need to say the words, lass."

"Yes, Dermott O'Malley. I would be honored to marry you."

One moment he was on bended knee, the next, he towered over her, drawing her to him. Wrapped in his embrace, she melted against him as his lips claimed hers, sealing their promise to one another with a kiss that befuddled her brain and stole every ounce of air from her lungs.

The sound of someone clearing their throat must have registered with her husband-to-be, because he took a step back and smiled down at her. "Trenchert will never get his hands on ye now."

A bleak thought wormed its way into her brain. Was Dermott only marrying her to protect her, or did he have feelings for her?

Dear God, had she avoided marriage based on the turn of a card, only to end up in one that would seal an honorable man's pledge of protection? Did Dermott feel even the tiniest speck of love for her, or was he only marrying her to keep the viscount from collecting his winnings?

He must have sensed her inner turmoil. Pulling her into his arms once more, he pressed a kiss to the top of her head. "Have faith, *mo ghrá.*"

She found her grit and her voice. "Thank you for the offer, but if you are marrying me as a way to protect me, I will have to take back my words."

DERMOTT LEANED DOWN, cupped the back of her head in his big hand, and drew her lips toward his. When they were a breath apart, he whispered, *"Mo chroí*—my heart—'twill be a pleasure to marry ye, lass. I'll make sure ye won't be regretting it."

"O'Malley."

He ignored the earl and pressed his lips to hers, this time adding a bit more of the feelings he'd been holding back on a tight leash—though not all. They weren't alone, and she was not yet his bride. Kissing her warmed his heart and heated his blood. The lass tasted of honeyed wildflowers. 'Twas a taste he would never get enough of and would cherish for the rest of his life.

He led her back to her seat and bowed over her hand. Turning to the earl, he asked, "Can the vicar marry us tonight?"

The viscount glanced from O'Malley to Georgiana and back, chuckling. "We'd best see to it that he does."

Dermott did not mind their laughter. The words that etched themselves in his brain when he'd found her filled his heart. Though he hadn't been a lad who lived by those words in years, he knew without a doubt that his ma was right—he'd found the lass meant to be the other half of his heart, and *he was keeping her.* The earl would see to it that they marry by special license tonight. What a tale they would have to tell their children and grandchildren of the brave lass he'd spied climbing a stone wall, tossing her portmanteau off, and leaping after it. That dawn patrol had changed his life forever. He could not wait to pledge his life to her, or seal their vows. But his conscience reminded him it was past time to set his mind where it belonged...on his duties and the threat to those under his protection.

Chapter Eighteen

VISCOUNT TRENCHERT STEPPED down from his town coach and brushed past the footman holding the door for him.

"Welcome back, your lordship."

He scowled in answer, storming past his butler and the servants lined up waiting to greet him. Without sparing the senior servant a glance, he tossed his top hat, gloves, and cane at him, grumbling when he heard his cane hit the marble floor. His servants were there to serve, be where he expected them to be. Didn't he pay them a fair wage to do just that? Each step he took rang out in the silence that surrounded him. Striding toward his study, and the full decanter of brandy that awaited him, he glared at the footman standing at attention by the double doors.

Fuming when the man did not move fast enough opening the doors to suit him, he did not allow the servant to close the door quietly. Trenchert grabbed hold of the edge of the door and slammed it shut, mumbling to himself about inefficient servants and lack of respect. Lifting the stopper from the crystal decanter, he poured a glass and downed half of it in one great gulp. "Time to hire a new staff…scullery maid to butler."

As he drained the glass, his anger did not lessen—it doubled. He poured a second glass and rang the bellpull. His summons was answered immediately, which did not please him—he should not have had to ring for a servant in the first place. They should know his preferences by now and appear before he had to ring for them.

The butler's face was pale and drawn, though his voice was steady. "Yes, your lordship?"

"Send word to Earl Lippincott that I will call on him in an hour."

"At once, your lordship."

Satisfied that his order would be carried out, he sipped the rest of his brandy. Feeling a bit more in control of the situation that had rapidly unraveled from the moment he won the hand of cards—and everything Eggerton prized—he strode from his study, calling for his valet as he approached the main staircase.

When the man appeared, he demanded, "Is the copper tub filled yet?"

His valet answered immediately, "Yes, your lordship."

"I will be leaving in forty-five minutes."

"Y...yes, your lordship."

He scowled at the way the man rushed around him to open the door to his bedchamber, frowned at the rough way his latest valet tugged on his arm when removing his frockcoat. "You can be replaced," he warned the man.

His words must have put the fear of God in the man, because he was far more careful removing the viscount's waistcoat. "Shall I assist you into the tub?"

Trenchert snorted with derision. "I do not have time for a full bath. You may shave me."

"But the footmen...the bath—"

"Is there a problem?" the viscount demanded. The sound of his valet sucking in a deep breath annoyed the bloody hell out of him. "Well?"

His valet answered, "No, your lordship. Please have a seat, while I place this heated towel on your face."

"Do not burn me, or you will be dismissed as your predecessor was," the viscount warned.

"I won't."

Trenchert's voice was silky smooth as he asked, "You won't

what?"

"Place a too-hot towel on your face, your lordship."

Trenchert settled in the chair and leaned back, letting his valet soften his beard in preparation to shave him.

Forty-five minutes later, he was shaved, dressed, and headed down the sweeping staircase. As expected, his carriage was waiting. He ignored the effusive way his staff treated him as he entered the coach and settled against the leather squabs. He was planning what he would say to the irritating earl who, his sources informed him, sheltered his bride-to-be.

He slowly smiled. If all went as planned, he would take what he'd won over the hand of cards…her virginity. Anticipating her resistance had him growing hard as stone. He could not wait to get his hands on Georgiana Eggerton, plunge through her maidenhead, taking what was rightfully his. Shifting on the seat, he rubbed a hand against his groin. It wouldn't be long now. If all went as planned, he would take what he wanted in the carriage on the ride back to his estate.

Chapter Nineteen

Dermott was two hours into his shift guarding the perimeter when he heard hoofbeats pounding toward him. Immediately on guard, he turned toward the sound, relieved to note it was Tarleton, one of the men Coventry had sent to add to their numbers. Tarleton had been responsible for keeping an eye on the comings and goings from the village, especially near Trenchert Manor.

The man reined in and dismounted. "Trenchert is on his way to pay a call on the earl."

"Is he now?" Dermott's temper threatened to flare as he remembered the late Lord Eggerton's warning not to let Trenchert anywhere near Lippincott Manor. "How soon will he arrive?"

Tarleton frowned, raked a hand through his hair, and shook his head. "Not long. He'll be arriving in his state coach. With a team of four, they'll cover the half a dozen miles easily...quickly."

"Did you notice anything else? Additional men arriving at Trenchert Manor?"

"Nay. I've been keeping close watch on the stables in particular. No new horses or carriages have arrived since I took up my position." He scanned the area around them, nodding to one of the large oak trees on the earl's estate. "One of my favorite perches is in the old oak tree near the corner of the house. It has the best view of the stables and the front door of Trenchert Manor."

"In a pinch, 'tis one of me favorite places to keep watch," Dermott agreed. "I've been known to climb a tree to get a better vantage point meself. Did ye chance to hear any conversation?"

"The stable master ordered the stable hands to ready the carriage and the team. The man in charge of the stables is not a young man. He moves a bit slower than I would think a man with Trenchert's reputation would be willing to make allowances for."

"Do ye think he'll be slow to respond to the viscount's order to ready his carriage?"

"I don't," Tarleton admitted, "but the stable hands seem to move at the same pace as the stablemaster."

"Good to know," Dermott said. "They'll be here soon, but we'll have time enough to set up our blockades and get into position."

"Do you need me to warn Varley and Stratford?"

"That would save time," Dermott said. "I need to go inside to speak to the earl before going to the perimeter where they're stationed to warn them."

When Tarleton mounted his horse and headed off to speak to the others, Dermott gave a sharp, short whistle. A few moments later, Sean was sprinting toward him from the outbuilding on the other side of the stables, Michael headed to him at a run from the west side of the manor house, while Garahan called down from the rooftop where he was stationed, "Do ye need me to come down?"

"Nay. We need ye up there to alert us when a coach and four approaches."

"Bloody hell," Garahan muttered.

Thankfully, Dermott's cousin did not shout out what he had surmised—Viscount Trenchert was planning to pay the earl a call. The O'Malley brothers stood side by side vibrating with anticipation. Dermott didn't waste any time going over their plans—they had formed them the day the earl received that first missive from Eggerton. Instead, he got right to the point: "Trenchert's on his way."

Garahan was already in his position on the roof, and the O'Malley brothers sprinted to the stables to get the pair of wagons they would use to block the north entrance and the south entrance that led onto the earl's estate. By now, Tarleton would be speaking to the two men guarding the perimeter. Dermott was to warn Flaherty, who was stationed inside near the back entrance. It would be up to Flaherty to get word to Bart, stationed on the second floor near the women, while Dermott spoke to the earl and the viscount.

Dermott ran for the back door, pulled it open, and rushed inside. Flaherty was standing at attention, braced for whatever was headed their way. "I heard yer whistle," he said. "Trouble?"

"Aye," Dermott said, "Trenchert's on his way. Is the earl in his study?"

Flaherty shook his head. "He and the viscount are in the library."

Dermott rushed along the hallway, nodding to Mrs. Wyatt as he passed the kitchen and burst through the door to the main side of the house.

Finch's surprised expression changed to one of determination. "Trenchert is on his way." It was a statement, not a question.

"Aye. Send word to the rest of the staff. I'll speak to their lordships before I return to me position between the stables and the house."

As planned, Dermott raced to the library, knocked twice, and opened the door. Lippincott and Chattsworth were already on their feet moving toward him. "Where is the bloody blackguard?" the earl demanded.

"On his way," Dermott said. "I'll alert Bart and the footmen standing guard by her ladyship's sitting room and the nursery."

"I'll head to the nursery," Lippincott said. "Chattsworth will go to my wife's sitting room. Don't worry, we'll protect

Georgiana as well."

Dermott's heart urged him to storm out of the library and warn Georgiana himself, but he knew that wasn't possible and would stick to their protection plan. He would assume his position, when under attack, at the back of the manor house near the stables. Stratford would be on guard for anyone skulking near the eastern tree line, while Varley would be patrolling the western perimeter. Though it pained Dermott to do so, when his heart urged him to go to the lass a second time, he shoved the need deep. Now was not the time to scrap the plans they had labored over, weaving their web of protection around the women and their lordships. It was time to defend!

GEORGIANA HEARD A commotion outside of the sitting room at the same time the door opened, and the earl and the viscount rushed in. "There is no reason for alarm," Lippincott said.

Aurelia narrowed her eyes, pinning her husband with her gaze. "Then why not knock politely, as you always do before entering?"

Calliope asked Aurelia, "Does this remind you of the time Wyndmere Hall was under attack and Edward rushed into Persephone's upstairs sitting room to warn us?"

"Yes," Aurelia drawled. "Right before he told us to stay put."

"Enough, wife!" Lippincott's voice sounded harsh to Georgiana. In the sennight she had been staying at the manor, he had not shown a proclivity toward violence, but she could not help but wonder if the earl would raise more than his voice.

Aurelia tilted her chin up, and in a clipped voice said, "I think you should leave before you say something that would curdle my milk!"

Calliope glared at her husband. "If you do not want our babe to have a sour stomach too, you should accompany Edward to wherever it is that you do not want us to go."

Georgiana was fascinated at the reaction of the men—both blanched at the mention of curdled milk and their wives nursing their sons. "Forgive our husbands, Georgiana, for forcing Calliope and I to speak of such things in front you," Aurelia said. "As an unmarried woman, you would not be accustomed to such talk."

"Do not give it another thought," Georgiana said. "When Mum was alive, I used to accompany her on the rounds to visit Papa's tenant farmers and their families. I am accustomed to being on hand during similar conversations while passing out soothing herbals and various remedies my mum would prepare as gifts whenever a new babe was born on our estate."

Aurelia turned to stare at her husband, whose color was returning. "Still, I would feel better if you say you will forgive me. Had my husband not vexed me in the extreme, I would have been more circumspect in my speech."

Georgiana agreed, if only to soothe Lady Aurelia. She had also learned at a young age not to upset women when they were carrying or nursing their babes. "Of course, your ladyship."

Odd that she would remember that fact years later. A warmth filled her as she recalled more memories from her time spent at Eggerton Hall—that was, until her mother died. From then on, Papa had insisted they spend more and more time in London.

"Bart and two footmen will be stationed outside, Aurelia." The earl's pained expression convinced Georgiana that though he was frustrated, and had been angry just a few moments ago, he would never lift a hand in anger toward his wife. "Please think of our babe and stay put."

Aurelia shook her head. "I think it would be better if we moved to the nursery now, rather than when Edward or William wake up hungry. You wouldn't want us dashing down the hallway, would you?"

The viscount shared a look with the earl before saying, "Excellent notion, Aurelia." The men motioned for the women, who quickly followed them to the door.

"Miss Eggerton," the earl urged, "hurry now."

Georgiana joined the others, and they were soon ushered into the nursery. Their ladyships' maids did not seem surprised to see their lordships escorting their wives. Was being in danger a common occurrence at Lippincott Manor? Before she could ask, Lady Calliope leaned close, and in a low voice told her, "Do not worry. Jenny and Mary Kate are accustomed to acting quickly when trouble comes knocking."

"Er... I am not worried." Georgiana managed to get the words out, but it was clear no one believed her. She realized her hands were trembling, and held them to her waist to still them. "Well, mayhap I am just a *tiny* bit concerned."

"If necessary, the men will fall back and stand guard inside," the earl assured her. "However, neither Chattsworth nor I believe that will happen."

"Thank you for soothing Georgiana's fears, my darling." Aurelia stood on the tips of her toes and brushed a kiss to her husband's cheek.

His voice deepened as he asked, "And have I soothed yours?"

Aurelia tilted her head to one side, studying the earl. "You may soothe them now."

Georgiana watched in fascination as the earl's gaze darkened, and he pulled his wife into his arms. As he bent to kiss her, a wail from one of the cradles had him pulling back to brush the backs of his knuckles to his wife's cheek. "Feed my son."

A second cry from the other cradle had both women bidding their husbands a hasty goodbye to take care of their babes.

With the closing of the door, Aurelia whispered to her maid, "See what you can find out, Jenny."

"I will try, but if anyone can pry information out of one of the duke's guard," Jenny said with a glance at Calliope's maid, "Mary Kate will be able to wheedle it out of Seamus Flaherty. He's stationed by the back door."

Mary Kate slowly smiled. "I can tell Bart that you require a special tonic for your monthlies—your woman's time—from Mrs.

Wyatt. That should embarrass him enough to allow me to scoot down the servants' staircase and return immediately."

Aurelia nodded. "Excellent notion, Mary Kate, but do not forget to bring up the dark brown bottle from the cupboard in the pantry."

Calliope's eyes twinkled. "Isn't that where you keep the blackberry cordial?"

"Of course," Aurelia said. "What else would soothe what a woman suffers once a month?"

"Whiskey," Calliope replied, causing both their ladyships to dissolve into laughter, which had their sons wailing louder.

A heavy knock on the door had Jenny moving to answer the door. Bart stood in the hallway, worry creasing his brow. "Do you need me to fetch Mrs. Wyatt or Mrs. Jones for her ladyship?"

The knowing look the countess shared with the viscountess had Georgiana realizing their plan to ferret information out of Flaherty was about to fall smoothly into place. "No thank you, Bart," Lady Aurelia replied. "Though I do need Mary Kate to bring up a special herbal from the cupboard in the pantry, it's for my—"

Before she could get the words out, Bart's face flamed and he stammered, "O-of course, your ladyship, whatever you need. I'll escort you to the servants' staircase. Flaherty will be standing guard at the bottom."

Aurelia beamed at the young man. "Thank you, Bart."

Mary Kate hurried out of the room as the heir to the earldom rooted around and latched on and began to nurse. As the viscount's heir did the same, a peaceful quiet descended in the nursery, until the only sounds were the creaking of the pair of rocking chairs and their ladyships' whispering to their sons.

A longing for something she had not thought she wanted to experience filled Georgiana. She'd only had one or two suitors that she had been interested in. The others were her father's idea of a proper husband. But when rumors of her father's penchant for wagering over cards started up again, and as no one could resist passing on gossip resurrecting his tendency to gamble in the past, the suitors vanished, both Papa's and her own. She was forced to set aside thoughts of marriage and family once and for all.

Jenny motioned her over to the pair of settees on the other side of the room. "Won't you sit down, miss? I need to set out clean linens and nappies. The little ones are always too hungry to wait to be changed before they eat."

A pair of brilliant green eyes and the handsome face of a certain Irishman filled Georgiana's mind, and she wondered if Dermott wanted to have a family. The sound of deep voices out in the hallway reminded her of the danger they were in. Should she even think about bringing a babe into this world when there was a very good chance Dermott may be injured—or worse—on a daily basis?

She listened to their ladyships quietly conversing while they burped their babes. The sight reminded her that her childhood dream, of a husband and half a dozen babes, was still something she wanted, that her heart longed for. Could she have that with Dermott, or would he refuse to consider having a family as long as he was a member of the duke's guard? What gave her the right to even ask?

She knew that Dermott was a strong, honorable man, and he had been patient and solicitous of her. Would he willingly leave the duke's employ, or would it require his suffering a grievous injury before he would even consider leaving the guard?

Georgiana needed to know the answer before they wed. But how in the world would she broach the question with Dermott without seeming as if she required him to make a choice between herself and his loyalty to the duke?

The light knock on the door interrupted her thoughts. Mary Kate returned with the bottle Aurelia requested. Her ladyship smiled. "I believe it's time we all shared a bit of Mrs. Wyatt's blackberry cordial. Don't you, Calliope?"

"Most definitely, although you and I should only have a small glass. The others can have more than one."

"Oh, I don't think—" Georgiana began, only to be interrupted by Aurelia.

"That is quite all right," Aurelia replied. "We've already decided for you, Georgiana. You need to settle your nerves—after all, you are going to marry Dermott later this evening."

Georgiana's eyes widened. "Are you certain that will still be happening?"

Lady Aurelia smiled conspiratorially with Lady Calliope. "Quite certain. As soon as the men have taken care of whatever is going on, we shall need to have the footman bring hot water to your bedchamber for your bath. We shall pamper you as a bride deserves to be pampered."

Jenny brought over the tray of glasses Georgiana had not noticed on the table beneath the window and proceeded to serve the cordial. When Mary Kate had passed out the glasses, Lady Aurelia raised hers in a toast. "To our husbands, and the men of the duke's guard, who diligently protect us with their lives."

Their lives. Would Dermott sacrifice his before they wed? The very idea had her hand trembling to the point where Lady Calliope told her, "Please do not worry. Our men and those in the duke's guard are stronger than you can imagine. They have wills of iron, and a deep, abiding faith to match."

Lady Aurelia added, "Dermott will be more than ready to do his duty to you tonight..." Her voice trailed off, and she tipped her head to one side. "As your mother passed away when you were young, was there a female relative who spoke to you about what happens in the marriage bed when you came of age?"

Georgiana felt her cheeks heat. "Er... No, though at Papa's urging, our cook was quite thorough in explaining what to expect."

"Do you have any questions?" Calliope asked.

Aurelia quickly added, "We would not want you to fear what lies ahead of you in the marriage bed. Contrary to what you may have heard, where there is respect and affection, after sealing one's vows, there is so much more two people who have pledged their hearts and bodies for the rest of their lives can experience." She sighed. "It is magical."

Georgiana blinked as a tiny spark of hope ignited inside of her. Perhaps she and Dermott would experience the same. "I confess I had not heard what you suggest, though it gives me hope for the future," she admitted.

"Well then, drink up, ladies," Aurelia urged. "Jenny will pour you another, and Calliope and I will have a tiny bit more—half a glass—while Mary Kate tells us what she found out from that handsome, auburn-haired guard with the dreamy blue eyes."

CHAPTER TWENTY

"WHAT IS THE meaning of this!" Trenchert roared from inside his carriage.

Sean O'Malley stared at the viscount before answering, "It should be obvious. The road is not open to visitors."

"Move that wagon at once!" Trenchert demanded.

Sean ignored the viscount and told the coachman, "Ye'll have to turn yer carriage around. Orders from the earl."

"Who does he think he is?" Trenchert bellowed, still seated inside his carriage.

Sean crossed his arms in front of him, stared down at the viscount, and replied, "The owner of this property. Edward Earl Lippincott, brother to His Grace, the sixth Duke of Wyndmere."

"Ignore that idiot, coachman!" the viscount said.

Trenchert had the door open and was about to step down, but Sean was already in position standing between the lead horses and had a hold of their bridles. "Easy now, lads," he crooned. "Ye'll not be wanting to crash into the earl's wagon. Walk with me now," he said as he led the horses onto the grass on the left side of the road, where there was plenty of room to turn around.

He chuckled, watching as the viscount struggled not to fall out of the carriage. Wouldn't it be grand now if the man fell on his face and broke his jaw? No one would have to listen to his bellowing then. A glance over his shoulder at the coachman had

Sean wondering if the man would suffer for his actions. Not much could be done about it now, as Sean was following orders, as the coachman no doubt was. He'd make a point to find out later if the viscount let the man go for insubordination. If the coachman had been, Sean would speak to the earl and ask to add the man to his staff.

He watched as the coach drove away, and signaled to the stable hand who'd been out of sight, waiting for the viscount to leave. "Take the shortcut through the woods," Sean said. "Let Michael know the viscount should be trying to access the manor via the south road, since he met with resistance here."

The stable hand mounted his horse and rode off to do Sean's bidding. Sean waited a moment before whistling—his signal for the footman who had accompanied him to the north entrance. While he waited for the man to approach, he wondered if Trenchert would brandish a weapon when forced to stop a second time. He should have said something to the stable hand before sending him off to warn Michael. But it was too late now, and he needed to remain in his position until word reached him that the situation had been fully handled and he could return to the manor house.

"As the viscount met resistance here first," Sean told the footman, "he's bound to try a different tack to get his way. While I know me brother will be ready for the man to try anything to get his way, I need ye to ride over there and warn him." He hoped his brother would anticipate being used for target practice.

TRENCHERT PUSHED THE carriage door open, leaned out, and bellowed, "You cannot refuse me! Do you have any idea who I am?"

"Aye," Michael O'Malley replied. "I've been given strict orders that no one—not even yerself—will be allowed entrance to the manor today. Ye'd best tell yer coachman to turn around and head back the way ye came."

Watching the viscount's bright red face darken to apoplectic purple, Michael added, "Oh, and don't be thinking to pull a weapon on me. I'm armed, and I have three men who have ye in their sights and will shoot at me command."

The viscount shouted, "I am not leaving until I speak to Lippincott!"

"That's *Earl* Lippincott," Michael reminded him. In a lightning-fast move, he reached for the rifle he'd stashed beneath the wagon seat, cocked it, and aimed for the spot between Trenchert's eyes. "And I have me orders—*no one* is to be admitted today."

Incensed, the viscount commanded, "Do not point that gun at me!"

Michael ignored him. "As soon as yer coachman turns the carriage around and heads back the way ye came, I'll put me *rifle* away. Until then, I am within me rights as one of the duke's guard to protect the duke's brother and his family to the best of me ability. That means keeping me weapon trained on ye until ye leave his lordship's estate. Ye should be warned nothing will keep me from fulfilling me duties."

The viscount frowned, but wavered under Michael's determined expression…and the rifle still aimed at his forehead. Finally, he capitulated and gave his coachman orders to turn back.

Michael did not lower his rifle, or his guard, until the carriage was out of sight. He whistled and waited for the men hiding out of sight to answer his summons. When the three of them appeared, he gave the order for one of the men to follow the carriage, for one to alert Sean of what happened, and for the third man to remain with him, in case Trenchert had a change of heart and returned.

⫸⫷

DERMOTT PACED, WAITING for one of the stable hands, or footmen, to arrive with the news that the viscount had indeed tried to push his way past—or through—the wagons his cousins were using to block the roads leading to the manor. All was quiet... And just like his ma never trusted when he and his brothers were quiet when they were young, Dermott knew that silence was not always indicative of retreat. He was confident in his cousins' powers of persuasion, and that eventually the viscount would do as they suggested.

He had no doubt Trenchert would realize he had no choice but to turn back, if only to return to his stables for his thoroughbred. A man could easily navigate the paths in the forest on horseback. A coach and four would never be able to follow one of the narrow trails through the woods to access the manor house from behind the stables. Besides, Stratford and Varley were guarding the eastern and western perimeters, and they were bound to send word that the viscount had tried to bull his way through one of the wagons—or returned to attempt access via the trails.

An hour after they'd assumed their positions, the man Sean assigned to follow the carriage returned, reporting that the viscount had gone back to his home. "And did ye observe him entering?" Dermott asked. "Did ye wait to make sure it wasn't a ruse, or that he expected to be followed?"

"Aye, O'Malley," the footman answered. "The viscount was shouting loud enough to be heard miles away. My gut feeling is that he'll return...with more men."

Dermott nodded. "It's what I would do. We'll need to ask Tarleton and the others to see what they can find out."

The man agreed and returned to his post inside the manor house. A short while later, Sean drove the wagon past the front of the house and around to the stables. Michael arrived a few minutes later, coming from the other direction. Leaving the stable hands to unhitch the horses from the wagons, they walked over to confer with Dermott.

Sean was the first to speak. "If he wasn't already, we've made an enemy of Trenchert."

Dermott shrugged.

Michael asked his brother, "Did ye have to brandish yer weapon, Sean?"

"Nay. I take it ye did?"

"Aye, he was half out of his coach when I aimed me rifle to the spot between his eyes. He didn't back down right away, just sank back into the carriage and continued to shout orders to let him pass. Stubborn bugger."

"That he is," Sean agreed.

"He'll not be giving up," Dermott murmured. "We'll have to send an escort to fetch the vicar when he comes to marry the lass and me later. If that bloody bastard manages to slip past us, the lass will be in imminent danger!"

"We'll not be taking any chances," Sean said.

"We'll send two of the footmen to fetch the vicar," Michael said.

"I'm thinking I should escort the man meself," Dermott told his cousins.

Sean shook his head. "'Twill never work—Trenchert is smart enough to eventually reason out that Eggerton had an alternate plan for his daughter that would involve marriage to someone else."

Michael agreed with his brother, adding, "We cannot risk having the viscount see yerself fetching the vicar and put a lead ball in yer back!"

Dermott scrubbed a hand over his face. "I cannot let that excuse for a man anywhere near the lass. I don't trust him!"

"None of us do," Sean assured him. "He won't be getting past us, and with our eyes and ears around Trenchert Manor, the bugger won't slip past our guard. We'll be ready and waiting for him."

The hard truth sat in Dermott's gut and burned. "The viscount will never give up a prize as beautiful as the lass. But while he no doubt planned to use her ill, and mayhap even destroy her reputation, he also does not realize how resourceful the lass is. She escaped him once...and suffered for it."

"She recovered," Michael reminded him.

"Aye, but she has a will to match me own and will never give up trying to escape the man. God forbid he manages to somehow get past our wall of protection around the lass—we cannot let that happen!"

With a glance at those surrounding him, Dermott blew out a breath. "I can never thank ye enough for adding the lass to those under yer protection."

"Yer thanks aren't necessary," Michael told him.

"Aye," Sean agreed. "After what ye said when ye brought her here. Ye found her..."

Dermott wasn't able to hide the emotions swirling inside of him as he finished his cousin's statement. "And I'm keeping her."

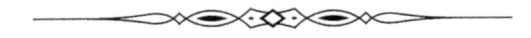

CHAPTER TWENTY-ONE

MARY KATE CONFIDED to the others, "Seamus narrowed his gaze at me when I asked what was going on. He has never done that before! Normally, I can get his attention—at least for a few moments—but whatever is going on has all of the guard on edge."

Georgiana's blood ran cold. "It has to be the viscount... He's coming for me!"

"Do try to calm yourself, Georgiana," Aurelia said. "That despicable man will never get past the duke's guard."

"Or our husbands," Calliope added.

Georgiana's belly churned at the thought that the viscount was nearby and could claim her as his bride! She had no doubt the man had already taken possession of her family town house in London...after he murdered her father during their duel. If Papa had not urged her to flee, she knew in her soul that the viscount would have claimed her as his intended. But she had thwarted him and escaped, although she could not recall what happened between the time she climbed into her father's carriage until she woke up staring into the brilliant green eyes of the man who had saved her.

Her mind raced while she sorted through the rest of her situation. If the viscount was in residence at Trenchert Manor, had he inserted himself as lord of Eggerton Hall as well?

Gathering her flagging courage, she asked, "Do you think he will try again?"

Aurelia frowned, and Georgiana imagined being carried off by the man her father despised, but not enough to avoid the man completely. She'd never know why her father agreed to wager at cards with the viscount. Finally, Aurelia answered, "Instead of worrying what might happen, I believe we should discuss the plans for your new home."

"I don't have a home. The viscount…" Georgiana trailed off as Aurelia's words sank in. "New home?"

Aurelia smiled. "The members of the duke's guard stationed here used to share quarters in one of the outbuildings. Up until Sean O'Malley married, the guards transferred to my brother-in-law's other properties every four months. His Grace decided to exclude the married members from the rotation. Once Sean and Mignonette married, Edward and I decided to have a cottage built for them on the estate. We planned to do the same for any other members of the guard if they married. After all, it would not be seemly for their wives to live in the guards' quarters, and nor would we expect them to. You will not be expected to after you marry Dermott, especially while Seamus is living there." She smiled. "My husband does enjoy planning ahead."

"I…er… Forgive me, I must admit that with all that has happened, I had not thought beyond marrying Dermott," Georgiana admitted.

"William and I wanted to build a cottage for Michael O'Malley when he married Harriet Mayfield," Calliope said, "but she and her son Bart did not want to leave their tenant farm where they had lived and worked the land for years before her husband passed away. They asked to stay. Of course, William agreed."

"Understandable," Georgiana murmured. "If my father had not gambled away everything…" She shook her head and lifted her chin. There was no point in belaboring something that could not be changed. It was better to look forward and embrace what could be, than to live in the past. Her future lay ahead...a future that included marrying the enigmatic Irishman who'd captivated her from the moment their eyes first met. "Thank you for the gracious offer, your ladyship, and please convey my thanks to his lordship. I am certain Dermott has already thanked you both."

"Now that we have settled that matter," Aurelia said, "I'd best find out how much longer we are expected to stay confined to the nursery."

Jenny was already moving toward the door when it opened. The earl's gaze unerringly met that of his wife's, and Georgiana could feel the strong pull between the couple. "I came to advise that the issue has been resolved. Is everyone all right?"

"We are all fine, but we have much to attend to before the vicar arrives," Aurelia replied. "You did send for him, did you not?"

"Of course, my darling. He's expected to arrive later this afternoon." He bowed over Aurelia's hand. "I am needed elsewhere."

Her mind awhirl with what lay ahead, Georgiana heard Aurelia and Calliope asking their maids to remain in the nursery. It struck her as peculiar that neither of their ladyships had engaged a nanny. She wanted to ask them why later, but did not feel comfortable doing so.

Soon she felt herself caught up in their ladyships' excitement and felt herself being swept along with their plans to pamper her before she married. Truth be told, left to her own devices, Georgiana was not certain she would have managed to do more than ring for tea to settle her nerves.

"Georgiana, hurry now," Lady Aurelia said. "The footmen should be arriving with hot water to fill the copper tub in your dressing room."

"I do not know how to begin thank you for everything you have done for me."

Georgiana's words were brushed aside as the countess and viscountess swept her along the hallway. As promised, the footmen were just finishing their task, while Mrs. Jones supervised.

"Now then," Aurelia announced, "hot bath first, then tea with some of Mrs. Wyatt's cream tarts to fortify us."

"Wait until you see the gown," Calliope told Georgiana. "Aurelia took in the seams and let down the hem so the gown would fit you perfectly."

Georgiana felt as if she were being swept along without anyone consulting her. "Gown?" She met Aurelia's steady gaze and asked, "When would you have had the time? Dermott only asked me to marry him today."

Aurelia slowly smiled. "I had a feeling he would ask. Always best to be prepared."

"A lovely shade of blue, with an overlay of lace," Mrs. Jones told her. "This way, Miss Eggerton."

Though Georgiana wanted to insist that she did not need a new gown, the truth was that her portmanteau had not been recovered. It was solely due to Aurelia's kindness that she had something to wear. The borrowed gowns had fit her surprisingly well and were the proper length. "I have only just realized something, and must plead the fact that I have not been thinking clearly since I was injured."

Aurelia and Calliope smiled, encouraging Georgiana to continue. "How is it that your gowns have been the proper length and fit? I am taller than you."

Calliope smiled. "My very good friend has a habit of having Madame Beaudoine leave extra material in all of her gowns to allow for adjustments—especially the length."

"That would make sense, of course, considering that after one marries, one may be expecting," Georgiana agreed. "But why the length, too?"

Calliope hugged Aurelia and said, "She saw to it that I had new gowns to wear until after I wed William."

Aurelia waved a hand in the air, indicating the topic was closed. "We have a wedding to get ready for."

Georgiana glanced at the lovely confection hanging in the wardrobe and could not help but stare. "Oh, it is lovely. Are you certain you do not mind my borrowing your dress?"

Aurelia laughed. "After the hours I have labored over altering it to fit you, the dress is yours, and the others you have been wearing are my gift to you."

Georgiana blinked back tears. "I cannot imagine why you would labor over seams and such yourself, your ladyship. The gown is exquisite. I could not possibly accept such a generous gift."

"My grandmother was a seamstress who taught my mother, who in turn taught me. Had Uncle Coddington not immediately come to fetch me after my parents were in that fatal accident, I had thought to someday be able to offer my skill as a seamstress." Aurelia smiled. "Then I met and married my darling earl. A moment in time—and a waltz—that changed the course of my life."

"Before my mum passed," Georgiana said, "she taught me how to sew a straight seam, though mending is the extent of my abilities. Not such fine needlework as your ladyship has done. Thank you for your generosity."

"You are quite welcome," Lady Aurelia said. "Besides, I could not possibly fit into it now that I altered it. I'm shorter and not nearly as slender as you. Do you know I am quite envious of your wand-slim figure? After taking in the seams, there is no way I could possibly squeeze into it."

Calliope chose that moment to interrupt. "We can discuss your gown, and whether you would like Jenny to do your hair for you, while you soak in that tub. I do hope you do not mind heather," she said with a smile. "A certain Irishman mentioned you had a preference for it. Lady Aurelia always has an abundance of it on hand." Calliope and Aurelia shared a glance before the viscountess continued, "It reminds her of her grandparents."

"Er...no. That sounds lovely. Thank you. Thank you both!" Georgiana followed Mrs. Jones into the dressing room and the waiting tub.

AN HOUR LATER, the tension between her shoulder blades and at the base of her neck simply melted away after her soaking in the hot, scented water. Their ladyships continued to fawn over her while they sipped tea and nibbled on currant cake and cream tarts. Georgiana felt replete, and was beginning to believe it was as simple as she had been told. She would have nothing to fear from the viscount after today. She would be married to Dermott O'Malley. Her formidable protector…the duke's mercenary.

Dressed in a gown more beautiful than she had ever owned, Georgiana sat before the looking glass while Lady Aurelia's maid pinned her hair into an elegant upswept *coiffure*. Turning this way and that, she could not believe how polished she looked. Hand to her throat, she stared at her reflection. "Thank you for pinning my hair, Jenny. I normally prefer the no-fuss topknot, but invariably strands escape until I am constantly brushing them out of my eyes or tucking them behind my ears."

"You look lovely," Jenny told her.

"Beautiful," Aurelia and Calliope agreed.

Georgiana felt the edge of unease sliding its way into her belly again. She could not stop the fear that Dermott deserved to marry someone without a tattered family reputation. They had yet to discuss expectations and how their marriage and future would unfold. Pinpricks of fear had her feeling flushed…hot. She said a quick prayer that she would not begin to perspire and ruin the lovely gown.

Reason returned, and with it the notion that of course they had not discussed children or which side of the bed he slept on, let alone whether he would set aside time in his busy day to remember that he had a wife!

Even with what the cook had told her, and Lady Aurelia and Lady Calliope's assurances, thoughts of marriage and the marriage bed were not a comfort and had tinges of uncertainty skittering up her spine again. Would he be sleeping elsewhere once they sealed their vows? How could he if they were being gifted a cottage? There would not be enough room for separate beds, would there? Did she dare ask if the handsome, broad-shouldered, heavily muscled man planned to share a bed with her for more than tonight?

Her mind whirled with questions only her husband-to-be could answer. She wondered where he was and what he was doing. Was he being swept along as he dressed for their wedding? Did he have anything to wear but the unrelieved black she had seen him and the other members of the duke's guard wearing?

Georgiana would not have long to wait to find out. Digging deep for the fortitude to hide her fears, she smiled and rose from the chair to thank everyone for their kindness.

A knock on the door had her breath catching in her throat when a footman arrived with the news: the vicar had arrived!

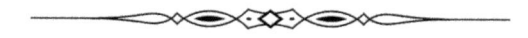

CHAPTER TWENTY-TWO

DERMOTT SCOWLED AT his cousins. Just because they were married did not make them experts. He wished one of his older brothers—Patrick or Finn—were here. They were happily married and had always been the voices of reason. Though, truth be told, he did not always listen to reason.

"Stand still, for *feck's* sake," Sean grumbled, about to slip a fresh black cravat around Dermott's throat.

"Leave off, Sean!" Dermott evaded the cravat and his cousin. "Why do I need to wear the bloody thing? Ye know it feels like a noose around me neck!"

Sean's frown was fierce. "'Tis because ye owe it to the lovely lass who has agreed to marry ye to show up looking yer best. Though even if ye clean up and wear yer best, she's bound to figure out that ye're a pain in the *arse* most of the time."

"Aye," Michael agreed. "The rest of the time, ye're a pain in the *bollocks*!"

Garahan and Flaherty snorted, trying to hold in their laughter, but couldn't. Dermott stared at the men gathered around him. Cousins by blood, brothers in arms. He nodded to Sean and let him tie the cravat around his neck. "If ye must know, I'm worried the lass will change her mind."

While the others scoffed at the idea, Sean nodded. "I know well the worry and the feeling. I could not help worrying that

Mignonette would change her mind, given me injury. I did not want her to feel obligated to marry me."

Dermott was surprised by the intensity in his eldest cousin's eyes. He hadn't ever known Sean to be worried about anything. "Did ye offer her a choice?"

"Aye, but despite the fact that I'd been severely injured and was likely to lose not only the use of me arm, but me arm entirely, she refused to go back on her word. Mignonette and our son Iain are me life, Dermott. Don't let yer pride have ye tossing away a chance at happiness with the woman who is meant for ye."

Unable to look away, or hold back the question burning inside of him, Dermott asked, "How do ye know she's the one?"

"I'd never felt the overwhelming need to protect a lass before, as if parting from her would be akin to taking a blade to me heart," Sean replied.

"Besides, 'twas plain to us the lass was meant for ye the moment we saw ye together," Michael said.

"How in the bloody hell did ye know that?" Dermott demanded.

"Sean and I recognized the determination in the set of yer jaw, and the possessive way ye held the lass," Michael told him.

"Never mind the fact that ye refused me help when I told ye to hand her to me so ye could dismount without dropping the poor lass on her head," Flaherty added. "But then ye just had to mention the one time ye had to carry me over yer shoulder in me face…after…" He grimaced. "Never mind the circumstances. 'Tis the fact that if ye had a third fist—since yer others were fully occupied holding the lass—ye'd have punched me in the gob with it for suggesting ye needed me help."

Dermott stared at his hands before lifting his gaze to the men surrounding him…his kith and kin. He may not have his brothers standing beside him, but he had his cousins: two O'Malleys, a Garahan, and a Flaherty. Ma would smack him in the back of the head for wishing for what was not there, instead of embracing the family with him. "Bugger it, but I'm an *eedjit*."

Sean chuckled. "Ye won't be getting an argument from me, boy-o."

"Nor me," Michael added.

"Well now, I have something to say," Flaherty said.

Garahan interrupted him. "Shut yer gob, Flaherty—we all know that ye wouldn't have been able to escape the wrath of the O'Leary brothers without Dermott here tossing ye over his shoulder and running like hell for his horse!"

Flaherty took a step closer to Garahan. "And I say 'tis *bollocks!*"

"Is this another family discussion?" Lippincott asked from the doorway.

Chattsworth moved to stand beside the earl. "Garahan, have you been refusing to share your flask again?"

The cousins shared a glance before dissolving into rumbling laughter, while Flaherty asked, "Faith, do ye not know Garahan well enough by now, yer lordship?"

The viscount smiled. "As a matter of fact, I believe I do."

The earl nodded. "He got the lot of you to smile and laugh as one."

"I stand corrected," Flaherty said.

The earl walked over to Dermott and asked, "Are you ready to marry Georgiana?"

Dermott tore his eyes away from his family and met the earl's steady gaze. "Aye, yer lordship. I promise to protect her with me life, while keeping me vow to His Grace and yer lordships to protect yerselves and yer families."

Lippincott nodded. "I never doubted that you would. Before we join the vicar in the downstairs sitting room, I need to ask you a question."

"Anything, yer lordship."

"Are you marrying Miss Eggerton solely to protect her?"

Chattsworth chose that moment to ask, "Do you have feelings for her?"

When Dermott did not answer immediately, the earl and the viscount shared a look. "She deserves to be loved," the earl told him.

"It's not too late for Lippincott or myself to ask the duke to assign someone else to guard her," Chattsworth reminded him. "You do not need to marry Georgiana to ensure she will be protected."

"I thought I made it clear when I told ye that I found her—" Dermott began.

As one, his cousins said, "He's keeping her!"

Dermott grinned. "Me cousins have the right of it and know me well. The lass stole me heart when she climbed atop that wall and jumped."

Lippincott smiled. "I believe you are ready to marry the lovely Miss Eggerton."

A sense of rightness filled Dermott as he replied, "That I am, yer lordship."

Finch stood in the doorway to the room at the end of the kitchen hallway. "Their ladyships beg your indulgence, and your attendance in the sitting room," he intoned.

"We'd best not keep them—or your bride—waiting, Dermott," Lippincott said.

"Lead on, Finch," Chattsworth told the butler before gesturing for the men to precede him. "Gentlemen?"

"Begging yer pardon, yer lordship," Garahan said. "Haven't we reminded ye numerous times that we aren't gentlemen?"

Dermott's cousins were smiling, still needling him, as they made their way to the main side of the house where the vicar was waiting. The group filed into the sitting room, and Dermott greeted the vicar. "Thank ye for coming under adverse circumstances."

"My pleasure, Dermott. The special license and circumstances are not the most unusual under which I have been asked to perform a marriage. Given the circumstances, I have absolutely no qualms, knowing His Grace and their lordships are standing in for Miss Eggerton's father." The vicar did not hesitate to add, "Lord Eggerton may have been tempted, or thought he had a good reason for placing that wager, but I believe he asked the Lord for forgiveness before he met the viscount at dawn. Rest assured, once you and Miss Eggerton exchange your vows, you will have the blessing of God and the church."

"Thank ye, vicar. But in order to ensure that no one can lay claim to me bride, we must seal our vows…tonight."

The vicar agreed, and the earl said, "We have the guest bedchamber ready and waiting for you at the end of the hallway," Lippincott told him. "You and Georgiana are to be our guests until your cottage is ready."

"I hate to impose on yer hospitality for that long, yer lordsh— Did ye say our cottage?"

The earl's smile widened. "Aye, Dermott. Chattsworth and I discussed it after you recued Miss Eggerton. Construction began shortly thereafter. We hoped to have it finished in time for your wedding, but plans changed. By the by, the duke heartily agreed with what we have offered to the men in his guard when they marry in the past, and he himself has done had a cottage built for your brother Patrick and Garahan's brother Aiden at Wyndmere Hall."

"Aye," Chattsworth agreed. "If Michael's wife changes her mind and no longer wishes to continue to work the tenant farm, I still plan to construct a cottage for them as I have for Garahan and his wife."

Michael sighed. "I have yet to win that particular argument with Harry, me lovely wife."

The men chuckled at the idea that one of them could not win an argument.

"The thatchers should be finishing the roof tomorrow," the earl added.

Dermott frowned. "How many men did ye take away from their farms to build the cottage?"

"I would think you would wish to know their names, so that

you can personally thank them."

Dermott stared at the earl and then the viscount. "Aye, yer lordship, that I will. Ye have me eternal thanks. Whatever ye need, never hesitate to ask—"

Lippincott interrupted, "Your vow to my brother and our family has been sealed with your blood—and the other members of the guard—already. We could not ask for more, Dermott."

At the sound of feminine voices, the earl turned toward the door. "Ah, Aurelia. I see you and Calliope have brought the blushing bride."

The earl walked over to where the ladies stood and bowed to them. When Georgiana hesitated on the threshold, the earl offered his arm. "Miss Eggerton, allow me to escort you to your husband-to-be."

⋙⋘

GEORGIANA COULD NOT feel the top of her head. It felt as if it were floating above herself. Nerves tingling, heart racing, she thanked the earl and laid her hand on his forearm. Her gaze swept the room, riveting on the man who had saved her life and captured her heart. The moment Dermott's eyes met hers, she felt a sense of rightness smoothing over her nerves, soothing them, and slowing her heartbeat to a normal pace. This was the man she would spend the rest of her life with, promise to love—and she would cherish any babes the Lord blessed them with.

In her wildest dreams, she'd never thought to marry someone whose very presence awed her. He wasn't a pink of the *ton*, nor was he a Corinthian—he was one of the sixteen formidable, honorable men who formed the duke's guard. Men who laid their life on the line daily protecting the duke and his family. The men who had bled for the duke, his brother the earl, and their distant cousins the viscount and the baron. Each and every member of the duke's guard were warriors proficient in all manner of weapons, as well as their fists.

"...And do you, Georgiana Hyacinth, take this man to be your wedded husband?"

Had she missed a vital part of her wedding vows?

Dermott bent his head to whisper, "'Tis the part where ye agree to marry me, lass."

She locked on the emotions swirling in his gaze: worry, anticipation, hesitation, and—dare she hope it—love? "Yes... Yes, I do, and promise to love him forever."

Dermott slid his arm around her waist, tucking her firmly against his side. Having already given his pledge, he asked her, "Haven't ye forgotten something?"

Appalled that she had, she met the intensity of his gaze, marveling at the way it softened from somewhat harsh to tender. "Forgive me—what did I forget?"

"Yer promise not to be climbing on, or leaping off, any stone walls, lass."

The laughter from Dermott's cousins, who stood in a semicircle behind them, warmed her heart. Thinking to add a little levity of her own, she paused before adding, "I think that would depend on whether or not I were chasing after our son or daughter."

Dermott's eyes widened before turning a darker, deeper shade of green. Their lips were a breath apart when he replied, "Well now, seeing's how ye'd be saving them from falling on their heads, like their beautiful, feisty ma, I'm thinking yer idea has merit, lass."

The feel of his firm lips pressed to hers had her heart racing all over again. The nearness of him, the heat of him, the heady scent of him—a combination of sandalwood, fresh air, and a hint of horse—had her head spinning.

Before her brain righted itself, he swept her into his arms. "Thank ye for standing up for me, lads. This leaves yerself, Flaherty, as the only unmarried member of the duke's guard in Sussex. When ye finally come to yer senses and recognize what's been standing right in front of ye, following ye around, and mooning after ye for nigh on six months now, I'll stand up for ye."

Flaherty's mouth gaped open, then snapped shut. The set of his jaw and temper in his eyes showed a man who knew he had not been able to hide his feelings from his cousins.

From the way Mary Kate spoke of the auburn-haired guard, Georgiana knew it would only be a matter of time before Seamus and she realized they were meant for one another.

Dermott thanked the earl and countess, and the viscount and viscountess, and Georgiana asked, "Aren't you going to put me down so I can thank them properly?"

"I included yer thanks with me own." His broad grin had his cousins chuckling. "Ah, lass, I'll never let ye go." He nodded to the others and strode from the room.

"What about the wedding supper Mrs. Wyatt prepared?" Georgiana asked. "Isn't it impolite of us not to attend?"

Dermott was nearing the main staircase when he answered, "The earl and the viscount approved of me plans. Don't worry, lass. I'm thinking they'll raise a few toasts to us and enjoy the meal." His eyes dimmed for a moment, and he leaned close to whisper, "'Tis for yer protection, lass. There's one more duty to see to."

Her throat tightened at the word *duty*. Did he only see their joining as such? She knew to expect pain in the marriage bed, but had hoped the act would be something more than a task to fulfill.

As he strode down the hallway to the last bedchamber, she wondered if she had pledged her life to a man so duty bound that he was unable to comprehend that she needed his assurance it would be more than duty when she lay upon the bed and willingly gave herself to him. A cold chill slithered up her spine.

He paused outside the guest bedchamber. "Are ye cold, lass?"

Unable to speak past the lump in her throat, she shook her head.

Understanding shone in his eyes. "Ye have no reason to fear

me, lass. I'll be gentle with ye."

Her heart clenched and her mind whirled, stumbling over unasked questions:

But will you... Do you... Could you possibly love me?

CHAPTER TWENTY-THREE

DERMOTT SET HIS wife on her feet next to the four-poster bed. He stared at it for a moment, feeling uneasy at the prospect of sleeping in one of the earl's beds. It was far too fine for the likes of him.

His bride noticed his hesitation and said, "It's a lovely mahogany bed. I used to sleep in one quite similar to this." She reached out to touch the pale blue bed linen. "So soft."

She looked up at him, and his heart began to pound. The woman of his dreams was standing in front of him, had exchanged vows with him. Suddenly he could not think of what to do next. He knew what he *wanted* to do, had been dreaming of doing, but he couldn't expect her to want to jump onto that fancy bed and let him sink into her softness. She was a maiden, after all.

He needed to woo her first. Bloody hell, he wished he had had the opportunity to court the lass before marrying her. Given her situation and the time constraints of his job, he had had little to no time to do so.

"Dermott, isn't this thoughtful?"

He hadn't taken his eyes off his bride from the moment she walked toward him with her hand on the earl's arm. Shaking his head, he finally noticed what she was looking at. The small table by the window facing the gardens had a silver tray with food to tempt their appetite—and did not require sitting down at a table to consume it. Mrs. Wyatt deserved a kiss and his eternal gratitude for understanding that they may not eat right away, and, if he could convince his bride, may be eating in bed!

He cleared his throat and his mind of such thoughts. She was nowhere near ready. "I was not expecting to be served a meal in our bedchamber, lass. This was kind of the earl and Lady Aurelia. We'll be certain to thank them when next we see them."

She frowned at him. "You make it sound as if we won't be leaving this room for days."

"If I had me way, I'd keep ye in that bed for a sennight."

Her laughter sounded like the tinkling of faery bells. "What could we possibly find to do to keep us there for seven days?"

Her innocence was a frustrating delight. He intended to show her how they could spend the time, but needed to reel in his impatience and need to claim her. Dermott walked over to where she stood next to the elaborate tray laden with everything from meat pies and slices of beef to trifle pudding and syllabub. She was reaching for the teapot when he moved to stand beside her. "Are ye that hungry, lass?"

She turned quickly and tumbled into his arms. Her cheeks flushed a lovely shade that reminded him of his ma's roses back home. Unable to resist, he brushed the tips of his fingers along the curve of her cheek. "Soft as the petals of a rose." Eyes wide with confusion and wonder tempted him to ask, "Has no man ever compared yer satin-smooth cheek to a rose petal before?"

"Erm... Not exactly."

She tried to turn away from him, but he nudged her chin with his knuckle until she faced him again. "Were the men courting ye blind?"

"Well... That is to say... Not exactly. It's just that..." Her voice trailed off again before she seemed to gather her courage and confessed, "If you must know, I did not take."

Dermott was confused. "Take?"

Her face turned red as a beet.

"I did not mean to embarrass ye, lass. 'Tis just that I do not understand yer meaning."

"Surely you've noticed my hair is a rather bland shade of light brown."

"When the sunlight shines on it, the silken strands remind me of honey."

From the expression on her face, his bride seemed to embarrass easily—mayhap she flustered easily, too.

"I do not have blue eyes," she said, as if to remind him.

"Is there a reason ye're pointing out what I can plainly see, lass?"

"I am tallish, and my curves are all but nonexistent."

Obviously the lass found fault where Dermott did not. "I'm thinking ye haven't noticed me height. I'd say ye're smallish." Sweeping his gaze from the top of her head to her toes, he smiled. "Ye've curves in all the right places, lass. I'm looking forward to discovering what magical taste I'll discover at the hollow of yer throat and beneath yer left breast."

Eyes wide, mouth hanging open, his wife was a delight. He knew he'd shocked her tender sensibilities, but he needed her to understand the man she married was not a fop, nor was he one to use a handful of words when one would do.

Cupping her face in his hands, he pressed his lips to her forehead, one cheek, and then the other, before placing a kiss to the tip of her nose. When she blinked, he lowered his head and rasped, "Kiss me back, lass."

When he felt her rise on her toes, he slid one hand to her waist and urged her closer. Her curves nestled against the hard planes of his body. When their lips were a breath apart, he whispered, "Ye're as lovely as a rose, slender as a willow, and beautiful as spring itself."

She opened her mouth to speak, and he took advantage, capturing her lips in a soft kiss, tracing the rim of her mouth with the tip of his tongue. When she sighed and melted against him, he took the kiss deeper and splayed his hand on her back, holding her captive while he sampled the flavor and texture of her sumptuous mouth.

※※※

GEORGIANA COULDN'T THINK—COULDN'T breathe! Dermott's mouth commanded her full attention, and participation, as he coaxed her to mimic the kisses he shared with her. His firm lips tutored her until she finally stopped thinking about *if* she was kissing him properly and poured what was in her heart into her response.

His lips trailed along the line of her jaw to beneath her ear, and she felt her legs wobble.

"Hang on to me, lass."

She could not do otherwise. She had lost the feeling in her legs when his talented lips and teasing tongue worked their magic. He was teaching her, while showing how much he cared for her. This man who stood head and shoulders above the rest towered over her, yet his callused hands were gentle; he was treating her as if she were as fragile as a butterfly.

She clung to her husband as he slipped his arm beneath her legs and held her against his pounding heart. Thank goodness she was not alone in the chaotic feelings rioting inside of her! Georgiana needed to show him she welcomed his touch, while he taught her what awaited her in the marriage bed. She slid her hands up and over his shoulders and trailed a path of kisses from beneath his jaw to the cleft in his chin. His eyes were dark with what she now recognized as passion. Pleased to be able to get a response with her awkward kisses, she nipped his chin and reveled in his deep groan.

"Ye're killing me, lass."

She froze and placed a hand to his heart. It pounded harder. "Forgive me! Why didn't you stop me?"

His rusty laugh surprised her as much as the tears she had to blink away in order to glare at him. "What is so funny?" Their eyes met, and he brushed her tears away.

"I'm humbled that ye care enough to cry over the thought of me dying."

She shoved against him, and would have ended up landing on her bottom if not for his lightning-fast reaction. He caught her and plundered her mouth with mind-numbing kisses until she could neither see, nor hear...but she could feel Dermott's lips and tongue! The strength of his hands, as they gently brushed away more tears that gathered, soothed her.

Finally, she found her voice and whispered, "Don't die, Dermott. Please?"

"'Tisn't as if I have any say in the matter, lass. Only God knows what plans he has in store for the rest of me life—and yours."

"From what I have heard and observed, you have a dangerous job. Would you promise not to take any unnecessary chances with your life?"

He studied her closely, as if trying to determine her thoughts. He'd never guess that her heart was breaking at the very idea that he would be taken from her. Not when she had only just found him!

"Aye, lass, ye have me word. Though ye must understand that what seems unnecessary to ye does not seem so to me—or the other lads in the duke's guard." He bent and captured her lips again, sending tingles of awareness to parts of her she had no idea were capable of feeling. "Seeing as how ye have strong feelings about me not risking me life, will ye let me make love to ye? I'll go slowly. If and when ye say stop, ye have me word that I will."

Georgiana could not control her breathing—she was panting as if she couldn't fill her lungs fast enough. Her head felt light over what he was asking, though in truth, she had agreed to marry the man. She could not very well expect him to walk away from her tonight, when he'd mentioned doing his duty before he carried her upstairs.

His kisses suggested that it was more than a duty to him.

Lord, please let him feel a smidgeon of what I hold in my heart for him. A peace settled over her, and she knew God had heard her petition. "Yes."

His emerald eyes gleamed as he walked over to the bed and stood her next to it. He removed his frockcoat, untied his cravat, and took off his waistcoat. "Are ye planning to make love to me wearing that fancy gown?"

She blinked and noticed that he was about to remove his cambric shirt. "I... um... What I mean to say is—"

"That ye've never disrobed in front of anyone before."

Affronted, she crossed her arms beneath her breasts and frowned at him. "Of course not!"

"I love a feisty woman. Turn around, lass, and I'll undo yer buttons."

Her arms dropped to her sides. Instead of speaking, she simply turned around. The heat of him seared her skin wherever they touched. His hands on her shoulders urged her to turn back around. "Do ye need me help taking yer gown off?"

Heart in her throat, she couldn't speak.

He trailed his finger from the scar high on her forehead to the curve of her cheek before pressing a kiss below her scar. "If only ye'd have listened and not jumped, lass, ye wouldn't have been so gravely injured.

"I never heard you."

"Would ye have listened if ye had?"

She shrugged. "Truthfully?"

"There will only be truth between us lass, never prevarications."

"I agree. As to that, Dermott, does my scar bother you? It is a mark I will bear for the rest of my life."

"Aye, lass, but only because of the pain it caused ye."

Heart in her eyes, she stared up at him. Seeing the utter truth on his face, she nodded.

"Now then, as to yer lovely gown, ye don't want to wrinkle it, do ye?"

His voice had deepened, and the rumbling vibration set off a chain reaction inside of her. She wanted—nay, felt *compelled*—to do whatever he asked when he spoke to her in that low register. "Erm... Yes, I could use your help. Lady Aurelia made the alterations herself. I've never heard of a countess sewing her own clothes before."

"There is much ye do not know about the family me brothers, cousins, and I protect," he said, gently lifting the gown up and over her head.

She felt painfully exposed standing before him in her borrowed chemise. The thin batiste did little to hide her body from his inspection. And the way his eyes took in every curve beneath the chemise had her breasts—and lady parts—tingling.

As if he knew his effect on her, he slowly smiled and tugged his finely tailored black shirt off, tossing it on the chair with his other garments. "Ah, lass, ye're a beauty to behold. I know I am not worthy of touching the hem of yer fine gown, but I've done that just now and plan to touch more of ye—with yer permission."

Georgiana knew what was expected of her, but the sheer size of him... Lord, the man was fit. His bulging muscles had her insides quaking. Would he accidentally crush her in the middle of the night if he turned over and ended up on her side of the bed?

"Whatever it is ye're thinking, lass, let it go. I gave ye me word to be gentle."

Needing to show him she would keep her word to him and allow him to seal their vows, she let her eyes travel from the top of his head to his too-handsome face. She snuck a peek and noticed his lips curving into a smile. Emboldened, she lingered on his impressive pectorals and lowered to his breastbone, then lower still to his belly and the waistband of his trousers.

"Lass, I cannot take much more of yer lusty looks."

"Lusty?"

"Yer eyes show what ye're thinking. 'Tis yer lips and yer tongue that are a bit shy. I can fix that." He tugged, and she fell against his massive chest. His heat seared through her, drugging her, until she was swaying on her feet. "Are ye ready to let me see all of ye, lass?"

She bit her bottom lip and dug deep for the courage to hear whatever comments he may have about her too-small breasts and barely there hips. Hadn't she overheard more than one gentleman at the last ball she attended saying the same, *sotto voce*? She had been near enough to hear their comments, as they no doubt intended.

"I'm ready."

Before she could change her mind, her chemise was gone, and her husband stood staring at her. She was wrong—she couldn't bear it if he found her form lacking. She closed her eyes tight and prayed he'd finish his intimate inspection quickly.

"Open yer eyes, lass."

She shook her head.

"Georgiana Hyacinth O'Malley!"

That had her eyes opening wide. "What did you call me?"

"Yer name. 'Tisn't Eggerton any longer, lass, and as soon as I make ye me wife, 'twill be part of yer past."

He scooped her into his arms, then gently laid her on the bed and joined her. His massive body, poised above her, covering her, made her feel tiny, fragile, though she knew she had nothing to fear from him.

He bent his head and kissed her gently at first. With each kiss, the intensity increased. His tongue traced the rim of her mouth again, but this time he nipped her bottom lip. Shock had her gasping, allowing his tongue entry to taste her fully. "Yer flavor is a heady combination of honeysuckle and heather, lass."

She'd never sampled either, and she wondered when he had. He slowly lowered his body so he was nestled between her thighs—the hard, hot length of him poised at the very heart of her. Pinned to the mattress, she did not feel as helpless as she thought she would. She trusted him. His heat seared her, as her passage wept and clenched of its own accord.

"Don't worry, lass—ye're not ready to receive me yet. I just wanted to feel yer moist heat before I began me first lesson."

She made a strangled sound in the back of her throat, but for the life of her, couldn't string two words together.

"Do ye want me to stop, lass?"

No! her heart cried. Unable to speak, she shook her head, and her husband lowered his head, capturing her breast in the wet heat of his mouth, swirling his tongue over her nipple, tugging on it, until she was squirming beneath him, begging him for something she did not understand.

"Do ye want me to stop, lass?"

This time she forced out, "No!"

His deep chuckle did things to her insides that she was certain were not proper at all.

"Thank God, lass!"

Chapter Twenty-Four

Dermott thought he would burst from the need to plunge into his bride, but he was not a beast. He had never taken a woman that had not been willing, ready, and nigh unto begging him. But the lass was innocent and needed to be treated with care, lest he injure her and have her dread the prospect of making love to him a second time.

Digging deep for patience, he found it and moved to lie on his side. He trailed the tips of his fingers from her shoulder along her arm to the gentle dip at her waist and curve of her hip. "Lass, ye're a feast for me eyes, with curves enough to drive me mad."

Her eyes revealed her innermost thoughts. She didn't believe him. Actions always spoke louder than words. He pressed his lips to her shoulder as he began his first lesson in lovemaking. Her quiet moan when he pressed his lips to her waist encouraged him. Still he asked, "Should I stop?"

Her breathy "no" was music to his ears. Dermott forged ahead to the curve of her hip, nipping it, drawing a louder moan from her this time. He moved to cover her with his body again, unable to hold back from pressing forward until he was at the entrance to her tight sheath. She coated him in her essence. The heat of her, the scent of her, drove him wild. He rasped, "Shall I stop now, lass?"

Her forceful reply would have had him chuckling, if not for

the stranglehold he had on his desire.

"If I'm to fit inside ye without causing ye too much pain, I need to stretch ye."

"I have no idea what you mean. How will you do that?"

In answer, he trailed his fingers over her belly, before brushing against her womanhood.

Her eyes rounded, and she bit her lip, nodding before he could ask permission.

He gently used one finger and then two to stretch her, kissing her lips, her neck, and her breasts while his hands worked their magic. She was writhing when he settled once more between her thighs. "Should I stop now, lass?"

Her eyes were dark with passion, lips swollen from his kisses, and nipples rosy from his suckling. "Don't you dare stop!"

The need to plunge into her warmth had him by the throat, and still he dug deep to temper the need. He took her breast in his mouth as he entered her, his lips and mouth teasing and suckling as he slowly pushed forward. He paused when he heard her whimper, kissed her deeply before switching to her other breast.

"Dermott?"

He stopped at the barrier between maiden and woman and dropped his forehead to hers. "I hate causing ye pain, lass, but—"

Georgiana cupped his cheek as she lifted her hips and urged him deeper. "We cannot make any babes if you stop now."

"Babes?"

"I'd like to start with a boy and a girl."

"God, I love ye, lass." He plunged deep and kissed her tears as she pulsed around him. "Let me know when the worst of it passes."

"You mean there's more?"

"Aye, lass, much more. The pain will recede, and pleasure such as ye cannot imagine will replace it."

He was on the verge of asking her if the pain had lessened when she lifted her hips again.

"Ah, lass don't move like that until the pain is gone."

She lifted them again and pressed her mouth to his throat. "It's gone. I'm ready for more."

Her husband's thrusts were powerful, but she reveled in his strength. Matching her rhythm to his, she sensed something was just out of reach. Feeling as if she would fly apart if she continued, she rasped his name. "Dermott? I can't."

"Ye can, lass, if ye trust me to take ye to the stars."

He plunged into her over and over until she felt herself soaring on a wave of feelings she did not understand. She cried out his name as he plunged into her one last time, pouring his seed into her.

Exhausted, they lay, legs tangled, hearts pounding, bodies slick with sweat. She'd never expected to enjoy lovemaking, thinking there wasn't much more to him entering her, tearing her maidenhead, and then pulling out.

Her loving husband took the time to ensure he would not cause her more pain than was necessary. She'd thought she understood what happened in the marriage bed, but she could not have been more wrong.

As sleep claimed her, her last thought was of her husband. Had she given him as much pleasure as he had given her? Yawning, she tensed her thighs and crossed her ankles behind his back, keeping him snug inside of her. Would he think her wanton and beyond redemption?

The lass didn't know how she tempted him to ease her onto her back and plunge into her tight sheath all over again. Gritting his teeth, he did not draw in a proper breath until she finally loosened her grip around his waist. She squirmed in his arms until he shifted her around so that her back was against his chest. Bracing himself while she settled in his lap, she finally sighed and relaxed against him.

His wife had surprised him with her passion. He looked forward to more lessons in lovemaking. His gentle wife had taught him something too—that her trust, once given, was all encompassing.

Now that the wicked edge of his desire had been satisfied, his mind would not settle down. The worry that his wife would be snatched from his arms plagued his thoughts. Would Trenchert cease his attempts to claim Georgiana? Would the viscount disregard the fact that she was well and truly wed to him? Should he confront the viscount with the news of their marriage and demand he cease and desist, or let Trenchert attempt to steal her away?

No. His retaliation had to ensure that the viscount—and not Dermott—would end up in irons.

He did not trust the viscount. Neither did Lippincott or Chattsworth. He would need to speak to them in the morning to come up with a plan... After he and the lass shared another lesson in lovemaking.

His worry resolved for the moment, he tightened his hold on Georgiana, loving the feel of her satin-smooth belly and breasts beneath his arm. He sighed and drifted off to sleep to the sound of her quiet breathing.

Chapter Twenty-Five

Dermott woke with a start and, for a moment, thought he was still dreaming. But no, the soft, warm woman in his arms was a living, breathing dream—and his wife.

Sensing she would be exhausted from their lovemaking, and a bit embarrassed upon waking beside him, he reached for the covers they had kicked off while they slept, and tugged them up over her. Unable to resist, he trailed his hand from her shoulder to her elbow and back. The contrast between her pale ivory skin and his ruddier skin tone bespoke of his years working in the elements, while she'd lived a more sheltered life...inside. Though it was well before dawn, he waited, watching to see how she'd react when she woke for the first time in their bed.

Her quiet murmur of pleasure was music to his ears as she rolled over onto her back, stretched her arms to the side, and gasped when her hand landed on his chest. Her eyes opened wide, but it was her expression of shock that had him struggling not to laugh. He swallowed the chuckle, not wanting to offend her sensibilities. "Did ye forget that ye're a married woman now and in bed with yer husband?"

She covered her face with her hands before answering, "Apparently."

He rolled over and tucked her against his side. "Since ye're already a bit embarrassed, I need to ask ye a personal question."

"How personal?"

"Intimately personal, lass. Are ye feeling tender?"

She covered her face with a pillow before answering him.

"What did ye say, lass?"

"You heard me!"

"Nay, not through the pillow. Are ye feeling tender?"

She lowered it to chin level. "Must you ask me such an intimate question?"

"Aye, lass, ye're me wife. I am duty bound to take care of ye."

Her exaggerated sigh was the signal that she would capitulate to him. He'd been called hardheaded, but it wasn't a fault in his mind, and nor did he consider the fact that she was a stubborn lass a fault. She reminded him of his ma, whose stubbornness was part of her charm.

"If you must know, yes, parts of me are feeling quite abused and tender."

The temper in her eyes changed to hurt, and he immediately felt remorse for finding her embarrassment amusing. After all, he knew she had never made love before and would be tender afterward. He had caused her uncomfortable soreness.

Before he could apologize, she asked, "Do you find this humorous, husband?"

Her miffed tone relieved him—her temper was back, snapping in her amber eyes. "Nay, wife—as sorry as I am that ye're feeling abused and tender, 'twas necessary. Though after our lovemaking last night, and the way ye responded to me touch, opening for me like a delicate rosebud, I didn't think ye'd be quite this embarrassed. Are ye regretting what we shared?"

She slowly lowered the pillow to the bed and reached out to touch his face. "No. I have no regrets, and would not change a thing... Well, mayhap *one* part of it."

He trusted that her eyes mirrored what she was feeling. "Ye may not believe me, lass, but last night felt different for me. And before ye ask, ye're not me first...but it has been some time since..." The way she narrowed her eyes had him realizing he'd already shared enough of his past with her. "Know this, lass—from the moment I gave me pledge to ye, on me honor, ye're the only woman on me mind, in me heart…and in me bed."

The stiffness left her, which was a relief to him. He'd rather not argue while sharing a bed with his wife. "I confess, I was afraid ye wouldn't want me to touch ye again, but ye surprised me with yer enthusiasm to me lesson. Ye need to know there's more to the act than joining as one, lass. There is so much more that I have to teach ye about lovemaking. 'Tis what is inside our hearts that links us now. Sharing me body with ye, and the gift of yer virtue, will be a memory I shall hold close to me heart for the rest of me life."

DERMOTT'S HEARTFELT WORDS had the tension leaving her body by degrees. "Last night was a first for me in so many ways. Do you want to know what touched my heart the most?"

"Aye, lass, if ye're willing to trust me with it."

"It was the tender way you treated me, as if I were fragile, though I'm not, and the way you would pause and ask me if I wanted you to stop."

"Do ye want to know what touched me heart, lass?"

Her gaze locked on his. "I do," she replied, before echoing his words: "If you are willing to trust me with it."

The devilment in his green eyes had her prepared for him to say something outrageous. She was not disappointed, "'Twas the way ye nearly shouted at me, 'Don't ye dare stop!' right before I made ye mine."

She studied the face so close to hers, marveling that his was what she would wake up to first thing every morning for the rest of her life. He wasn't smiling, and he was not laughing. Dermott meant every word. She owed him the truth, too. "I may have sounded a bit autocratic at the time, but my body was on fire, and

I felt as if something was about to swallow me whole."

He pressed his lips to her forehead beneath her scar first and then her nose before his mouth molded to hers. His kiss stole her breath. If she hadn't already given him her heart, he would have stolen that too.

When she had no breath left, he slowly ended the kiss. Her breathing was ragged as she gulped in air as if it were water. Georgiana had never imagined that a kiss could convey more than words. She wondered what other hidden talents her husband had.

"Now that ye've caught yer breath, there's one other intimate thing I need to tell ye." He seemed to be waiting for her to comment, but she decided to wait for him to continue. "I'm thinking I should take care of yer tender parts and make sure I haven't damaged ye."

She could not stop her face from flaming when she said, "Did I forget to tell you that I feel fine?"

"What manner of husband would I be if I didn't take care of me wife? Ye need tender care, lass. Please, let me see to ye?"

His plea had her falling deeper in love with the man. *Love!* He had told her he loved her, but she did not remember telling him how she felt. He had laid his feelings bare, and she should do the same. He was her husband and deserved to know what she held in her heart for him. He also needed to know that she trusted him in all things. If that included the embarrassment of his gently bathing her, and checking to ensure she was still in one piece and not irreparably damaged, she would agree. But first she needed to share what was in her heart.

"There is something important that you need to know."

He stiffened, and she wondered what was going on behind those brilliant green eyes when he drawled, "Is there now?"

"Aye," she answered, imitating his brogue. "There is." Cupping his face in both hands, she pressed a kiss to his forehead, one cheek, and then the other. His eyes met hers as she pressed her lips to his in a kiss that she hoped would convey how she felt, though she still needed to say the words. "I love you, Dermott O'Malley."

He drew her to him and held her against his heart. "Ye have no idea what yer words mean to me, lass. I was worried that ye changed yer mind after our loving."

"I did not think it was possible, Dermott, but I love you more than yesterday."

"Ah lass, ye are *mo ghrá*," he rasped, "me love." His lips brushed hers. "And ye are *mo chroí*," he whispered, "me heart," before he claimed her in a devastatingly tender kiss. "We should eat supper after I bathe ye. Ye'll be needing yer strength before we move on to the next lesson."

True to his word, Georgiana's husband bathed her carefully as if it were of the utmost importance to him. She nearly asked him why he was so at ease walking around without a stitch of clothing on, but refrained when he held up the linen cloth and asked if she'd help *him* wash. Mortified, she could not find her voice to reply.

He was laughing when he steadied her on her feet. "I didn't think me question would cause ye to swoon, lass. Well, there was a time or two when the lasses used to faint at me feet, but that was before I came to England."

After having a laugh at her expense, he gently patted her dry with a featherlight touch. Then he helped her into the nightrail and dressing gown Lady Aurelia had thoughtfully laid out for her. He donned his trousers, took her by the hand, and drew her over to the table. And in a gentlemanly act that surprised her, he pulled out her chair and waited for her to sit before taking a seat next to her.

Though she tried not to stare, her eyes kept drifting back to the broad, impressively muscled chest in front of her. His body was as disturbingly distracting as his thorough, yet gentle, touch had been. She needed to thank him before she forgot her own name! "Erm... Thank you, Dermott, for taking care of me, though I'm certain I could have taken care of the task myself."

"'Twas me pleasure. I'm looking forward to joining ye in that copper tub in the dressing room, in the morning when they deliver the hot water for our bath."

"*Our* bath?"

She shivered, wondering what that would be like, sharing a tub with Dermott. Would they both fit? Would he want to wash her intimately again? Would he expect her to wash *him* intimately?

Her husband distracted her thoughts, holding a forkful of meat pie for her to sample. The flavors ignited her appetite, and she was soon offering him a taste of the tender sliced beef.

As they devoured the delicious spread Mrs. Wyatt had arranged for them, Dermott said, "Me da instilled the importance, and the responsibility, of caring for our wives into me brothers and meself. Reminding us to treat our wives with tender care because, God willing, they would bear our babes...the next generation of O'Malleys."

His words burrowed into her very soul. Munching another bite of the perfectly seasoned meat pie, she murmured, "I am sorry I will not be able to meet your father—he sounds like a wonderful man. I do hope to meet your mum one day."

"I'm not sure when that could be arranged." He nipped a bite of the tender beef when she held out her fork to him. "Be assured that I'd be proud to introduce ye to me ma—she'll love ye as I do. Until then, I'll be introducing ye to me older brothers, Patrick and Finn, their wives, and daughters...and me younger brother Emmett."

Recalling that the duke had a number of estates, she asked, "Where are they stationed?"

"Patrick, the eldest, is head of our guard and stationed at Wyndmere Hall. He's married to Gwendolyn, who's nanny to the duke and duchess's twins. They have a babe—she must be walking by now—a daughter, Deidre."

"Where is Finn?"

"He's stationed at Penwith Tower on the coast of Cornwall.

Finn's married to a feisty Irishwoman, Mollie. Their babe is a bit younger than Patrick's—her name is Boadicea."

"Like the ancient warrior queen?"

"Aye. After going through the birthing with Mollie, me brother promised she could name their daughter."

Georgiana set down her teacup to keep from spilling it as she held back her laughter at the very idea of a man by his wife's side while she brought their babe into the world. It simply wasn't done, was it? She smiled. "I think that was a lovely gesture on your brother's part. What of Emmett? Where is he?"

Holding out a cream tart for her to take a bite, he waited until she did before answering, "Me younger brother is in London at the duke's town house. Rumor has it that he's met his match, but there is a bit of mystery—and more—surrounding the lass."

"That is keeping him from telling her how he feels?"

"Aye. 'Twould be dangerous to the lass…and me brother. Though with the help of Captain Coventry and Gavin King, I'm certain they'll soon be discovering a way for me brother to marry the lass without her being in danger."

"I hope Emmett will be careful."

"As the healer in the family, ye can count on it."

"Who is the captain, and who is Mr. King?"

"Captain Coventry is the duke's London man-of-affairs, and much more. King is a higher-up with the Bow Street Runners, and has a number of men reporting to him."

"I see. It sounds as if His Grace is connected to influential people."

"'Tis essential in order to keep his family—and extended family—safe." Reaching for her hand, he asked, "Have we emptied the teapot?"

She lifted the lid and nodded.

He rubbed her thumb across her knuckles, distracting her. "I wonder what we can do to pass the time now that we have eaten every crumb and drained the teapot? 'Tis a few more hours until dawn, and we need to digest our meal."

She sighed and admitted, "I'm full."

He laughed. "Faith, I am as well. What do ye say to sitting up in bed and deciding on names for our sons and daughters?"

"Sons and daughters?"

"Were ye not the one who said ye wanted half a dozen children?"

"Well, yes, but—"

"And did ye not entice me to continue making love to ye, after breaching yer maidenhead, with talk of *our* son and daughter?"

She was becoming used to his plain speaking, getting right to the point and not mincing words because she happened to be a woman. Happiness radiated from deep inside of her. She'd never thought to be happy again when her memory returned and she remembered the viscount, the wager, and learned of her father's death. Everything changed the day she opened her eyes to find the handsome man currently holding her hand watching her, waiting for her to waken.

"Er... Yes," she admitted, "I did." She squeezed his hand and slipped hers free. "Let me stack the dishes and place the tray—"

"Have ye not considered that ye could be carrying our babe this very moment? Ye'll not be lifting anything heavy until we know for certain that ye're not with child. I'll set the tray outside our door."

She blinked and bit the inside of her mouth to keep from arguing with him. Years ago, Mum had cautioned her to pick her battles after she'd heard her parents arguing. She diligently straightened the tray, stacked the dishes, and smiled at him. "Thank you, Dermott."

He grunted in reply, hefted the tray, opened the door, and placed it in the hallway. Closing the door, he surprised her by sweeping her into his arms and kissing the breath out of her. He placed her on the bed, and she scooted toward the headboard. When her back was leaning against the pillows, she waited for him to sit beside her.

"Now then," he said, "should we start with names for our sons or our daughters?"

Chapter Twenty-Six

"Have ye seen our cousin this morning?" Sean asked.

"Ye mean the *eedjit* walking around with a smile plastered on his face?" Flaherty snorted with derision. "Aye, the bugger."

Sean chuckled. "Well now, if I were to be giving unsolicited advice about married life, I'd remind ye that I already pointed out who is right in front of yer nose, Flaherty... Mary Kate Donovan."

Flaherty's face flushed a deep red. "I didn't ask yer advice."

Sean frowned. "Do ye still not trust that the lass isn't pining after Garahan?"

Flaherty's fist clipped the edge of Sean's jaw.

Sean rubbed his face. "*Bollocks*, Flaherty! If I hadn't been up all night, with Iain cutting a tooth, ye would have missed by a mile!"

"Ye've been slow to react ever since ye got married," his cousin countered. "Ye'll not see *me* leg-shackled! One of us needs to remain alert and in full fighting form."

It was only by the grace of God that Sean was able to rein in his considerable temper. O'Malleys may not have tempers as volatile as their Garahan cousins, but no one ever made the mistake thinking they were mild mannered. His fist stopped a hairsbreadth from Flaherty's chin. Vibrating from pulling his punch at the last second, and angry with his cousin for questioning his ability to protect the earl and his family, Sean warned, "Don't question me abilities, cousin. I won't be pulling me punch next time."

He shoved Flaherty out of the way with his shoulder, and got shoved back. The two men stood facing one another like raging bulls.

"Next, ye'll both be pawing the ground with yer big feet," Dermott said, walking over to where his cousins stood, poised and ready to start throwing punches. "I've only been away from me duties for two days and ye're already thinking to start a round of bare-knuckle sparring without me?" When no one answered him, he sighed. His cousins were well into the staring part of their competition. Insults would be next, followed by Sean's right cross, countered by Flaherty's uppercut. "Does the earl know what ye're about?"

That comment got through to Sean, who scrubbed a hand over his face. "Leave off, Dermott. Flaherty, ye're a minute late for yer shift patrolling the perimeter. We can spar later."

"Count on it, Sean." Flaherty pushed past Sean and muttered to Dermott. "Quit *fecking* smiling!"

Dermott opened his mouth to speak but closed it again at the warning glance from Sean. Waiting until Flaherty was out of earshot, he asked, "What did I miss?"

Sean shook his head. "Flaherty's *bollocks* are in a knot over Mary Kate, and he refuses to acknowledge how he feels about her."

"I thought he was courting the lass," Dermott said.

"We all thought that, but whenever Garahan shows up, Flaherty suffers a change in personality—and his mind, ignoring the lass and acting like a jealous *eedjit*."

"But Mary Kate only has eyes for Flaherty."

"Aye," Sean agreed. "But Flaherty is so twisted up in love with the lass that he can't see past his jealousy of Garahan being the first man to rescue her when she was forcibly shoved out of the side door of Lady Kittrick's town house and landed on her knees."

"I've heard that tale more than once. Garahan was there to help her to her feet and bring her to the duke's town house," Dermott said. "But Flaherty was the one to rescue her and Lady Calliope when their carriage slid on ice, landed on its side, and threatened to roll onto its roof as it teetered toward the ditch on the side of the road. Flaherty had to climb on top of the carriage, reach inside, and pull Mary Kate and Lady Calliope out."

"Aye."

"Well then, what the *feck* is his problem?"

Sean sighed and stared at Dermott, who slowly realized what his cousin wasn't saying.

"*I'm* his problem? How did ye come to that conclusion?"

Sean snorted with laughter. "Did ye see yer reflection this morning when ye shaved yer ugly mug?"

"Of course I did," Dermott grumbled. "How else would I keep from slitting me throat with the straight blade?"

"Ye should have looked closer."

"Ye aren't making a bit of sense." Dermott took a moment to really look at Sean and noticed lines of exhaustion on his cousin's face. "Is little Iain cutting another tooth?"

"Aye."

"Kept ye and Mignonette up all night?"

"Right again."

Dermott shook his head. "I'm afraid I don't understand what yer lack of sleep and Flaherty's *bollocks* in a knot over Mary Kate have to do with me."

"Ye're *fecking* smiling!" Sean all but shouted.

Dermott chuckled. "Well now, ye'd be smiling too if ye were up all night with yer lovely wife in yer arms…instead of a wailing babe." Energized from another night spent in his wife's arms, making love to her, Dermott easily avoided his cousin's punch. "With Coventry's men and the rest of the Sussex guard here, our web of protection is well manned. Take a break and get an hour or two of sleep."

"Did ye forget who was in charge of the duke's guard here at Lippincott Manor?"

"Not in this lifetime, boy-o, as ye're always ready to remind us. Not shut yer gob and go lie down in our quarters."

"But—"

"Don't even try to argue. Those few seconds yer punch was off could be detrimental if the viscount dares to show his face. I'll send one of the footmen to let Garahan know he's to take yer shift on the rooftop. He's more accurate with the rifle than you."

Sean glared at him. *"Feck* yerself, Dermott."

"Faith, did ye forget I'm a married man now?"

Sean took another swing at Dermott and missed—again. Staring at his hands and then his cousin, Sean admitted, "Ye're right. Thank ye for making me see sense."

"Any time. Oh, and Sean?"

"Aye?"

"Be sure to lie down in *our* quarters in the outbuilding, not in yer cottage with yer lovely wife and son, or ye'll be useless to us for the rest of the day."

"Not if I'll be lying down beside Mignonette to sleep," Sean called out as he walked away.

Dermott laughed. "As if ye'll be thinking about sleeping the moment ye walk in through the door to yer cottage."

Sean did not turn around or answer him, but from the rigid set of his shoulders, Dermott knew he'd made his point. He continued to watch his cousin stalk toward the outbuilding where they stored their weapons and ammunition. They had slept there until exchanging vows with the loves of their lives. It was large enough to house all sixteen men in the duke's guard. Flaherty bunked there at the moment with the men Coventry had sent to protect the earl's family.

Dermott watched until his cousin entered the building, then sprinted back to the house to send a footman to alert Garahan of their slight change in plans for the next few hours. With a fighting force armed and ready, he had no worry that anyone would breach their lines of defense.

His mind raced over the one worry that ate a hole in his gut: Viscount Trenchert. Although he should no longer pose a problem, the thought of his gaining access to the lass was constantly on Dermott's mind. He would have to eliminate the problem...though without doing too much damage to the viscount. The duke had rules that must be followed.

Dermott could admit his thoughts to prevent the viscount from getting his hands on the lass included his favorite weapons...his fists included. Reason returned, and with it the knowledge that Trenchert had no legal claim to the lass now that Dermott and she had wed. He had not agreed with the earl at first when he insisted they inform the vicar of Georgiana's circumstances. In the end, he saw the wisdom in the advice.

Lippincott had made him see past his anger toward Trenchert to the fact that the vicar would never condone the wagering of any lass's hand in marriage over a hand of cards. Once he accepted that fact, Dermott agreed with the earl that the vicar needed to be apprised of the rest of the situation: the loss of her family home in London and estate in Sussex, her inheritance and dowry, the duel, her father's death, and her injuries fleeing from the viscount. The dire circumstances behind the duke's request for the special license, and Dermott's promise to protect the lass with his life and his name, convinced the clergyman. The vicar had been rightfully incensed on Georgiana's behalf and eager to marry them immediately. It always helped to have those in positions of authority on your side.

Convinced they had thought of every possibility to protect his wife, Dermott wondered what could possibly happen now that he'd wed and bedded the lass.

Two hours later, his question was answered when all hell broke loose.

DERMOTT AND FLAHERTY ran toward Tarleton before he fell off his horse. Noting the trickle of blood dripping onto the man's hand, Dermott asked, "What in the bloody hell happened?"

Tarleton swayed in the saddle. "Heard the crack of a rifle... Felt the lead ball slice through my arm." He clenched his jaw and closed his eyes. Then he rallied, opened his eyes, and said, "Had to warn you. Three men on horseback, armed with rifles, are headed this way."

Dermott's whistle alerted the footman standing guard at the rear entrance to the house to warn those inside. Garahan, Michael, and Sean ran toward him from their positions.

Sean took over command, barking out orders: "Dermott, warn their lordships to gather the women and their babes in the nursery. Michael, head to the north entrance and warn Stratford. Garahan, head south, alert Varley. Flaherty, ye're on the roof. I'll take Tarleton to Mrs. Wyatt."

The men took off on foot and horseback to spread word to tighten their net of protection around their lordships and their families.

Dermott sprinted past Sean and Tarleton and yanked open the rear door. Having been warned by Dermott's whistle, the footman said, "The earl and the viscount are in the earl's study."

Next Dermott sprinted down the hallway, past the kitchen, and through the servants' door to the main part of the house. The urge to shout a warning filled him, but that would only frighten the women and the staff...and wake the babes.

The door to the study burst open. "Trenchert?" the earl asked as he intercepted Dermott.

"Where are the women?" Fear licked up his spine, but he ignored it. "We need to get them to the nursery. Three of Trenchert's men are headed this way. Sean executed our exterior plan. Our men are warning those on patrol to the north and south."

"Calliope is in the nursery with Mary Kate and Jenny. Aurelia and Georgiana were in the downstairs sitting room discussing taking a turn around the gardens—"

Dermott's blood froze at the realization that his wife and Lady Aurelia were outside. He locked gazes with the earl. "Do not go outside without me!" Turning to the viscount, he said, "Make certain Lady Calliope and—" The viscount didn't wait for him to finish. He raced to the staircase shouting his wife's name.

Running to catch up with the earl, Dermott called to the footmen stationed in the hallway, "Tarleton's been shot. Sean may need a hand getting him into the room by the pantry. See that Mrs. Wyatt has enough help to tend to his wound." He was grateful that the men immediately responded. They'd gone over their plans numerous times until everyone involved knew where to go and when. Dermott reached the sitting room as the earl was about to open the terrace doors. "Yer lordship! Let me go first."

The earl hesitated, then yanked the doors open, shouting for his wife.

Lady Aurelia's answering cry had the hair on the back of Dermott's neck standing up. From the sound of it, the women were near the back of the of the garden by the roses climbing the stone wall. "Bloody, *fecking* hell!" He leapt over the stone bench on the path and raced toward the wall.

"Let her go!" His wife's angry voice and command seared through him, surprising him.

He vaulted over a second bench and finally spotted the women by the door in the wall, being held by two men. He heard more than one horse, but didn't see them—they must be on the other side of the wall. In a heartbeat, he decided to use his fists first, pistol second. He couldn't take the chance that his shot could be deflected by the thug holding Lady Aurelia, or that the miscreant would pull her in front of him and take the lead ball meant for him. "Unhand her ladyship!"

The man turned and aimed his blunderbuss at Dermott's gut. With a superior sneer in his voice, he demanded, "Which one are you?"

Dermott slowly closed the distance between them, ignoring

the fact that at this range, the man could fire a round that would blow his guts out through his back. A calm washed over him as he countered with a demand of his own: "Let her ladyship go, and I'll tell ye."

The sound of a pistol cocking behind him was expected, and added the element of surprise Trenchert's men had not counted on. The man's gaze shifted toward the sound, and Dermott saw his chance. Using the distraction to his advantage, he yanked the hand holding the blunderbuss over the thug's head and disarmed him.

The earl swooped in, clubbing the blackguard on the head with his pistol. When the man dropped like a stone, the earl pulled his wife into his embrace, swept her into his arms, and strode toward the terrace, out of range.

Dermott blocked out everything but the need to subdue the second intruder. He delivered a lethal left cross, which stunned the would-be abductor. He quickly bound the man's hands behind his back as the eerie sensation that something was not right registered. Where was his wife? Was there a third man? "Georgiana!" He shook the prisoner, intending to ask him, but the man was unconscious. He dropped the man and spun around. "Lady Aurelia, where is me—"

His wife's angry shout was music to his ears. "Let go of me!"

Sprinting toward the sound, he prayed he would reach his wife before her abductor spirited her away. His prayers must have fallen on deaf ears, as the sound of hoofbeats pounding on the path on the other side of the garden wall reached him.

He ran toward the stables as if his life depended on it…but it wasn't his life in jeopardy, it was his wife's! The realization that he may not catch up in time to follow them had a fear such as he had never known churning, building inside of him, until his vision grayed. He immediately set aside the fear, clearing his vision. He pushed for more speed as Bart called his name. The lad was riding toward him, leading a second horse. No words were necessary, as his cousin's stepson tossed the reins to Dermott, who leapt onto the horse.

"They passed me a few moments ago," Bart said. "They're headed toward the woods, and the path that leads to the village."

Dermott, leaning low, whispered in the gelding's ear, "We have to save the lass again!"

Both horses took off like a shot, hooves thundering, as they responded to the urgency in Dermott's plea. Reaching the narrow path, they were forced to ride single file. "There!" Bart called from behind him. The pair were just ahead of them, riding double, which slowed them down. Relief filled Dermott until he saw the lass quickly glance his way before turning back to jab her elbow into her abductor's face. The man cried out as blood poured from his broken nose. He released his hold on her, and she shifted sideways off the horse.

"Hang on, lass!" Grateful for the narrow path, and tight fit, Dermott brought his mount alongside the other horse, reached out, and wrapped his arm around his wife's waist. "I've got ye, *mo ghrá!*"

"Move ahead of him, O'Malley, and I'll take care of the bloody bugger," Bart called out.

"Aye, Bart!" Dermott shifted his wife onto his lap and urged his mount forward.

"Who are you calling a bugger?" the man shouted. "I'll show you—"

Dermott snorted with laughter. Bart's punch had stunned the man long enough for the boy to tie his hands behind his back. "Excellent form, lad. Ye've a fine jab. I can tell ye've been practicing."

Bart grabbed the other horse's reins and said, "My aim's improving with the rifle Michael's letting me use, too."

"I'm grateful to have ye guarding me back, lad. I'll be letting the duke know when we send our latest report to him. Thank ye, Bart."

Now that their prisoner was secured, Dermott glanced into eyes the color of the finest whiskey. He tamped down the need to shout at her, demanding to know what in the bloody hell she'd been thinking going outside without alerting anyone. Conquering that, he struggled not to act on the desire to shake some sense into her.

"I'm fine, Dermott." The breathless sound of her voice surprised him. He was about to ask if she'd hurt her ribs when she rasped, "You're squeezing the breath out of me."

He reacted instantly, loosening his hold on her. "Forgive me, lass, I was—"

"Trying to decide whether to shout at me or shake sense into me?" she finished for him.

His mouth gaped, and he quickly snapped it shut. "As yer husband, 'twould be me right."

"Don't you want to know why the two men grabbed hold of Lady Aurelia?"

Her question startled him. Dermott had been so focused on rescuing them that he'd forgotten the man had a hold of the countess first. The attacker had only grabbed Georgiana when he had been forced to let go of Lady Aurelia. "Aye, what did the man say?"

His wife's eyes welled with tears.

"Ye have nothing to fear now, lass. Thanks to Bart's quick thinking, ye're safe."

"It's not that. The viscount has given up on me."

"Are ye certain about that?"

She nodded. "The man who grabbed hold of Lady Aurelia told me I was useless to the viscount now that you've..." Her voice trailed off.

Dermott tightened his hold on his wife, tucking her head beneath his chin. "I've got ye, lass. Now tell me what the bloody bastard said."

She rasped against his cravat, "Now that you've taken my virtue, I have nothing of value."

The need to grab hold of the viscount and demand he cease maligning his wife had him by the bollocks. He cleared his throat and said, "Ye have infinite value to me, lass. Ye're me wife... Me life. Tell me what else he said."

"The countess would be worth her weight in coin."

Her stifled sob told him more about the lass's compassion than words. She feared for Lady Aurelia's safety. "Go ahead and cry, lass. Ye'll feel better for it."

She surprised him by sniffing and lifting her head. Tear-drenched amber eyes blazing with anger held his. "I'm glad I broke that man's nose. I was so afraid that they would keep her ladyship prisoner and little Edward would be beside himself." Her words indicated that her courage was equal to her compassion.

"The path widens just ahead," he told her. "We can turn around and head back to the manor, and ye can see for yerself that the earl has taken care of her ladyship."

"Thank you for rescuing me again, Dermott."

"I'm hoping this is the last time," he replied as he urged their mount to turn back the way they'd come. Bart followed his lead and did the same. "Ye can have a bit of a rest when we return, lass."

"I'd rather have a bath to scrub everywhere that other man touched me."

Dermott's temper shot straight to boiling. "Where did he touch ye?"

She did not answer him.

"Ye'll be telling me now, before we reach the stables."

"We cannot always have what we want, husband."

"Are ye defying me, lass?"

Bart's laughter irritated the hell out of him. "She sounds like my mum."

"Does she now?" Dermott asked. "And how does me cousin react when she defies him?"

"He raises his voice until Mum gets that look in her eye."

"Then what happens?"

"I'm consigned to mucking out the stalls and cleaning the barn."

"Why would they send you out to the barn?" Georgiana asked.

Dermott met Bart's gaze and smothered his need to laugh outright. "I'll explain it to ye later, lass, when—"

The crack of a rifle had him swearing and scooping his wife off his horse and onto Bart's. "Ride like hell and warn the others!"

The lad wrapped his arms around Georgiana and said, "But—"

"NOW!"

※※※

BART CURVED HIS body around her and urged his horse into a gallop, never letting go of the other horse with their prisoner. As they rode toward the manor, more shots sounded, and her heart hammered with fear for Dermott.

She struggled against him, demanding, "Take me back!"

He tightened his hold on her, as fierce at following orders as her husband and his cousins had been.

"Bart, please?" she said. "You do not know how many men were lying in wait for us. Dermott could be killed."

"He vowed to protect the duke and his family."

Frantic to convince him to turn back and help her husband, she elbowed him in the stomach. "At the cost of his life?"

Bart grunted, absorbing the blow, loosening his hold on the reins. The prisoner gasped, slid sideways, and fell off his horse, but Bart kept going and answered, "Aye. My stepfather and the others promised, too."

Tears streamed from her eyes. Ignoring them, she shifted and almost succeeded in loosening his grip. *Almost.*

They rounded the bend in the road, and Bart let out a short, sharp whistle—like the one Dermott had used. She stopped struggling as Sean and Michael ran toward them. Before either man could ask what happened, Bart jumped off the horse and faced them. "The prisoner I was leading back here fell off his horse just up the road. His hands are tied behind his back, and his nose is broken, so he won't get far."

Sean nodded. "Where's Dermott?"

"We were ambushed... I heard more than one shot in succession. Had to be three men—no one can load that fast."

"Where?" Michael asked.

"Follow the road to the path in the woods. We were attacked just beyond where it narrows."

Michael lifted Georgiana off the horse and set her on her feet. "Go inside with Bart, Georgiana—Dermott's life depends upon it."

"I will. Hurry! Dermott's outnumbered!"

Michael mounted Bart's horse and shouted, "Now, Bart!"

Bart tugged on Georgiana's arm, urging her to run, as Sean rode past at a gallop.

She looked over her shoulder and stumbled, but Bart steadied her and kept going. Nearly out of breath, she struggled to ask, "Will they get to Dermott in time?"

He grunted in response, yanked open the door, and pulled her inside. The earl met them there. "Where's Dermott?"

Unable to speak past the pain in her heart, she sank to her knees as Bart replied, "The viscount's men ambushed us!"

Her knees were still wobbly when Bart and the earl helped her to her feet. "Sean and Michael are due to be changing shifts," the earl said. "Who went after Dermott?"

"Both of them, your lordship. I heard three distinct shots, too close together—"

"Three men," the earl said with a nod. "The type of odds my brother's men prefer."

Stiffening her knees to hold her up, Georgiana demanded, "How can anyone defend themselves when they are outnumbered?"

"The O'Malleys, Garahans, and Flahertys have faced and conquered those same odds more times than you would imagine," the earl replied.

"But—"

"We'll speak of this later," he interrupted. "I have to warn the others."

Georgiana let herself be led to the kitchen. Mrs. Wyatt was filling tart shells, and paused when she heard them approach. She brushed her hands on her apron and nodded to Bart. "I have her."

His duty complete, the young man turned on his heel and sprinted toward the back door.

"Sit down before you collapse on me. We're going to need all hands to be ready for however many wounded walk through that door. Compose yourself while I pour you a cup of tea."

The housekeeper walked into the kitchen, took stock of the situation, and said, "Brandy, Mrs. Wyatt."

Ashamed that she had nearly fallen apart in front of Bart and the earl, Georgiana drew in a deep breath and slowly exhaled. Willing her hands to stop trembling, she accepted the glass and sipped. She could feel the warmth spreading from her lips to her belly.

Mrs. Jones shared a knowing look with Mrs. Wyatt and said, "Tell us what happened."

CHAPTER TWENTY-SEVEN

D ERMOTT FELT THE lead ball penetrate his upper arm. He absorbed the impact and bent low over his horse, galloping toward the man who shot him. The other man's mouth dropped open in shock as Dermott launched himself out of the saddle into the sharpshooter, taking him to the ground.

Anticipating the others would take aim and fire, he rolled until he was lying beneath the blackguard who'd shot him. The man stiffened and moaned in agony as a shot was echoed by a curse. Dermott shoved the man off him, reached for the knife in the sheath at his waist, and hurled it at the closest attacker. The man's eyes widened in shock as he stared at the knife embedded in his shooting arm and dropped his rifle.

Instead of going for one of the rifles, Dermott reached for the knife in his boot and aimed for the third sharpshooter. Unerringly, the knife hit its mark, disarming the third man. Dermott shoved to his feet, bent down, and retrieved the first rifle. The man moaned, and for a moment Dermott thought about letting the man bleed out.

"*Bollocks!*" The earl and the duke would have his hide if they found out that he'd failed to render aid to one of his prisoners. He reached into his frockcoat pocket, withdrew a rope, and bound the man's hands behind his back. In his waistcoat pocket, he found what he needed, and used the spare cravat as a temporary bandage to wrap around his attacker's arm. "How much is Trenchert paying ye to kill me?"

Not bothering to wait for an answer, Dermott moved to the next man, surprised that his vision had dimmed. Had the sun gone behind a cloud, or had he imagined it was bright where it filtered in through the trees? He wiped his eyes with the back of his hand and noticed the blood. *"Feck* me! Lord, I'll be needing a bit of a hand here. I need to tie up the other two thugs and see to their injuries before I pass out."

The sound of hoofbeats coming from the direction of the manor were the answer to his plea. "Thank ye, Lord." He managed to tie the man's hands behind his back, and remove the knife, but was struggling to tie the knot in the cravat he'd wrapped around the man's arm.

"Dermott!"

"Over here, Sean."

His cousin knelt beside him, and before Dermott could ask, Sean assured him, "Bart brought the lass back safe and sound."

Dermott nodded to where Michael now tended to the third man. "If they hadn't winged me, I would have had all three tied up nice and tidy when ye arrived."

"Never would have expected less from one of the Cork O'Malleys," Sean replied, nodding to Dermott's injury. "Can ye lift yer arm, or should I cut off yer sleeve?"

Dermott started to lift his arm, then stopped. "Cut me sleeve off."

Sean sliced through his cousin's coat sleeve with his knife, tossed it to the ground, then cut off the shirt sleeve and sheathed his knife. "Ye've two wounds—entry and exit. He shot clean through yer arm."

"Felt like it. Bind it up, would ye?"

Sean made short work of the task and said, "We should head back right away. The way ye're bleeding, we won't be able to sear yer wounds with a hot blade." Dermott groaned, and his cousin nodded. "Ye'll be needing threads to close it."

"Bloody hell."

Sean glared at their prisoners. "Not that I give a damn as to yer preferences, but the chances are a bit greater that ye'll bleed more if ye're facedown, hanging over the saddle. Now, his lordship and His Grace *do* care, so I'm giving ye a choice—ye can either ride sitting on yer horse, or draped over it."

Michael grumbled, "Why would ye be giving them a choice? Did they give her ladyship or Dermott's wife a choice?"

"Ye have the right of it, boy-o. Help me drape them over their saddles." Turning to Dermott, Sean asked, "Can ye hold yer seat on the ride back?"

"Aye."

A few moments later, Sean, Michael, and Dermott held the reins to their prisoners' horses, leading them back to Lippincott Manor.

SEAN WHISTLED AS they rode toward the stables. Flaherty was waiting for them. He lifted the prisoners off their saddles and lined them up against the water trough by the stables as Sean and Michael dismounted and rushed to help Dermott.

"I can get off me *fecking* horse without yer help." He shrugged their hands off and promptly stumbled and fell on his *arse* when his legs gave out.

Garahan walked over, hefted Dermott over his shoulder, and strode toward the house.

"I can walk, ye bleeding *eedjit*!"

Garahan snorted with laughter. "I'm not the one who's bleeding...or an *eedjit*."

Helping hands were already opening the door and motioning for Garahan to lay Dermott on the cot. He struggled against his cousin's hold. "I can bloody well sit!" Garahan set him on his feet. When Dermott wobbled, his cousin used the tip of his finger to keep him from falling on his face.

"Sit, then." Garahan used a bit more force, and his cousin sat.

"Where's me wife?"

"She's sitting with her ladyship," Mrs. Wyatt answered as she began to cleanse the area around Dermott's wounds.

"Were either her ladyship or me wife injured? Did ye check for bruises and cracked ribs?"

"Both women are fine," the physician assured him as he entered the room and walked over to the pitcher and bowl, washing his hands. "Thank you, Mrs. Wyatt." He studied Dermott's arm and nodded. "Excellent—the lead ball went right through your arm. Although the exit wound is a bit ragged around the edges—"

Dermott interrupted, "'Tis better than ye having to dig the lead ball out of me arm."

"I do believe I have spent more time here in the last fortnight than I have tending to the villagers."

The physician was tying off the last of the threads when Georgiana rushed into the room.

"Dermott!" She skidded to a stop, and her eyes filled with tears. "I knew they would shoot you."

"I'm glad Bart was able to get ye to safety. 'Twas a bit chaotic for a few moments before I had everything under control."

"But you were shot!" She walked over to where he sat, waiting for the physician to finish bandaging his arm.

Satisfied, the doctor nodded. "As you have no doubt heard my instructions numerous times before, O'Malley, I don't believe I need to repeat them."

"Would you, please, repeat them for me?" Georgiana said. "I have helped tend to injuries in the past, when our tenant farmers were injured, but no one was ever shot."

The physician nodded and began to explain the cleansing, bandaging, and diet he expected Dermott to follow. When the doctor left, Georgiana laid a hand to her husband's cheek and rasped, "I didn't want to leave you."

The others followed the doctor out of the room. When they

were alone, Dermott reached for his wife's hand and tugged her onto his lap. "'Tis a paltry wound, lass. I've had worse." He brushed away her tears and kissed her gently. "I'm proud of ye."

"For what? Not fainting when I walked in a few moments ago, or for following orders?"

He smiled. "Now that ye mention it, both, lass." When her eyes met his, he lowered his mouth to hers, kissing her more deeply this time. When she sighed, he tucked her head beneath his chin and felt himself relax for the first time since she was captured. Dermott was well used to dealing with those who thought they would succeed in abducting those the duke, his family, or the women his guard loved. The man who'd abducted his wife was currently waiting for the constable, along with the three men—including the one he'd used as a shield against the attackers' rifles—who were about to be tended to by the physician.

Cradling the lass to his heart, he wondered if he would ever be able to forget the gut-wrenching fear that threatened to consume him when she had been taken from him. When she started to cry, he resolved to think about it later. "This time listen, lass, and cry it out. Then I'll carry ye to our bedchamber."

She shoved against his hold, and he eased back. The temper in her eyes surprised him. "What's wrong now?"

"You will not carry me upstairs. You have been shot!"

"Won't I?" Dermott rose to his feet with her in his arms, and walked out of the room. He nodded to the footman stationed in the hall. "I could use a hand opening the door to the servants' staircase."

The footman obliged, holding it open for him.

As he ascended the staircase, Dermott whispered, "If ye're up to it, lass, I'm thinking I'll need ye to soothe me wounds by making love to me."

Her gasp had him chuckling.

"This is not a laughing matter, Dermott."

He reached the top of the stairs. "I agree—making love to ye is a serious matter. Open the door for me, lass."

She did as he bade her, and did not speak to him again until he paused in the doorway to one of the guest bedchambers. He crossed the threshold, and she demanded, "How can you even *think* about making love to me?"

He kicked the door shut behind them. "Ah, lass, how can I think of anything else when today could have ended far differently?" He walked over to their bed and gently laid her on it. "Now then, I could use a hand taking off me clothes."

When they had shed their clothing, he lay on the bed and pulled her on top of him. "Now then, lass, I'm thinking 'tis time to teach ye another way to make love."

Her eyes were wide until he kissed her deeply, passionately, letting her know without words that he needed the affirmation that they were alive by burying himself deep inside of her. Sliding into her warmth, he felt his world realign. Here was love—here was his *life*. "Mo ghrá?" She opened her eyes, and he confessed, "Ye have me heart and me love forever, lass."

"Mo ghrá," she whispered, "you have had my heart from the moment I opened my eyes and you were there. I will love you forever."

They made slow, sweet love until exhaustion claimed them, and they drifted off to sleep.

CHAPTER TWENTY-EIGHT

A SENNIGHT LATER, Dermott was well on the road to full recovery. Though he did not agree with the earl's decision to stay in the guest chamber until the physician proclaimed that he was ready to resume his duties, Dermott gave in because of his sweet wife's worry.

He shook his head, remembering the way she had looked at him. He'd noticed the fear in her gaze when she stared at him before she could hide it. Was the lass committing his face to memory because she had so little faith in his ability to uphold his vow and duties to the duke as part of his guard?

"Want to tell me what's on yer mind?"

Dermott shrugged. How should he answer Sean? He thought being married would be like any other day performing his duties to the duke and the earl. He would accept the assignment and fulfill his duties. Relaying orders was part of his job. "Same as yerself—if I give an order, I expect it to be obeyed."

Sean followed Dermott back to the wagon in front of the cottage to unload more furniture. "Well now," Sean drawled, "I'm here to tell ye that although our wives may appear to be gentle, agreeable women, they've got spines of steel and a will of iron to match our own. What did ye tell the lass that has set her back up?"

Dermott rolled his shoulder to ease the ache in it. He was

pushing himself harder than he should for the amount of blood he'd lost. Bloody hell, he was an O'Malley, and O'Malleys never sat and watched others working—they pitched in and did their part! "I told her she was not to leave the manor house, or our cottage when we moved in, unless one of us accompanied her."

Sean snorted. "I can see why the lass would be upset with ye, Dermott. She's so wrapped up worrying about ye being shot that she hasn't considered that the threat against her isn't over."

"And I cannot help that me temper heats up every time she treats me like I'm half a man. Did Mignonette do that to ye?"

Sean snorted with laughter. "Oh, aye. That and more."

"How did ye find a way to get her to treat ye like the strong, capable man that ye are?"

He clapped Dermott on the back. "Just remember her worry is because she loves ye, has only just found ye, and hasn't learned the most important part about being an O'Malley."

"Oh, and what's that?" Dermott asked.

Sean's green eyes narrowed as if he were sizing up his enemy. "We O'Malleys may get knocked down, but faith, we bounce right back up again...battered and bleeding, but ready to fight!"

Dermott looked up as the cottage door opened, and the lass stood on the threshold, a look of love in her eyes until she took in the table they were carrying. Her expression changed, and the lass stomped toward them.

"What do you think you are doing?"

With Sean's words echoing through his mind, Dermott appreciated the fire in her eyes and the worry-tangled love behind it. "Moving the table into our home," he said.

"You are supposed to be resting for an hour in the middle of every day," she reminded him. "Doctor's orders."

He slowly smiled as he set his end of the table down. "Well now, wife of mine, I'll be happy to rest—if ye want to call it that—after me cousin and I finish unloading the furniture." When she opened and quickly closed her mouth, he could not help teasing her. "Can ye not wait that long to get yer hands on me, lass?"

Her face flamed and she spun around so fast, he thought she'd fall. But she did not—she marched back to their cottage, walked inside, and slammed the door.

Sean picked up his end of the table and nodded to Dermott. "Ye need to work on wooing yer wife over to yer way of thinking, boy-o, else ye'll be sleeping on a pallet in front of the fireplace—or with Flaherty and Coventry's men in the outbuilding."

Dermott picked up his end of the table, surprised when Bart rushed over. "The door's closed," the lad said, "I'll open it for you."

Dermott motioned Bart closer and confided in a low voice, "Ye'll need to knock first, Bart. If me wife thinks it's me, she may end up clobbering ye on the head by mistake with whatever's handy."

Bart's mouth dropped open. He stared at Dermott and shook his head. "Miss Georgiana would never do such a thing. She's a kind, loving, and giving woman."

Dermott knew the lass was probably inside with her ear to the door, straining to hear what they were saying. He called out loud enough for her to hear, "Would ye open the door for us, Bart? I don't want me wife to think I'm letting down me guard, allowing a stranger to walk into our home."

Sean struggled not to laugh while Bart shook his head and walked over to the door and knocked. "Mrs. O'Malley? It's Bart. Sean and Dermott are ready to bring the table inside."

The door opened with a flourish, and the lass stood beaming in the doorway. "Hello, Bart. Thank you for helping the men with their chore."

Dermott knew he'd never understand the lightning-fast shift in his wife's moods if he studied her for the next fifty years.

In a honeyed voice, she said, "Please set it over there near the stove."

When they did, the lass smiled and walked over to him. Laying a hand to his arm, she lifted to her toes and pressed her lips to his cheek. "Thank you, Dermott. I'll have your lunch ready and waiting after you help Sean return the wagon."

He looked into the amber eyes that by turns bewitched him and bedeviled him, and decided not to question the carefully worded order. The lass expected him to help his cousin with the wagon and the horse and to return immediately after. Deciding what was good for the goose was good for him as well, he nodded.

Sean was already out the door when Dermott pulled her close and kissed the breath out of her. "I believe I'll be taking that rest after lunch, lass."

THEY NEVER HAD the opportunity to rest because of the commotion that invariably occurred whenever Lady Aurelia and Lady Calliope had to bid one another goodbye—no matter that their estates were only half an hour apart. The earl and the viscount patiently waited for them to finish before Chattsworth settled his family into their carriage to return.

Dermott nodded to Michael and Garahan as they flanked the carriage, while the three additional men Captain Coventry had assigned to add an extra layer of protection for the viscount's family sent one man ahead of the carriage and two behind.

Watching them leave, he leaned toward Sean. "How long can we keep Tarleton, Varley, and Stratford?"

"Until the matter has been handled," his cousin replied.

Dermott nodded. As long as Trenchert still resided at his nearby country estate—a reminder that the man had yet to collect the last of his debts—the matter would remain unsettled.

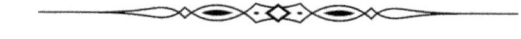

CHAPTER TWENTY-NINE

IF LIVING ON tenterhooks were not enough, Dermott was dealing with his wife's willful disregard of his orders to remain indoors unless accompanied by one of the duke's guard. He was accustomed to being obeyed. Given his wife's circumstances prior to losing her memory, he knew he should not push her. He would have to encourage her to come around to his way of thinking slowly. The lass had suffered greatly when her father told her that he'd all but gambled her life away! Her home, inheritance, and dowry were a huge loss, but the greatest of them all was Lord Eggerton's untimely death. He knew intimately what the loss of her da must have felt like.

"He's thinking again," Flaherty said loud enough to break through Dermott's reverie.

Sean was quick to agree. "Aye. Ye'd think he'd have paid attention to how his da handled his ma when she was wont to disagree."

"Aye," Flaherty agreed. "Aunt Bridget is a strong-minded woman, not unlike me ma—or yours."

"That she is, and she listened to Uncle Patrick," Sean said.

"Used to... Da's gone," Dermott mumbled. It hurt to say the words even after all this time. He hid his sorrow behind the glare he leveled on his cousins. "Need I remind ye that Ma's people were Flynns, and they were even-tempered people...until they weren't." Thoughts of his ma and his three brothers-in-law had him smiling. She was surrounded by men who'd take care of her and not tease her, as he and his brothers could not resist doing.

But Da used to tease Ma. He wondered if she missed the teasing. His brothers-in-law were a serious lot, given the fact that first Patrick and Finn—then Dermott and Emmett—had entrusted Ma into their care when they left to find better-paying work.

The money they sent home monthly would see that their mother would want for nothing. Their brothers-in-law would tend to the land and the farm. If not for the urgent need of coin, they would have stayed in Ireland and married stubborn women just like his sisters.

The realization hit him right between the eyes. "*Feck* me, I've gone and married a woman as stubborn as Grainne, Maeve, and Roisin combined!"

Sean and Flaherty snorted with laughter. "And ye didn't notice that until just now?" Sean asked.

"How in the bloody hell would I when I was consumed with worry for the lass since I lifted her limp and bleeding body into me arms?"

"Remind me not to rescue any more lasses," Flaherty grumbled.

"Yer heart is safe," Sean told him.

"Oh?" Flaherty asked. "And why is that?"

"Mary Kate Donovan has held it in her hands since the moment ye climbed on top of the carriage, opened the door, reached in, and lifted her to safety."

Flaherty's face lost all expression. He turned his back on his cousins and stalked toward the stables.

Dermott shook his head; he wasn't the only one bearing the brunt of their cousins' teasing. "Ease up, Sean. Flaherty's got enough on his mind, seeing as how ye assigned him the midday shift patrolling the road from the estate to the village and back. Besides, don't be forgetting that with yer wife, plus Garahan's and

Michael's, spreading the word of Trenchert's terrorizing tactics and near abduction of Lady Aurelia and me wife, we have the villagers on our side."

"Aye," Sean agreed, "and two estates' worth of tenant farmers looking out for us, too."

Dermott nodded. "Flaherty still needs to check his temper and keep his wits about him. Plenty of places for a sharpshooter to hide and catch him unawares."

Sean grinned. "But he's so easily riled."

"Which is why ye should stop," Dermott said. "I'm thinking he's so in love with the lass that he cannot see straight. We need every man on their guard, or have ye forgotten because these few days have been quiet?"

"I haven't forgotten."

"I for one do not trust the viscount not to try again—and soon," Dermott said.

Sean sighed. "Ye have the right of it. By me calculations, the viscount should have tried something yesterday."

Dermott's mind was awash with visions of the lass being taken from the manor—hidden somewhere on the viscount's estate or in his attic.

Sean continued, "I know ye were counting on the earl to approve yer plan to infiltrate Trenchert Manor at midnight and confront the viscount in his bedchamber. Ye'll need to understand there is more at stake than the need for retribution."

Dermott turned toward his cousin. "I do. 'Tis just that thinking about how satisfying it will feel when I club the blackguard in the mouth, and hold me blade to his throat, brightens me day."

"I'm not certain the earl will be agreeing to yer plan if he were listening to ye right now."

"'Tisn't just me wife who is in constant danger," Dermott replied. "They tried to abduct and hold her ladyship for ransom!"

"Which may be the deciding factor that sways his lordship to our way of thinking."

"Ye're with me on this?" Dermott hadn't wanted to push his

cousin, but he hadn't given up hope that Sean would side with him.

"Aye! It could just have easily been Mignonette, Harry, or Melinda in the viscount's cross hairs."

"Or Lady Calliope," the earl said, interrupting their conversation as he approached the two men. "I don't like the idea of holding a member of the *ton* at knifepoint—no matter what he has said or done. If either of you, or any of my brother's guard, choose to use that as a means of forcing his hand, there will be an uproar that will taint my family's name, and that of my wife and sister-in-law."

"What would ye have me do?" Dermott asked.

The earl slowly smiled. "My brother dubbed you his mercenary, did he not?"

"Aye, but if ye won't support me going in under the cover of darkness—"

The earl interrupted again. "You have my full support, and that of Jared, to do so."

"But if I cannot go in armed—"

"I never said you had to go in unarmed. I merely stipulated that you cannot hold a knife to the viscount's throat."

"What would ye have me do if I cannot threaten him with me knife? No doubt ye won't be wanting me to club him on the back of the head with the butt of me pistol."

"You are correct. Use your imagination."

Sean snorted with laughter. "He's newly married, yer lordship, and using his imagination for other things right now."

"What would Dermott be using it for if not for convincing the viscount to cease his attempts to abduct my wife—or his?"

Sean turned to Dermott and asked, "How long have ye been married now?"

"Are ye wanting to know in minutes, hours, or days?"

The earl shook his head. "I stand corrected and remember being newly married myself. Sean, help jog Dermott's memory, meet with the others, and have a new plan ready by teatime."

"Aye, yer lordship."

Sean and Dermott watched Lippincott stride toward the rear entrance to the manor. "When he thinks no one is looking," Sean murmured, "his lordship's eyes devour her ladyship."

"'Tis as it should be," Dermott remarked. "Da was the same way, and I know for a fact yer da still is."

Sean nodded. "The earl approved of your going in under the cover of midnight. There's bound to be more than one window or door ye can slip through unnoticed."

"What can I do to make the earl see reason and agree to me plan?"

"Abduct the viscount," Sean said.

"That was me plan, but—"

"Not at knifepoint," Sean reminded him, "nor should ye knock him on the head with yer pistol, nor hold one to his belly."

"That was the entirety of me list," Dermott grumbled.

"Concentrate on yer strengths, boy-o…without the need for weapons."

"He'll never hear me coming."

Sean smiled. "And?"

"I've mastered a number of knots sailors use."

"Ye'll have no trouble throwing him over yer shoulder once ye've tied him up, but—"

"I'll need to gag him."

"Aye. A blindfold might help, too."

"I'm thinking yer plan is brilliant," Dermott said.

"Our plan," Sean reminded him. "And how will ye render him unconscious?"

It dawned on Dermott that Sean remembered what he had forgotten… "I'll wrap me arm around his throat… Only takes a few moments and a bit of pressure."

"I knew ye'd remember once ye were able to stop thinking about the stubborn lass ye married."

"I'll go tonight," Dermott said.

"Not alone," Sean told him.

"'Tis best if I go alone. I can be in and out before ye miss me."

"Ye'll be taking two men with ye to stand watch."

"Fine! I'll Ask Stratford and Varley."

"Coventry's men? What of meself or Flaherty?"

"Don't ye trust Coventry's men?" Dermott asked.

"'Tisn't the point," Sean replied.

"What in the bloody hell *is* yer point?"

"One of our guard should accompany ye," his cousin reminded him.

"Coventry's men are part of the duke's guard—his London eyes and ears."

"Bugger it," Dermott swore. "I'll take Flaherty and Stratford. Ye can let Stratford know—I'll have a word with Flaherty."

His cousin stared at him without speaking. Finally, Sean nodded. "Ye'll go in armed to the teeth, but ye won't be holding a knife to the viscount's throat, or a pistol to his belly."

"I already said I wouldn't." Dermott turned to leave but paused. "Don't say a word to me wife. I don't need her getting any ideas from their ladyships. I won't have her following after me. 'Tis too dangerous."

"Aye. Do ye want one or two men guarding yer wife?"

"Two…three if ye can spare a man."

Sean nodded. "Done."

"Done," Dermott agreed.

"I'll let his lordship know the plan for tonight. He may want to send a missive to His Grace."

"Whatever ye think is best, Sean."

***

GEORGIANA'S SENSE OF prevailing doom grew exponentially as another day without incident passed. She wanted to ask Dermott if he was planning some sort of retaliation against the viscount for the attempted abduction of Lady Aurelia—and her own brief capture. But her husband had been in a pensive mood that morning, and barely said two words to her upon rising.

She sighed. She missed seeing him throughout the day as she had when she was staying at the manor house, and had looked forward to his visits in between his shifts guarding the interior and exterior of the manor. The only time she spent there now was during her cooking lessons. Which were going well enough, but apparently not as well as her husband had hoped. *He could have asked if I had any experience in the kitchen before he asked me to marry him.*

She laughed remembering his expression of astonishment when they'd moved into their cottage and she burned their breakfast the first morning. She'd told him she had years of experience in the kitchen…snitching berry tarts. Apparently Dermott had not found it as amusing as she had.

The only reason she knew how to brew tea was due to their cook's giving in to Georgiana's constantly pestering the poor woman to give her something to do. She had hoped to be given the task of helping make the pastry for the tarts, but the cook had been horrified at the notion.

Dressed for the day, she straightened up their cottage. Looking about her, she could not help but notice how huge it seemed without Dermott's commanding presence in it. He took up so much room with his broad shoulders and deep chest. She sighed, remembering how they had spent the hour before dawn. *All of those lovely muscles.* She had caressed and pressed her lips to those very same muscles.

Her face heated and her heart raced. The unexpected pleasure of his lessons in lovemaking, and time spent locked in his arms, had her losing her train of thought at odd moments during the day.

She scolded herself as her thoughts wandered back to earlier that morning. Recalling the desire in his eyes, and the emotion and intention in his expression, had her shivering all over again, and not from a chill.

"You are going to need to pay attention this morning," she said aloud. Mrs. Wyatt had reminded her yesterday that the pies and tarts she was to bake under the cook's supervision would be sampled at teatime. She did not want to disappoint the earl or Lady Aurelia by burning their pastry, as she had two days earlier. In order not to repeat that unhappy performance, she needed her wits about her, and her head firmly attached to her shoulders—not in the clouds daydreaming of her handsome husband.

She opened the door to their cottage and stepped into a bright spring day. The air was soft, the sun warm. Reveling in the birdsong, she inhaled the subtly sweet scent on the breeze. Lifting her face to the warmth of the sun, she sighed and took another breath, this time taking in the scent of freshly turned earth from the nearby tenant farm. A pang of sorrow pierced her breast at the thought of never walking along the lane that wound toward the brook that edged Eggerton Hall leading past their tenant farms with her father again.

Instead of heading toward the manor house and her cooking lesson, she turned to the right. Lost in thought, she didn't remember passing by the first farm or the second. It wasn't until she heard a horse and rider approaching from behind that she looked around her, surprised that there were no farms in sight.

The look of disapproval on Flaherty's face had her sighing. Her husband would hear of her disobeying his dictate that she stay put. The man's blue eyes were riveted on her as he reined in his horse. "Where are ye headed, lass?"

The edge in his voice and intensity in his eyes reminded her of Dermott's, though her husband's were a brilliant green. "Just walking."

It was a bit unnerving how much taller Flaherty appeared sitting on his horse. "Were ye now?"

Miffed that he would question her as if he had the right to, she did not bother to respond. She turned her back on him and continued walking. One moment she was on her feet, and the next she was sitting in front of Flaherty on his horse.

"How dare you!"

"Ye'll not disappear on me watch, lass."

Dermott had warned her not to go anywhere without an escort. The realization that she could very well have been spirited away by another of the viscount's men had her trembling. "I did not mean to go so far," she explained. "When I opened the door and felt the warmth of the sun, I could not help but follow my nose toward the scent of fresh-turned earth."

She supposed his grunt was an answer.

Needing Flaherty to understand that she wasn't trying to make his job more difficult, she told him, "I used to walk the fields with my father early in the morning and stop and visit our tenant farmers... I do hope they won't be forced off the land they've farmed for years," she rasped. "Do you think the viscount will make them leave?"

Instead of answering, he said, "I'll have yer word ye won't be leaving unescorted again. Dermott would have me hide if he knew ye were out here...alone."

She frowned at the guard. "Nothing happened. I don't see why—"

A shot rang out. She felt Flaherty's big body jolt a heartbeat before he curled himself around her, protecting her. He leaned low over his horse and rasped, "*Rith*, laddie!"

Georgiana did not understand the word, but she understood the horse's reaction—he took off at a gallop! The echoing sound of more than one set of hooves behind them—chasing them—had him urging her, "Keep yer head down. We'll outrun them."

She prayed he was right, because she could feel the warmth of his blood soaking through her shawl onto the back of her gown. When she felt him leaning at an angle, she shifted to wrap an arm around him. A second shot rang out, splintering the tree branch hanging over the road. The third shot, and echoing grunt of pain, had her praying she could keep Flaherty from falling off the horse. The reins went slack, but she grabbed hold of them before the horse slowed his pace.

"I can see the back of the stables up ahead," she said. The sound of riders approaching from the direction of the manor was the answer to her prayer. "Help is coming, Flaherty. Hang on!" His weight threatened to topple them off the horse, but he managed to keep his seat until strong hands pulled her free. Flaherty groaned, bonelessly slid off the horse, and landed face-first in the road.

Two men raced past them, chasing after their attackers, who had spun around to retreat. Sean set her on her feet before lifting Flaherty off the ground onto his shoulder and draping him over the other man's horse. "Stratford, take Flaherty. I'll take the lass."

Stratford nodded, put a hand to Flaherty's back to keep him from falling, and raced back to the manor house. When Sean lifted her onto his horse, he swore, staring at his bloodstained hands. Before she could explain, he mounted behind her, pulled her tight against him, and followed behind Stratford. He reined in by the stables and leapt off his horse. "Why didn't ye tell me ye were shot, too?"

She was about to answer, but he swept her into his arms and ran toward the house. "It's not what you think," she protested. "I can walk."

"'Tis the blood loss that has ye thinking ye can, lass. Bart went for the physician," Sean started before Dermott shouted, "Georgiana!"

The sound of her husband's voice should have soothed her, but the edge of concern added another layer to her guilt.

Sean answered for her, "In here, Dermott!"

Her husband burst into the room by the pantry and jolted to a stop. "God, the blood!" Looking over his shoulder, he shouted for Lady Aurelia's maid. "Help me get this dress off her, so I can see where me wife's been shot."

Georgiana started shaking now that the danger was over. Tears welled in her eyes. She grabbed hold of Dermott's hand. "It's not my blood…it's Flaherty's!" As soon as the words were out of her mouth, she burst into tears. "It's all my fault. The morning was so lovely, you see…and I just started walking."

Sean motioned the maid over. "Jenny's here, Dermott—best to have her take a look, then. She could have been grazed by a lead ball."

Dermott nodded to the maid, who stared at the blood on Georgiana's gown before quickly nodding to him. "We'll be right back."

"Me wife stays here," Dermott growled. "Ye can go behind the dressing screen in the corner. If not for the others in the room, I'd undress me wife meself!"

Jenny tugged on her arm and did as she was bidden. Georgiana should have been relieved that she was not injured, but instead, it was all suddenly too much to bear. The guilt and the embarrassment twisted inside her. She had walked farther than she intended and been caught off guard when Flaherty raced toward her. The sound of riders approaching and the shots fired would keep her awake nights.

The weight of her guilt hit her, and she crumpled to her knees and sobbed. *Flaherty had been shot protecting her!* Dear Lord, it was her fault that he lay bleeding.

"They've stopped the bleeding, lass. Flaherty's strong as a horse," her husband murmured as he lifted her into his arms. "The physician is on his way to remove the lead ball and stitch him back together."

"I have to tell him I'm sorry!"

"Tell him after ye've washed the blood off and changed yer gown."

The lack of inflection in his voice had her sniffing back her tears and looking into his eyes. She hoped her husband did not blame her for his cousin getting shot. She needed to apologize. "I didn't mean for Flaherty to get shot."

"Ye'll not be left to yer own devices again until we've taken care of the viscount and his men once and for all."

She wondered if her husband planned to lock her in one of the guest rooms upstairs, or put a guard at the front of their cottage and another at the back. His fierce frown had her swallowing the question.

He carried her up to the room they had shared, set her gently on her feet, and warned her, "Do not leave this room until I come back for ye." With a nod to the housekeeper who had been waiting for them, he stalked from the room. Georgiana sank into the nearest chair and knew she'd rather be locked away for a sennight than have her husband angry with her.

The knock on the door had Mrs. Jones moving to open it. Several footmen entered carrying containers of hot water to fill the tub. Georgiana watched and waited for them to complete their task without speaking. When the housekeeper closed the door, she turned and held out her hand to Georgiana, who let Mrs. Jones pull her to her feet and lead her to the dressing room where the hot bath waited.

When she was in the tub, her tears started again. "Will Flaherty die?"

"He's a strong man, Georgiana—all of the duke's men are."

"But he was shot in the back like my father." She lifted her gaze to the housekeeper's. "Papa died."

⇶✖⇷

DERMOTT'S JAW CLENCHED as he stood listening outside the door to the room where his wife wept into the bathwater. He turned and walked away, vowing, "I'm coming for ye tonight, Trenchert. Ye'll pay for setting this travesty in motion, trying to take me wife and her ladyship...and for ordering yer men to shoot me cousin!"

Chapter Thirty

The air was still as Dermott dismounted and hid his mount in a copse of trees near the side entrance of Trenchert Manor. He motioned to Stratford and Varley—Flaherty was out of commission until he healed. The first lead ball had struck him in the back, high enough on his shoulder that it didn't crack the bone. The second had grazed his upper arm.

Setting the worry for his cousin aside, Dermott led the way to the north side of the house. Varley had reported that the window to the small breakfast room was never locked. Dermott prayed the information held true. He needed a quick way in and out. Leaving the two men to stand guard, he made his way over to the building. The Lord and the fates were with them, as no one was about. He raised the window and silently slipped over the sill inside.

As his eyes adjusted to the darkness, he navigated around chairs and tables into the hallway. Though he expected to be stopped, he wasn't. An eerie sense of foreboding threatened to distract him. He ignored it and forged ahead to the door to the servants' side of the house. Ascending, he made sure to step to the side—and not the middle of the steps—to avoid any creaks.

He paused at the top, opened the door, and slipped through. Counting the doors from where he stood, he noted all but one sconce had a candle burning—the one outside the viscount's bedchamber. A whisper of sound had him prepared for attack.

The moves were swift as he exchanged blows with one of the viscount's men. Time was short. He kneed the man in the bollocks. The man moaned, and Dermott quickly silenced him, adding pressure on the man's neck until he collapsed unconscious.

He straightened and stood, poised on the balls of his feet, more than ready to take on the two men who rushed him. After dispatching them as he had the first man, he drew in a breath and slowly exhaled. Time to beard the dragon in his den.

He was surprised that the door was not locked as he slowly turned the handle and opened it a crack. His gaze swept the room, lingering on the darkened corners before settling on the lump beneath the covers. He'd forgotten how rotund the older man was. From the scent wafting toward him as he approached the bed, he resigned himself to the fact the viscount was sotted, stank of brandy and sweat, and was in dire need of a bath.

The man was easily rendered unconscious, given his drunken state. Hefting him over his shoulder, ignoring the God-awful stench, Dermott retraced his steps. The men he'd overpowered in the upper hallway were stirring. He quickly made it to the servants' staircase and descended. A guttural sound had him striking out with his fist to his left without looking. The satisfying groan that followed had him quickening his steps to the room he had used to gain entry. Knowing he was minutes away from discovery, he locked the door behind him and rushed over to the still-open window. Instead of sticking his head out to see if the coast was clear, he shoved the viscount out first.

He snorted, swallowing his laughter when a man dove out of the shadows and tackled the viscount. Grateful for the cover of darkness, he slipped out of the window and snuck up behind the guard, taking him out with the same silent method he'd used on the others. Expecting attack, he hefted his smelly burden over his shoulder and raced toward his horse. Stratford was waiting for him. "There's a man right outside the side window. Grab him and bring him with us. He was the one who tackled the viscount and pummeled him, thinking he had captured an intruder. We'll need him to confess that to the earl. We cannot let the viscount think I was the one who laid a hand on him. He'd use it to his advantage against me."

Stratford ran toward the house, returning by the time Dermott had secured the viscount's hands and had him lying across his horse. With a nod, Stratford did the same. They urged their mounts to a walk, only increasing to a trot when they met up with Varley and were well away from Trenchert Manor.

"What of the others?" Varley asked. "Will you be sending a contingent of men back for them?"

Dermott shook his head. "We can, though once they discover that we have the viscount, they'll scatter to parts unknown and disappear, like the scum they are."

Varley moved his horse alongside Dermott's. "You don't believe they'll retaliate, and try to free the viscount?"

"From all that we've heard about Trenchert, and what we've seen of those he's hired, they will not feel any allegiance toward the man."

The rode the rest of the way in silence, approaching Lippincott Manor as the sky began to lighten. Sean was guarding the perimeter when they arrived. He rushed over to Dermott and lifted the moaning burden off the horse. "God help us, what is that *smell*?"

Dermott sighed. "'Tis the viscount." He lifted his arm and gagged. "And 'tis on meself from carting the man from his bedchamber." He dismounted and sniffed his gelding's neck. "Ye poor laddie. Ye reek of his stench too."

Sean and the others snorted with laughter as the rear door to the manor house opened and the earl strode toward them. The look on his face had Dermott chuckling. "Before ye ask, the odor is from the viscount—and I did not lay a finger on him!" Nodding to the man struggling against his bonds and Stratford's hold on him, Dermott added, "Knowing he would have guards patrolling outside, I had the viscount go out of the window before me."

The earl stared at Dermott. "Willingly?"

"Ye might say that I convinced him to precede me. That's when the thug Stratford brought back tackled the viscount and started punching him. I did not want to interfere before I climbed out of the window." Dermott nodded. "Yer man here never heard me approach him until I had me arm around his throat."

The earl sighed. "I see that he doesn't have a mark on him."

"Not a one," Dermott agreed.

"We'll have to tend to the viscount's injuries before we summon the constable."

"I'm afraid I cannot let ye do so inside yer home, yer lordship—or have ye forgotten that he gave orders to abduct yer wife and mine, and orders to shoot anyone who tried to stop them?"

The earl put his hand on Dermott's shoulder. "I have not, and I was about to suggest we head to the outbuilding, where I know you have a ready supply of fresh linens, ointments, and herbals."

"Aye," Dermott replied, "and whiskey."

AN HOUR LATER, the constable arrived and was escorted to the outbuilding where they were holding the viscount and one of his men.

"I've been waiting for word that you were holding the viscount for questioning since I received the missive from His Grace about the attempted abduction of her ladyship and Mrs. O'Malley, and the shooting of one of the duke's guard."

The earl sighed. "Did you receive my message about *another* attempted abduction of Mrs. O'Malley, and that the viscount's men shot and seriously injured another member of the duke's guard?"

The constable stared at the viscount, whose face was bruised and battered. "Aye. If I were you, I'd expect the viscount to level charges against one of your men for the beating—"

Lippincott interrupted, "One of the viscount's guards was responsible for the injuries. The man who inflicted the beating on the viscount already confessed."

"It is not that I do not credit what you have told me, your lordship, but I must satisfy my superiors that I have questioned everyone and ascertained the truth of the matter."

"Be my guest."

The constable extracted the information he needed from the viscount's man and returned to the earl. "I see that you have rendered aid to the viscount. Even after all he has done to Miss Eggerton—"

"Mrs. O'Malley," Dermott interrupted.

"Ah yes, congratulations, O'Malley," the constable said before continuing, "I commend you and your men for doing so. I shall pass the information on to the powers that be."

Sean helped the constable load the two men into the back of his wagon, and the earl asked, "Would you like an escort back to the village?"

The constable shook his head. "I checked their bonds, they are secure. But thank you for the offer. I shall be in touch."

The earl turned to his men. "Thank you for your efforts today, men. I do not believe Trenchert is known to run in Prinny's circle. With God's grace, he will remain in custody, facing the punishment for what he has done."

Sean walked over to stand next to Dermott, leaned close, and sniffed his shoulder. "Ye're in sore need of a bath, boy-o. Do ye prefer the horse's trough, or a hot tub?"

Dermott sighed. "I'd best start with the horse's trough. It's going to take more than one soaking—and soaping—to rid me of this stench."

The earl shook his head and said, "I'll have hot water delivered to the guest room—through the outer dressing room door. We don't want to wake Georgiana. She was still crying when Jenny left her two hours ago."

Dermott digested the news, asking, "Did ye not let her speak to Flaherty after the doctor patched him up?"

"I did," the earl was quick to respond. "Apparently she is

worried that you will end up like Flaherty and not come back to her."

Dermott changed direction and headed toward the back of the manor house. But the earl raised a hand to stop him. "You'd best take that bath first."

Dermott lifted his arm to his nose and gagged. "Aye, yer lordship. If the lass is awake, please tell her I'm on me way to see her."

"I will."

Chapter Thirty-One

Dreams of being pursued and abducted by the viscount plagued Georgiana. She was alone, with no one to save her, as the viscount dragged her into his carriage and shut the door. She tugged her hand free and shrank from his grasp.

"Did you think I would not come for you?" he snarled. "Your father never should have wagered everything on that hand of cards."

She crossed her arms in front of her, making herself as small as possible. When the viscount reached out and touched her, she cried out.

The door to the carriage swung open, and suddenly Dermott was there…

"Open yer eyes, lass," he urged. "Ye're safe now. He'll never bother ye again."

She struggled to free herself from the nightmare and the viscount's clutches, and slowly opened her eyes. "Dermott?" she whispered. "Am I dreaming, or are you really here?"

"Who else would be sharing yer bed, lass?"

Tears welled in her eyes. She hadn't thought she had any left after crying buckets yesterday. She tried to answer, but could not push the words past the lump in her throat.

"Ah, lass," he whispered. "Please don't cry. I'm here and will always protect ye."

His warmth surrounded her, seeping in through the last vestiges of the nightmare. "Flaherty is going to recover."

"Aye."

Dermott placed a hand to her back and urged her closer. She burrowed into his embrace, but needed to be closer. She shivered as need tangled with the remnants of fear that she would never feel his loving arms around her again.

He kissed the top of her head. "The viscount will be made to pay for his crimes, lass. Trust me and let go of yer fear."

She stared into the emerald eyes she knew so well, then lifted her mouth to brush against the sculpted lips that by turns teased and tormented her. She poured all of the love in her heart and joy in her soul into her kiss, pressing her body to his until not a breath was between them.

"Ye're exhausted, lass. Ye need sleep, not loving."

She slid her arms around his neck and pulled his mouth back to hers, silently willing him to understand that she needed proof that she was still awake and not dreaming. She needed to feel him inside of her, filling her until they were both mindless with passion and overcome with desire until they wrung every ounce of pleasure from one another.

"Love me, Dermott."

"Ah, lass, I do."

"Show me," she whispered.

THE LAST THREADS of his control snapped as he rolled her beneath him and drove into her. Need to reaffirm that they were both alive had him plunging into her warmth over and over until she cried out his name, on the edge of reaching fulfillment. He claimed her mouth in a mind-numbing kiss as he drove into her and released his seed, following her over the edge into oblivion.

Fearful of crushing her, he rolled over until she was lying on top of him. She settled onto him and sighed. Clamping a hand to her lush bottom, he held her to him, praying that a babe would come from their loving. Creating a new life from the remnants of the old. Leaving behind the terror and sorrows the lass had suffered. A daughter with soft brown hair the color of meadow flower honey and amber eyes. Mayhap a son who looked like him, carrying on the strong blond-haired, green-eyed O'Malley genes.

Still deep inside of her, he said a prayer of thanks for the gift of love the lass had brought to him, along with her gentle laughter that reminded him of faery bells. As he drifted off to sleep, he thought he heard his da's voice welcoming her to the family.

Epilogue

Nine months later...

"Quit yer pacing, Dermott—ye're driving me to drink."

He didn't bother to turn around as he handed his flask to Sean. Worry arrowed through him until he thought he'd go mad. "Why won't they let me in to see her?"

Sean placed a hand to his shoulder. "The lass is fighting like a warrior to birth yer babe."

Dermott held out his hand. "Give me the bleeding flask back!"

Sean shoved it into his hands, while Flaherty blocked Dermott from reaching for the door to the bedchamber he'd been summarily shoved out of a few moments earlier.

Dermott glared at Flaherty first, Sean second. He raised the flask to his lips and took a gulp of whiskey, shoved his cousins out of the way, and pounded on the door. "Let me in! I need to see me wife and babe."

The eerie silence that followed his demand shook him to the core. Sean clamped a hand on Dermott's right shoulder, Flaherty his left. "Ye'll not barge in there until ye're bidden," Sean said.

The guttural cry he recognized instantly as his wife's had Dermott's blood running cold. "Ye'll not keep me from me wife!" The flurry of movement and hushed voices had him imagining the worst.

The physician stepped out of the room and shut the door behind him, holding on to the doorknob. "O'Malley, I need you to stop shouting—you are upsetting your wife." He stared at Dermott and pitched his voice low, saying, "The babe is stuck—we have to turn him, and need your patience and prayers, not your demands and interruptions."

God help him, Dermott was raised on a farm... He knew what it meant. His heart began to pound.

Flaherty gripped Dermott's shoulder and bowed his head to pray. "God, please grant Georgiana strength."

Sean echoed his words, adding, "But hurry."

Grateful for his cousins' prayers, Dermott added his own: "God, I need the lass. I cannot live without her. Spare me wife... Take me instead."

"Have faith, Dermott," Sean rasped. "The Lord and yer da are watching over the lass."

Dermott stared at the door, willing their prayers to reach the Lord's ears, and eventually heard the lusty cry of a newborn babe. He shrugged out of Sean and Flaherty's hold and headed for the door. It swung open, and he stumbled into the room. "Lass! Are ye all right?" He knelt beside Georgiana, willing his strength into her. She looked so fragile to him. "I swear I'll never touch ye again. Please forgive me for putting ye through this agony."

"Did you see them?" She did not sound tired—she sounded exultant.

He glanced down at the babe—nay, *babes*—in her arms and felt every drop of blood drain from his head. The last thing he heard was his wife calling his name.

"Easy now, O'Malley," the physician said, helping him off the floor. "Happens more often than you might think—the shock of witnessing your wife's pain and seeing your twins for the first time."

Dermott blinked, and the lass was no longer wan and fragile—she was triumphant and glowing. "Twins?" He couldn't feel the top of his head.

The next time he opened his eyes, he was lying on the floor beside the bed where his wife gave birth. "Did ye say twins?"

There it was again, the sound of faery bells ringing as the lass's laughter filled the air with hope. Sunlight filtered in through the window, adding a halo to the babes in Georgiana's arms.

He sat up and stared at his babes. "*Two* of them?" His head cleared and worry filled him. "Is that why ye had such a hard time birthing them?"

The physician rolled down his sleeves before donning his coat. "I'm going to be leaving your wife in the excellent care of Mrs. O'Leary, the cook, and the housekeeper. Between the three of them, they looked after the countess when her babe was born. O'Malley?"

"Hmmm?" Reluctantly, Dermott shifted his gaze to look at the doctor. "Aye?"

"I have strict instructions to be followed to the letter. Your wife will need to stay abed until I am satisfied that she is out of danger."

"Danger?"

"It is not uncommon for a woman who has had a difficult birth to hemorrhage."

He felt his eyes roll back in his head a third time before everything went black.

<hr>

AFTER THE PHYSICIAN assured her that Dermott would be fine, he left. She turned to the midwife. "Are you certain my husband did not fracture his skull the third time his head hit the floor?"

Mrs. O'Leary smiled at her. "He'll have an aching head, but he'll survive. Between the doctor and myself, we have not lost a husband yet."

Moisture filled Georgiana's eyes as she confessed, "I thought I was going to die without bringing our babes into this world."

The midwife mopped Georgiana's tears. "I have assisted the doctor on many occasions. Between us, we have delivered hundreds of babes over the years. I have never lost a babe, nor mother, when I have had to turn one that needed the gentle touch and guidance of my hands to embrace life outside the womb."

"Will I hemorrhage?"

"Not if you follow our strict instructions, especially once the urge to be intimate with your husband returns—and it will with a vengeance. Your body needs to heal, and you need to recover your strength, which will be taxed by nursing two babes. Promise me, you will rest, eat, and ignore those dark and desperate looks your husband will be sending your way once he sees you on the road to recovery."

Georgiana laughed. "I promise." She glanced at her husband, who was beginning to stir again. "Do you think his cousins counted how many times he hit the floor?"

"His O'Malley and Flaherty cousins?" Mrs. O'Leary asked. "Aye, they'll feel duty bound to never let him forget it."

Georgiana was enraptured by the beauty of her daughters—two of them. She still could not believe there were two.

Dermott's moan had her glancing at him as he sat up next to the bed. "Bugger it…again?"

She smiled. "Aye. Are you ready to let the family meet our daughters?"

He started to shake his head, and groaned. "Oh, me aching head. The Lord must have decided I needed to share a tiny bit of yer pain by whacking me head on the floor…three times. Lass, I never dreamed that ye'd have to endure such—"

"It's over now, and our daughters are beautiful, aren't they?" When he just stared at her, she asked, "Aren't you going to kiss me, Dermott?"

"Aye, as soon as we name the wee lasses in yer arms."

"I was thinking Bridget after your mum, and Mary in memory of mine."

HE PRESSED HIS lips to Bridget's tiny forehead first, Mary's second. With tears in his eyes—tears he was not ashamed of—he kissed the lass…the love of his life, the other half of his heart, the mother of his children. "*Mo ghrá, mo chroí*—ye are me love and me heart, lass. We'd best be letting me cousins in, as I intend to name them guardians and protectors of our babes. Are ye ready?"

"Aye, Dermott. Have I told you today how very much I love you?"

He snorted with laughter. "As a matter of fact, ye cursed me name, the day I was born, and me manhood. I cannot say I recall ye saying anything about loving me."

He cut off her immediate protest with his lips, pouring everything he felt for the lass into his kiss. When he eased back, she was smiling, and he heard Sean and Flaherty calling his name. "Time for our wee lasses to meet the first of their family. Come in, lads, and meet the newest members of the family ye're bound to protect with yer life!"

LATER, WHEN THEY were alone, Dermott lay beside his wife, who cradled Mary to her heart, while he cradled Bridget to his. "I'm thinking 'twill be best to teach the lasses how to climb at a young age."

"Why in the world would we do that?"

His eyes twinkled with merriment as he kissed the scar on his wife's forehead. "I have a feeling that they'll be as stubborn and beautiful as their ma, climbing and leaping off stone walls."

"Can you forgive me for the things I said right before Mrs. O'Leary barred you from the room? She saved my life and that of our daughters, doing what had to be done."

His heart hammered as he remembered the fear that had had him by the bollocks. "Aye, if ye promise not to bring up that particular part of the birthing again until I'm old and gray."

Georgiana leaned against him and sighed. "I look forward to growing old with you, Dermott."

"Aye, lass, Lord willing."

"Lord willing, Dermott."

About the Author

In case we have not met yet, here is a little bit about me:
   I write Historical & Contemporary Romance featuring: Hardheaded Heroes & Feisty Heroines.

I fell in love at first sight, when I was seventeen, with the man who will hold my heart forever. DJ and I were married for forty-one wonderful years until my darling lost his battle with cancer. We have three grown children—one son-in-law, two grandsons, two rescue dogs, two rescue grand-cats, and one rescue grand-puppy.

My Hardheaded Heroes and Feisty Heroines rarely listen to me. In fact, I think they enjoy messing with my plans for them. BUT if there is one thing I've learned in dealing with my characters for the past twenty-nine years, it is to listen to them! My heroes always have a few of DJ's best qualities: his honesty, his integrity, his compassion for those in need, and his killer broad shoulders.

I have always used family names in my books and love adding bits and pieces of my ancestors and ancestry in them, too. I write about the things I love most: my family, my Irish and English ancestry, baking and gardening.

Happy reading!

Sláinte!
CH

C.H.'s Social Media Links:
Website: www.chadmirand.com
Amazon: amazon.com/stores/C.-H.-Admirand/author/B001JPBUMC
BookBub: bookbub.com/authors/c-h-admirand
Facebook Author Page: facebook.com/CHAdmirandAuthor
GoodReads: goodreads.com/author/show/212657.C_H_Admirand
Dragonblade Publishing: dragonbladepublishing.com/team/c-h-admirand
Instagram: instagram.com/c.h.admirand
Twitter: @AdmirandH
Youtube: youtube.com/channel/UCRSXBeqEY52VV3mHdtg5fXw